Caribbean CROSSROADS

a novel

CONNIE E. SOKOL

ALSO BY CONNIE SOKOL

Motherhood Matters
Faithful, Fit & Fabulous
Life is Too Short for One Hair Color
Life is Too Short for Sensible Shoes
Are You Ready for a LIFEChange?

Caribbean CROSSROADS

a novel

CONNIE E. SOKOL

Published by Sokol Publishing 865 S. Oak Dr. Woodland Hills, UT 84653

DEDICATION

To my fabulous and hilarious family, who gives me unintentional yet continual writing material. And to all talented, clean romance writers everywhere for their gift and inspiration.

CHAPTER ONE

The blind date was late.

Megan sat on the edge of the couch and glanced again through the window, watching and dreading the promise of another awkward evening. She moved her tennis racket to check her watch. Five more minutes, and counting. Dates got a max of ten minutes wait time, no exceptions. But why even wait? This tennis date was another one of Jillian's ideas, not hers. Then again, it was still better to trust a well-intentioned roommate than her own intuition right now.

Through the window a movement on the opposite balcony caught her eye—a group of animated college students headed toward the stairs. The perk of many apartment complexes at Nevada Groves University was the fishbowl square, allowing each apartment—at a glimpse—to know their neighbor.

Who was that? Was it... Megan jerked forward, a quick dread filling her stomach. Could it be *Jackson?* She carefully noted the gait and size—no, it wasn't him. Not supermodel enough, just a blond guy with Jillian and jolly company. Megan exhaled, relieved, and automatically plied the tennis racket strings with her fingers, straightening the small squares. Unbelievable that after all he had put her through, she could still react to the possible sight of him. Megan sat up and took a deep breath. That was six months ago and she was a whole different Megan now.

Wasn't she?

The chatting group moved down the stairs, laughing and talking like they were at a cocktail party. Jillian led the pack with all the confidence of a congresswoman. Megan frowned. She used to have confidence too. Before ...

Nope. Not going there.

The small herd of people now headed toward Megan's apartment. A few minutes later the door burst open and the crowd of people crammed in, throwing out greetings—"Hey Megan, lookin' hot," and, "Are you getting stood up?" Finally, a throaty "Hi, Meg," from Damon, who looked her up and down in a way that made her wish she had dressed in a muumuu.

She turned away from him.

Men.

Jillian entered last, talking to another coed in a too excited tone—the kind of tone that usually meant work. As in, "Let's put on a benefit concert to raise $100,000" or, "Let's save the blue dung beetle and fly to Africa for a rally." Megan braced herself.

"Megs, you're still here," said Jillian.

"Not for long." Megan checked her watch again.

Jillian funneled the group to the small kitchen while she wrapped her straight blonde hair into a French knot at her nape. "Come on, Megs, it's Robert Gentry. What if he just got a flat tire?"

"He'll have to carry a spare next time."

"You're ridiculous. But glad you're here, we need to talk." Jillian tugged Megan's arm and with the new girl, stepped into the tiny hall separating the front and back of the apartment.

"It's no, whatever you're pitching this time," said Megan.

"Okay, this is big. Very large. Supersized." Jillian stood close, ignoring Megan's words. "Are you listening to me? Focus. We need you, this very summer, in fact right now ... *to take a cruise.*" She smiled triumphantly.

"A what? You mean, go on a trip?"

"Yes—sort of—but better than that. You get to"—she paused dramatically—"perform! And, *you get paid*, just like me!"

"What? What are you talking about? Perform? Summer cruise star is your gig, not mine." What was Jillian thinking this time? Megan was definitely not the glam performer type.

Jillian and the new girl bobbed their heads. "You're perfect. You've done this kind of thing before, and you're athletic, and enthusiastic—okay, decently enthusiastic when you're not in a severe depression which is, thankfully, just about done. And you are almost done with it, right? See, you're exactly what we're looking for."

Megan stared at both girls. "Jillian, you know me, that's not my forte. I mean, I did some dancing a few years back, and one singing group, but it was completely cheesy stuff."

"That's perfect! That's all we do is cheesy stuff—lots of makeup, big hair, cheesy moves. They already have the main people doing the hard stuff. We're sort of the ladies of Vegas with the big headdresses."

"But fully clothed," the new girl clarified. "It's a family-friendly tour."

Megan shook her head. "No can do. If I want to go full-time with the temp agency I have to start the hours next week." Another watch check—two minutes to go. She looked back at Jillian, more like a sister than her own, and almost smiled. Oh, to have her carefree attitude about life! When would that come back to her, or would it ever?

"Megs, come on—that's not a real job."

"It's safe."

"What's happened to you—where's my old Megs? She would have jumped at the chance."

"Well, the Old Megs was a pushover. Welcome to the New Megs who is done with the looks-good-on-the-cover opportunities." Jackson came unbidden to her mind and she quickly pushed him out.

Jillian put her hands on her hips, intimidating in the small hallway. "Megs, it's a *temp agency*. She can get a fill-in for you, that's what she does. Besides, we don't leave until Tuesday."

Tuesday! "Jillian, NO—I seriously don't think that word is in your vocabulary." Megan felt between laughing and yelling. "Do you know how many of these things you've roped me into? The dancing bear for the hospital kids? Blowing up two-thousand balloons, with a broken tank? My lips were sore for a week. No, Jillian, this time I won't be reeled into your next big project."

"No, no, no," said Jillian in a soothing tone. "This isn't about me, it's about you—getting outside of yourself, serving others."

Megan made an exasperated sound. "You really need to run for office. I can't believe you're even asking me this. Used to dance, can you please hear what I'm saying? I'm done with humiliation, on all fronts." How could she help Jillian understand? It all seemed so simple to her. She was happy-go-lucky, in love, and bent on getting Megan *out there*, meeting people and "back in the scene." Because, of course, that's what you did with formerly engaged girls who got dumped by their fiancé. What would Jillian truly know about that? She was sky high with Derek, at the beginning of the Love Roller Coaster with no idea how that ride could end.

Jillian pouted. "Now you're safe *and* sorry."

And staying that way, thought Megan. "Making me mad will not get me to say yes."

"How can I then?"

"Promise me that all my troubles will go away and I'll come back deliriously happy."

"Done. Look at your life. You just graduated, you've got no serious prospects, and your spring contract is almost up. And seriously Megs, a cruise ship. Don't you remember me talking about the gorgeous men and awesome food? I met Derek, didn't I? And you, in this state of couldn't care less how you look in a swimsuit—not that it matters, as you look sickeningly great—I ask you: if that doesn't define bliss, what does?" Jillian switched to a pleading tone. "Listen, it's absolutely the chance of a lifetime. Marla is out with mono and we are in need—"

"—desperate need—" added the friend.

"—and you don't even have to audition, I've already spoken for you. Trust me, people would give their eyeteeth for this opportunity."

Megan felt the beginning of suspicion. She wasn't the best choice by far. Why were they so intent on her? Clasping the racket to her chest, she leaned back against the narrow hallway wall. "People giving their eyeteeth, huh? Why not ask *them*?"

"Because we need it signed today."

Pause.

Megan looked between them. "And?" she said slowly.

"And ... you're the only one we know that we like." Jillian's eyes pled.

"And who has the cash," said the new girl.

"Cash? I thought I got paid." Megan looked hard at Jillian, who gave the girl a look and turned back with a shrug.

"You have to put down a deposit. Non-refundable."

"How much?"

"A thousand dollars."

Megan shook her head and began walking away.

"No, listen for two seconds," Jillian said, grasping her arm. "It's for plane fare to Florida and a costume deposit, which is reimbursed—absolutely. And, you get paid six thousand dollars for the three months' work—dancing, Megs, *dancing*."

Megan plucked at the small string squares. She could care less about the men offerings or "chance of a lifetime," but the logistics were compelling. A summer spent on a cruise ship and getting paid for a few dances, compared to a dead-end but steady paycheck that had nothing to do with her degree. And then there was not going home for the summer, dealing with Jackson. And Kara. It was a no brainer. She had no other job offers in the wings, but that was her fault. For the past year all she'd done was the agency job and, of course, cleaning the guys' apartment part-time. Her stomach twisted. For the last six months she hadn't been planning a career, she'd been preparing for a future, one that didn't look at all like now. Still, past experience with Jillian showed that anything could happen, especially if that anything was inconvenient, frustrating, or unexpected. And it usually was.

Megan shook her head slowly. "Jillian, I want to help—you know I do— but I'll end up saying, 'What was I thinking?'"

Jillian jumped on the softening tone. "Megs, if you don't do it, they might cancel the tour, and Derek and I will spend the summer apart. And he is this close"she showed half an inch with her fingers—"to popping the question. Do you really want that on your conscience?"

Megan gave her a look—cancel the tour my eye—and checked her watch one last time. "Time's up. I'm off to the library." Turning back to Jillian, she smiled and added, "I'll think about it."

In the late cool of the evening, Megan lay on her cranberry colored duvet, immersed in the soothing lamplight of the apartment bedroom. Ultimately, the Blind Date had called with a legitimate roommate emergency—she could hear the intercom announcement for a doctor in the background—so she had stayed at the apartment, being spared her typical Friday-night trek to the library.

Gazing at her bulletin board to the right, she reached up and fingered a tarnished gold running medal hanging from a silky blue ribbon. Next to it, she traced down her "My Goals" list. It seemed an era ago, though it was just last fall. Megan had felt the same senior zest as her friends, knowing this degree was it, unless she inherited a fortune. Already she had taken longer than most to finish, paying her own way through. But education and all that went with it made her tingle—it was opportunity and adventure, and she was zealous to make it count. Or had been. Megan stared at the goal sheet, line after line of overactive sentences in red: Learn Italian, Climb the Alps, Get a Master's Degree.

And then he had come, softly padding through her life like a patient predator, waiting. Promises and playing her, pulling her in, making her feel that she was everything—loved, adored, The One. His world became her world until she'd lost sight of her own horizon. And she had forgotten those goals, at first for the joy of him. But then, with the betrayal, and numb shock of the truth, she'd been unable to conceive of achieving anything at all.

Megan rolled over, her back to the bulletin board. Tuesday—three short days. A once-in-a-lifetime experience, Jillian had said. People gave their eyeteeth for it, she had said. Three days to a new start and another world, or at least avoiding the old one. It wasn't a tough choice. This was the New Megan after all. So what was stopping her?

A gray feeling settled on her, suffocating her potential summer joy. Megan closed her eyes. She hated this feeling that obstructed her happiness just when something new or good entered her life. The past was over, done. That was then. She could move on—needed to move on—but an invisible hand grabbed at her waist and held her back from happiness, making her doubt herself and unable to trust those she loved. Or wanted to love. Or thought she loved.

She could still see him, sitting there on the couch, arms spread out across the back, his legs relaxed, like he was enjoying himself. Smiling that smile, with the dimple, telling her it was over. He'd made his choice and it wasn't her, or the three others she hadn't known about. Then he had told her, easily, about dating all four of them at the same time—for an apartment contest, no less. How he and his roommates had ranked them on a list of *essential* things—body shape, cooking, cleaning, income potential after marriage. And described the cartoon racing lanes with little magazine swimsuit bodies, and moving them toward the finish line.

She had stared at him, disbelieving, her emotions fluctuating through surprise, disgust, anger, and then numbing shock. His expressions, his arrogance, his cool deliberateness about it all. It was beyond her understanding. He had pursued her, lured her on the pretense of love, even talked to her about marriage and family. Jackson had been everything to her, had made himself everything.

When she'd found her voice and asked why, he had laughed outright. It had been a game, he said. Too bad the girls had taken it so seriously, and she had lost, didn't she get that? That's when he had shaken his head. Pathetic, he had called her. Naïve. And to make sure to clean the bathroom as it was Thursday.

She had turned and left then. Days later she had still sifted through the shrapnel. He had been her first true love. Shell-shocked, she had tried to comprehend this new Jackson she had only now seen—cold, callous, completely foreign. And suddenly, she was ten years old and being told that Daddy had left and wasn't coming back. Those same feelings had washed over her—stunned, betrayed. At the time she hadn't known how to react. Following her mom's lead, she stuffed her feelings far down inside, avoiding difficult emotions and putting her energies into non-emotional things—track, tennis. Facts she could record, things she could hold onto, or hit. Or pretend to run away from.

Megan cringed. She still regretted going back to Jackson at all, returning the next week to follow through on her commitment to the cleaning contract. But mainly it was to prove he hadn't won, that he hadn't devastated her the way he thought or seemed to relish. At first, showing him the same ambivalence he had shown her, she had cleaned. But it had felt wrong—this wasn't her way of doing things, and playing his game only made her more like him. That had been the moment of realization, of understanding just how much he had influenced her. So she had quit, and made sure he got the message loud and clear.

And yet, even after saying so, even after finally leaving, he still had some kind of hold on her that she couldn't figure out. With any other guy she wouldn't have put up with being treated that way for a minute. But she had taken it, and that's what bothered her. Where had *she* gone? How had she, Megan, lost herself in this man, without even seeing it?

Well, it wouldn't happen again.

Megan took a deep breath and opened her eyes. It had taken months to get to back to where she was. Now she was faced with a new reality, a possible cruise ship full of those same kinds of people, those kinds of men. Superficial. Stage performers. Say one thing and do another. Had she learned enough yet? Could she trust herself to recognize hypocrisy, to be safe from making the same mistake?

Megan sat up, clearing her mind and clinging to the facts. This cruise tour could be the opportunity for a fresh start. With the money earned she would have options, even to create a new life somewhere else—no distractions, no detours. And the truth was clear: it was either a cruise and The Unknown, or a summer dealing with the presence of him, the Must Forget.

I can do this, can't I? Megan tried to recapture her old bold self. I can do this until I know what else to do, to find the real me, to trust myself again.

But after Jackson, was that possible?

Before more doubts cascaded down her mind, she picked up her cell phone and dialed. "Jillian? Okay, you win. I'm in."

CHAPTER TWO

Mammoth.

Megan had never seen a cruise ship up close, and that was the first and only word that repeated through her mind. Turning from the 15-story-high ship, she faced the expansive concrete dock that was about the size of two football fields. It teemed with masses of people, luggage, and uniformed help in all shapes and sizes, shouting in various languages and competing with the squawks of birds overhead. Smaller vessels were tied up farther down the pier while seagulls flew constantly in search of leftovers. Various groups of people clustered around tall signs announcing names of companies, and young children laughed and chased one another in between the moving humanity. So much stimulation—every sense and nerve felt strung like the rope on the gangways.

But the salt air was heavenly, and she breathed it in. For the past few days, Megan had finally begun to feel ready for this new phase, wrapping her mind around performing. A few painful and very long days in the dance studio had yielded sore muscles and the need for a lot of ibuprofen.

"Last call for Premier Performers," a voice blared from a megaphone.

Megan moved toward the sound and away from the vast ship. A crowd of 20-somethings gathered—tanned, pert, and talkative. She shook her head. Of course that was them.

Jillian saw her first. "Megs, over here!" Notifying the group, she hurried over to Megan, giving her a quick hug. She eyed the one small suitcase and Megan's normal-sized purse. "This is it? Good thing there's outlet shopping at two of the ports."

"I don't shop anymore."

"Uh-huh. Just keep saying it like a mantra." Jillian moved her through the crowd toward the group where a silver gray-haired man with a deep tan stood next to a woman in an obvious black-hair wig and red sequin show dress. The woman directed a blond, nicely built young man in a mango colored T-shirt carrying stacked boxes labeled "Premier Performers." Megan smiled as the woman couldn't decide where to put them and the young man patiently acquiesced to her repeated change of mind.

"Come on now, gals and gents," said the tanned man. With a charming smile he carried himself like he'd been a catch in his day. "Welcome. We're so glad to see so many familiar faces, although Kyle, we'll be confiscating any contraband fireworks *before* boarding this time." A spiky brown-haired young man waved to the laughing group.

"And we welcome someone new to the Premier Performers team this year—Miss Megan McCormick, thanks for joining us." He made a slight bow toward her. She returned an awkward smile, feeling 20 pairs of eyes suddenly on her. "Very pleased to have you here, Megan. And hope you brought bunion pads and Band-Aids, you're gonna need 'em."

Some laughed, some nodded seriously.

"I'm Clint—as in Eastwood, except I'm much younger of course—and this is my wife, Minerva. But only I get to call her Marvy," he said, winking at his wife. "Well, we're all here now, and I've just a few bits of vitally important information that can't be missed, which means you will keep right on texting."

A chuckle rippled through the group.

Megan glanced at the human sea of tan and sparkle, noting a few differences here and there. One guy stood playing on a handheld video game with an intense focus and junior high hairstyle.

Definitely crew.

She scanned to a slim peroxide blonde sinuously shrugging her shoulders as she spoke to the guy next to her. Megan leaned into Jillian. "Okay, that's a Tiffany, Bambi, or a Brittany."

"Straight up," said Jillian out of the side of her mouth. "Brittany Shay Weller."

"Seriously?"

"Don't forget the Shay. She doesn't like that."

Clint began detailing luggage information and meal times. As Megan listened, she felt a slight pressure close in on her, like someone watching her. Discreetly turning her head, she saw a caramel blond-haired surfer wannabe staring at her through the listening heads. Megan squinted, recognizing the mango T-shirt he wore. Was it the same box mover guy? *He* was part of the performance company? The surfer continued to unabashedly stare but not in an interested way, more with a perplexed look. She couldn't tell what it meant. Not that she cared.

Megan turned her attention back to Clint. After a few minutes she glanced sideways. Surfer Boy still looked at her.

What is his deal? Megan ignored his distinctive jawline and checked her T-shirt and khakis—no, no stains. She looked up and saw him chuckle, as if he knew what she had just done. She scowled.

Men.

Inwardly, she mocked his tousled hair just to make herself feel better: that wavy kind of casual thing as if he'd just gotten out of bed. It reminded her vaguely of a magazine cover. She shifted her gaze to appear mesmerized by a seagull standing still.

She could feel it. He still looked at her.

Totally uncalled for, and frankly, downright rude. Probably from California, where the "rolling stop" originated. Abruptly, she turned her head toward him and stared right back, telepathing, "You. Are. A. Jerk."

He smiled. A wry, knowing smile.

Was he telepathic?

Narrowing her eyebrows, she telepathed, "Leave. Me. Alone," and turned away.

"We'll have a cast orientation and first rehearsal in one hour—"

A collective groan went through the group.

"That's right, on the Coral Stage. My Marvy will hand out your cabin assignments. I've already got mine," he said, looking at his wife.

"Go on." She sheepishly smiled back then clapped her hands, ample bracelets jangling as she distributed slips of paper. The group dispersed amidst friendly chatter with roommate assignments in hand. Jillian took the paper and hurried over.

"Vista Deck, cabin 535. We're in the same one, isn't that perfect?" Jillian was breathless, her ponytail bobbing behind her so that she looked sixteen instead of twenty-three. "There are four to a cabin, minimal space. But don't worry," she said, immediately scanning the crowd. "There's more room for makeup and stuff in the stage closet. Oh!" Jillian was up on her toes. Apparently she'd seen Derek.

"I'll be right back."

Megan had a feeling she would hear that phrase most of the summer.

That pressured sensation of being watched came again. This time, Megan turned with her hand on her hip, only to see Marvy walking towards her.

"Hello, dear." She gave Megan a hard peck on the cheek then took her hands and pulled them out to survey her. "Lovely to have you here. I've heard such rave reviews about you." The sunlight glanced off the sequins on her polyester dress. "If you should need any little thing, just let Clint or me know."

Marvy tugged Megan's shirt at the shoulders, fitted it at the waist, then ran her hand down the side of her pant leg and pulled at the khaki pant cuffs as if assessing an imaginary fit. Megan looked around awkwardly.

"Um, yes, I will," said Megan.

"Well then, a delight, a wonder, a treat to have you." She pulled Megan's chestnut hair to the side, checking it as a different style, then shaking her head, smiled and moved onto to the next unsuspecting person.

Recovering from the on-site fitting, Megan had almost reached the gangplank when she stopped.

The paper. Her room assignment. Jillian had it, meaning it was long gone in a starry-eyed haze. Well, the cabin couldn't be that hard to find.

Stepping on the short black bridge from the dock to the ship with her ID card ready, Megan paused. This was it. Now or never, no turning back, no crying to Mama—though she would never do that anyway. Gazing up at the massive ship and back down to her small feet, she breathed in the salt air, adjusted her luggage hold, and strode across the gangplank.

Somewhere behind her, Megan felt that same impression of someone watching her. But this time, she tossed her head and walked on.

Megan searched the hallway signs for "Vista Deck," trying to remember Jillian's breathless information on the dock. If only she had the paper. For no reason at all, a tall, blond man in a mango T-shirt came to mind.

Jerk.

Mentally, she continued to deride him for five more minutes, noting the way his white teeth had stood out against his tanned face. Why had he looked at her that way? It had been so odd—and yet compelling. Megan shook her head, ignoring a small flutter in her stomach. It didn't matter, anyway. She had more important things to focus on. Like not making a complete fool of herself at the first rehearsal. And finding her room.

After a few more minutes of wandering hallways, Megan paused. Angry sounds echoed from around the nearest corner and she edged closer for a look.

A large man standing with his back to her wearing bright shorts and black socks berated a maid standing at her cart.

"I said fresh towels. Does it look like I have fresh towels?"

"No, sir, bery sorry. No one say to me." A Latino girl—maybe in her early twenties—standing next to a cleaning cart handed him a stack of white towels. She bowed her head apologetically.

"And I asked for them ten minutes ago. What's wrong with you people?"

The man stomped away in the opposite direction while the girl wiped her eyes and began placing golden wrapped chocolates in a decorative bag.

Megan wasn't sure what to do until the girl looked up at her and gave a hesitant but courteous smile.

Megan walked toward her. "Are you okay?"

Her eyes watered slightly but she nodded.

"You must work very hard," said Megan, not knowing what else to say.

"Yes, I work bery hard," she said it quietly, as a statement. But there was a confidence to her, and an optimism in her tone.

13

Megan took in the light sheen of perspiration on the girl's skin and the dark puffy circles beneath her eyes. "Thanks for all you do. I'm sure there are some long days. Hopefully you know the passengers appreciate it."

With a shy smile the girl passed Megan a chocolate, which she accepted. "Thanks. I mean, 'gracias.' I don't remember much of my high school Spanish. But your English is very good."

The girl nodded as a little child. "I teach you. My name. You say, 'Cómo te llamas.' Okay? You try?"

Megan unwrapped the chocolate. "Cómo te—was it llamas?"

"Rosa. Mucho gusto. Dat means, nice meet you. I speak only English, dat is good, no? So I ask you, what your name?"

"Megan McCormick."

"Very pretty name for pretty girl. Now, how help you? Are ju lost?"

Megan felt the watched feeling again and looked around the fluorescent-lit hallway, barely wide enough for the cart and another person. She thought she saw a blur of mango color at the hall intersection but maybe she was wrong. "I'm trying to find the Vista Deck, and I think room 535."

She nodded knowingly. "Dis good news. Dis Vista Deck. All singers and dancers stay on dis floor, no? Boys here, girls dere. Make it separate, good idea, no?" Rosa shared an earnest look that made Megan laugh.

"Good idea, yes," said Megan. "Thanks, these chocolates are really tasty. I mean, gracias for la chocolate?"

Rosa's smile spread over her face. "Bery good, Megan McCormick." She handed Megan several more chocolates and pointed to the right hallway with her other hand. "Buena suerte. Dat good luck." She entered the open room door behind the cleaning cart.

"Buena suerte, Rosa." Megan turned and walked a few feet to the end of the hallway when she saw a familiar back of a head walking away from his room—the video gamer with the junior high hair cut from dockside, it had to be. He would know where the Coral Stage was.

He turned the corner and she hurried after him only to smack into Surfer Boy.

"Oh, I'm so—*you?*" Megan blushed.

14

"Still me, last time I checked." He just stood there—a six foot two, massively attractive mango road block. How long had he been standing there—was he the color blur from earlier? Possible, but realistically, what reason would he have for watching her talk with a maid?

Megan needlessly adjusted her shoulder luggage strap. "I meant ... I mean—" She couldn't gather her thoughts. Looking down at her, he wore a particular smile—less arrogant than before, this time more gentle and appraising. As Megan tried to get by him they sidestepped a few times before she finally put her free hand on his chest to stop him.

In a shocking second, something of a tingle passed through her, like the first seconds of immersing her cold body in a hot bath. Touching a man—it had been a while and she had forgotten how it felt, like this.

No.

She did not want to feel that, to feel anything.

"Okay—I'm passing on the right," she said.

"Need help with your—"

"Nope, I'm good." She had already moved beyond him, striding down the hall without looking back. She refused to think about the hot bath tingle.

A few minutes later she found room 535 but realized in the surprise meeting of Surfer Boy, she still didn't know the location of the Coral Stage. Megan groaned. After pulling out her dance wear, she quickly stowed her luggage in the cabin's miniscule drawers and—as she was the only one present—chose the left bottom bunk. Jillian was apparently still with lover boy and there was no sign of her other roommates, except for an expensive-looking set of baby blue embossed suitcases. Megan located a ship's map and after changing clothes headed in the right direction.

By the time she entered the theater doorway, Megan could see that most of the cast and crew members sat down near the stage in the cool, dimly lit room. Clint was talking to a few of the cast, and though she couldn't clearly see, one of them looked like the surfer boy. To her immediate right she noticed Marvy standing a few rows close to her, holding onto some costume pieces and looking perplexed at several large boxes on the ground.

"Can I help with something?" said Megan.

"Ah, Michelle." Megan smiled at the mistake but said nothing. "No, I'm—well, yes, maybe you can, just for a minute." She stole a glance at the stage. "I need to find the matching waist sash to this one skirt but my silly sciatica is acting up right now. Makes it hard to bend. I don't want Clint to know because he'll make a big tadoo about it and think I need to go lie down, like I'm an old woman or something."

Though she'd spoken lightly, Megan could see the deep lines in her face beneath the stage makeup Marvy typically wore. For the first time Megan thought how hard it must be for a woman to age in this business.

"Not a problem," said Megan, keeping her voice private and surveying the blue skirt. "It's probably more about these boxes, sitting down on the floor like this." She lifted up one of the narrow but deep boxes onto the seat. Though heavy it was doable, and she quickly sifted through for the match.

"Bingo," said Megan, handing her the blue ribbon sash that had slid near the bottom.

Marvy smiled and thanked her, seeming suddenly shy and embarrassed. "Just my silly back. Sometimes it has a mind of its own." Megan gave her a comforting smile then hurried down to the front, scanning for Jillian, who was in earnest conversation with Derek, and sat beside her.

Amidst the murmur of chatter, Megan looked around the medium-sized hall which appeared fairly new and able to hold maybe 150 or more. She was about to mention this to Jillian when someone plopped down next to her. The scent of ocean surf and man hit her first, and then the realization.

Megan stared at him. Where had he come from? She did not want to think about men, especially hot performers who were likely I'm-too-sexy-for-my-shirt kind of men.

She took in his easygoing manner as he settled back in the chair. Unfortunately, he didn't seem like that kind of person. In fact, he reminded her of her brother, Sam. A smile started on her face, then she stopped. No, she would not think that. Just because he looked fairly harmless meant nothing. Like a mantra, she must remind herself of that very point, several times a day. It was crucial she kept up her guard, *especially* in this environment where looks could definitely be deceiving.

16

He turned and smiled—relaxed, and completely unaware of the stomach flutter he caused in her again.

Megan shifted to a cool demeanor. "You again?"

"I was actually given a Christian name."

"St. Annoying?"

He showed no response and bent a knee over his leg, tanned calves showing below khaki shorts.

"Bryant, actually. And this is Chad." He thumbed to the person next to him.

The video gamer guy. Still intent on his game, he nevertheless looked up. "Hey," he said, and returned to his game.

"A pleasure," Megan said to Bryant, her voice syrupy. His wavy caramel-colored hair touched a shaving knick along his strong jawline. For no reason Megan smoothed her hair.

"So, what did Marvy need?" He had a kind of bemused, interested look on his face.

Marvy? Had he been watching them? "Oh, nothing, really. Just girl chat." His eyebrows raised and Megan faced front, her face beginning to get warm.

Clint and Marvy now entered stage left, parading out and touching hands like it was opening night. He gave her a slight twirl, and they took a mock bow to the applause.

"Sorry we're late getting started—it was my toupee. But don't say anything, Marvy still thinks it's real." He raised his eyebrows in a dramatic gesture. "All right folks, thanks for coming on time and seeing as we don't have much of it, we'll cut to the chase. Marvy?"

With a slight flourish she moved to center stage. "You all look lovely, truly lovely." She beamed. "Now, remember, rehearsals are today and tomorrow, that's all we have. Then it's show time, as they say. Matinee performances are at 4:00 on sea days and night performances at 8:00 and 10:00 p.m. Green room is an hour before performance, but of course it all depends on your makeup and costume needs." She gazed meaningfully at a few people.

Clint stepped up beside her. "Thanks, Marvy. Now people, your orientation packet has all the details but I want to emphasize the basic rules. Don't forget that you've all been hand-picked—the best that west coast Christian schools have to offer. That means you're gonna see a lot of things happening on this ship that you're not to participate in."

Some shifted uncomfortably in their seats, a few mumbled, and two girls turned to each other and laughed quietly at a private joke.

"Yes, I know, I'm the happy God-fairy who gets to make all your restrictive dreams come true. I have to answer to the board, but more worrisome than that, to your parents. I don't care if you're over 21—you know what's expected so let's go through the short list. No going anywhere on excursions without a buddy, especially in Jamaica. Curfew is at midnight, one a.m. on performance nights. And there is no, and I mean absolutely, don't mean maybe, NO dating of cast members. Did you all catch that last sentence? Jasmine, take out your earbuds. What did I just say?"

A red-haired girl with a bored expression took out one earbud. "Buddy. Curfew. No messing around with the hired help." She put the earbud back in.

"Right on cue, Jaz," said Clint.

Megan leaned over to Jillian. "But isn't that how you met Derek? I thought you said this was the place to meet guys. But if you can't date . . . I mean, not that I'm interested, just that—"

Jillian whispered back. "It's the biggest joke. Fifteen marriages and counting, but we all get that it's 'the rule,' for the parents' sake. And the board's."

Megan shrugged her shoulders. Show biz.

"Okay, ladies and gents." Clint clapped his hands. "Everybody up onstage. Let's do a run-through with the salsa number first. Grab your partner and to your marks—sound crew to the booth. Lighting and stage crew, you know what to do. Tape is on the floor, so look for your color."

Everyone seemed to know what to do, except Megan. Following Jillian, she nervously moved to the outside of the stage, a black half-circle outlined in lights. Clint walked to the center of the stage with what appeared to be the star performers—the girl named Brittany was there. And Bryant.

So he was a star performer. Hmm.

She didn't know why she was surprised. He seemed on the ball, but her idea of a star performer was all charm and no conscience. That didn't fit him. Well, what she had seen of him anyway.

As the cast gathered on the stage, Megan tried to look more confident than she felt. She glanced around the room, noting the minor performers in an outline on the frontal half-moon and guessed her spot. The recent hours of dance practice evaporated into a blank screen. She fought down the panic.

Jillian scooted up to her. "Just like we rehearsed. Be natural. No stress. Breathe." Then hurried back to her position. Megan nodded and smiled, but swallowed down momentary reflux.

After a few minutes of cueing the music and testing the lights, hot salsa beats exploded from an excellent sound system. Megan's stomach clutched—it *had* to be the salsa. It was the toughest dance in the lineup.

Marvy took on an intense countenance—clapping beats, shouting directions, correcting dance steps. Megan partnered with Garrett, an amiable young man with shoulder-length dark hair. Together they managed the tempo and moved fairly well. Just as she started to get it, they entered a complex series of movements, and passed through an X-formation with each other, moving like Vegas performers but doing salsa steps and turns. Megan tried desperately to keep up.

Bam. Megan slammed right into a perfectly coiffed guy.

"What are you doing?" he yelled over the music, and with a disgusted sound, hurried to his rightful spot. She didn't have time to apologize, though it wasn't necessary—she bumped into him several more times before the rehearsal was over.

After two hours of non-stop practice, the sweaty and thirsty minor performers took a needed break off stage while Clint worked with the stars.

Outwardly, Megan appeared attentive on the workings of the group, but found herself unwittingly gravitating to Bryant. Sure, he was good looking—she begrudged him that. But something was different—a typical golden boy but to a point. And though he had to be mid-twenties at least, he had a kind of freshness about him. Like the nine-year-old boys at the door with gelled hair and tubs of homemade cookies to sell for camp. Endearing. But, still, something about him seemed odd—his expression, maybe, or the square cut of his jaw.

Bryant was doing a song-and-dance number with Brittany. He turned and dipped her, hand on her waist, close. She moved with him, gripping his arms tightly and keeping constant eye contact.

Hmm. Pretty chummy. Not that it mattered.

Megan felt suddenly aware of her old capri dance pants and white T-shirt, and the realization that she couldn't hope to move half as smoothly as Brittany. With luck, she could melt into the background dancers and it wouldn't matter.

"Hey there, I'm Chalise." A curvy girl with dark hair slicked back like a Spanish dancer stuck out her hand and gave Megan's a quick squeeze. "Listen, don't mind Tag."

It took Megan a second. "Oh, him. I feel so bad. I think he must be sporting some serious bruises by now."

She laughed. "You're fine. He tends to take things just a *bit* seriously, especially on the stage. He's looking for a big gig this year—had a couple of offers for the fall if things go well here, sooo—"

"—give him a lot of room and make him look good."

"You got it." She looked back at the center performers. "And I think I'm your roomie, officially. With Jillian—you know her, right?"

"Yeah, we've been roommates at NCU in Nevada. I think we have a fourth but I'm not sure who."

"Oh, that's her, right over there, the one dancing with Bryant." Megan followed her gaze.

No.

"Her name's Brittany Shay Weller." Chalise turned back to her and spoke in a low tone. "Used to be tight with Bryant, so I don't know how that's gonna work out this year. Awkward," she said in a sing-song voice.

Brittany and Bryant?

"What happened?" said Megan before she could retract it. She immediately tried to look bored.

Chalise had turned back to the dancers. "I'm not sure, I was on another ship. All I know is that it got messy for a while. Jillian would know the details.

But, by the look of it, they've kissed and made up." She gasped. "Oh, I'm on." Chalise hurried to her mark.

Kissed and made up. What exactly did that mean? Well, they did make the perfect Barbie and Ken couple. But what did it matter, anyway?

At the conclusion of several more exhausting rehearsal hours, the three girls changed before the dinner buffet closed.

"I'm starving, completely ravenous," said Chalise, as she quickly finished powdering her face. Megan read a book on her lower bunk. She had showered first and simply pulled her wet straight chestnut hair back into a small ponytail holder.

"Khaki pants and T-shirt again?" said Jillian, looking away from the mirror. "C'mon, Megs, you used to always look chic. How about a blouse? Borrow my turquoise one, you'll look amazing."

Megan looked up from her book, smiled, and went back to reading.

Jillian tisked at her and finished layering mascara. "As God as my witness, you will wear a skirt this summer."

"Thank you, Scarlett," Megan said, still reading her book.

"Come on, get something to show your legs a bit."

"No way." Like she needed that. She was just fine with her basic khaki with T-shirt outfits—who was she here to impress? Suddenly a white smile and tanned face came to mind, looking down at her in the hallway, making her feel ...

No. She was here to work and get back to Being Megan. End of story.

"Just the lower half, Megs, it's not going kill you," said Jillian, finishing her mascara. "You're not sending the wrong message, but you'll be about ten degrees cooler. And much more feminine, I might add."

"And this is important because?"

"Well, you might want to be back into men someday."

"Please, we're about to eat," said Megan and turned the page. No need to let Jillian in on her flutter issues. That would only make her relentless in trying to stir up romantic waters.

Jillian paused, capped the tube, and walked over to Megan. "You know, not every guy is like that."

Allowing the sincerity to stay, Megan nodded. Jillian had been there for her through most of the Jackson fiasco, which was likely why she was hadn't yet forced on her a cruise list of datable guys. "I know," said Megan. "There are still guys like Derek, after all, so I haven't lost complete faith." She hesitated then gave Jillian a meaningful look, grateful for how their friendship had deepened over the many years. "I know what you're trying to do, and I appreciate it, I really do. But it's just not for me, not right now. Not for a very long while yet."

Jillian thought for a moment then smoothed Megan's hair. "He's out there, Megs, he really is. And he's wonderful. I just know it. You've got to let go and try again, despite what's happened. You'll see. Something good is right around the corner, I can feel it."

Megan smiled. Jillian had said it earnestly, genuinely. Like a comforting mother who knows best, and you almost believe her because you really, really want to. Jillian kissed the top of Megan's head and headed back to the mirror. Brittany had not yet arrived but her suitcases had been meticulously unpacked and stowed somewhere out of sight.

Minutes later they headed for the food. Chalise led them down the serpentine hallway which opened into the enormous mezzanine. It overflowed with people, casino entryways, and buffet entrances, spanning the size of a stadium floor. The girls made their way through the first food line. Every few minutes Jillian surveyed the place for Derek who said he'd meet her there.

Tonight's buffet—celebrating the first evening of the cruise—was an elaborate Asian theme. Four enormous banquet tables held platter after platter of seafood and meat dishes, egg rolls, noodles, rice and more, all displayed with ornate Chinese decorations of red and gold lanterns and stationed Terra Cotta army statues. Between the platters wound a luscious full-length version of the Wall of China made from chocolate fondant cake.

"This is my favorite perk of being a Premier Performer, baby," said Chalise, piling a bit of everything on her plate.

"Where do you put it?" said Megan.

"High metabolism, much to the ship's dismay," she said, spooning on some Szechwan shrimp.

The abundance made Megan feel full before she began, and by the line's end she only had a few entrees on her plate. They made their way to a cozy table by a wall, the dull roar of five hundred people's animated conversation in the background. With the stimulation of the day, the afternoon's rehearsals, and now the evening noise, Megan's head throbbed a steady beat.

As they settled into the seats in a section with a table sign labeled "Premier Performers," Chalise called out, "Hey Britt, over here."

The stunning peroxide blonde paused at the table, while a Latino man stopped behind her, carrying a tray of salad without dressing, a palm-sized piece of grilled fish, and a small bowl of lemon slices.

"Leesy, sooo good to see you." Brittany leaned down for an air kiss on her cheek." She glanced and smiled to the girls at the table.

"Good rehearsal today, ladies." She paused at Megan. "You're the new girl—is it Megan?"

"Yes, that's right."

"Can't believe it was your first rehearsal, you did a really great job. And don't worry about Madame Helga. She gets sort of point and shoot out there but she's really a big marshmallow."

Megan nodded in appreciation. Wow, disarmingly nice. Megan felt a momentary pang of guilt for her earlier Barbie and Ken judgment. She obviously had a lot to learn about performers.

Chalise pointed to an open chair. "Come sit with us."

"Thanks, no, Manuel is seating me with Mrs. Van De Morelle."

Chalise stopped. "She's here, on the *ship?*"

"Oh yes, and about *five* board members. She's supposedly coming to a performance, though no one knows which one." Charlise's hand flew to her chest. "I know. Word is they're making new decisions on staff, performances, casinos—lots of things." Brittany smiled abruptly at another table. "Hey, good to see you!" then did a princess wave.

Megan noticed that her teeth were perfectly aligned, standing at attention like little alabaster soldiers. Her lips naturally sat up slightly higher than her gums so that her smile gave the constant impression she had just been crowned Miss America.

"Who's Mrs. Van De Morelle?" said Megan.

"She's the big cheese decision maker," said Chalise. "And connected to *everyone*, right up to the president of the United States, I swear. Fingers in lots and lots of money and the x-factor in who stays and who goes. But what gives, are they firing anyone?"

"No, no, nothing like that," said Brittany. "Actually, great news. My mom heard from the board that they're shaking things up to better compete with the other cruise lines. But that's not the best part." She leaned in closer to the table, taking in all the girls one by one. "They're looking for new star performers for the Intrepid."

"Are you serious?" Chalise practically shouted.

"That's what I heard. So, no pressure for performances but, this could be the summer." She smiled fully at the girls. "Ta-ta, ladies."

And she was off, her lithe body in a white camisole shift moving nimbly between the tables while Manuel followed submissively behind.

Chalise watched her leave. "Isn't that Bryant over there—with that dark-haired kid?" She squinted for a better look then turned back to her generous plate. "He's such a catch, but then so is Garrett, that shoulder-length wavy hair. You're so lucky to partner with him for the salsa, Megan. He was on the Discovery with me two years ago. Maybe it's time to revitalize the friendship." She gave a sly smile.

Jillian checked her watch and looked around again, a dark expression fleeting across her face. She dug into her plate. "I can't believe they're back on a boat together."

"Who?" said Megan.

"Brittany and Bryant. Such a soap opera."

Megan found herself ridiculously hoping for more information. What was wrong with her?

"So what's the skinny on those two?" Chalise scooped up a forkful of rice. "Weren't they an item?"

"Oh yes. I only remember the major turns because I'd just met Derek and was otherwise occupied." She eyed the room quickly. "But it was the total scuttlebutt for a while."

Megan remained impassive but something in her stomach remembered the tingle. Absurd, she thought. I don't even know him.

Jillian talked through a mouthful of food. "If I'm right, she and Bryant had dated before coming on board—danced together for some sort of group at Three Pines College. That's where the Premiers started."

"So he wants to be a dancer, like a career?" Megan couldn't help herself. For some reason, he just did not seem like the lifelong performer type.

"No, he was some basketball star at his college or something, but Marvy's sweet on him—they know each other through some old family connection. He was sort of her go-to dance guy."

"But he's already graduated, hasn't he?" added Chalise.

"Yeah, a few years ago, and took his sweet time doing it too. Apparently he's been doing this and that, working, and then went on some service mission for Community Builders, like a Habitat for Humanity deal, for about a year."

"Really?" said Megan. Good looking and with heart. Was that possible? A warning sound began very softly in her brain. No, she would not go there. Looks can be deceiving, she repeated in her mind.

"It was actually his mother's encouragement from what I understand." Jillian chewed a piece of beef and broccoli. "They own some building business or something, I can't remember. Anyway, so it was pretty strong for a few months but then they both left after the cruise tour was over—she went back to college and he went back with Builders as promised. But he was only supposed to go for like six months or something. Then Bryant extended his tour for some reason. The next spring Brittany went on a ship alone, and lo and behold met Mr. Fantastico—get this, from Monte Carlo." She chewed carefully while she talked, pointing for emphasis. "A distant relative of Prince Rainier and absolutely loaded. I remember *that* part, let me tell you. They got engaged within weeks, you should have seen the rock."

"So she and Bryant had broken if off before they left?" asked Chalise, almost finished with her plate by now.

"Noooo." Jillian waved her fork in the air. "Apparently, they were still hitched in some form, no idea the extent of foul play. All I remember is that Bryant flew to the Cayman Islands where she was at port—actually, it was pretty romantic—to find out what was going on. Which was not so romantic, at least for him. She tells Bryant it's over, that she's found her true love and he jets it back to South America to build some more homes."

"Whoa, that's like a low-budget movie." Chalise had pushed her plate aside. "Ooh, I think I ate too much."

"That's not the half of it," said Jillian. "Next thing we see is Brittany back on the Love Boat without the Love Bug."

"Her fiancé ditched her?" said Megan. She knew all too well how that felt.

"Worse, he was a *fake*." Jillian punctured the air again. "He thought *she* had money, which apparently they do, but not like he had been led to believe. It's Mrs. Van De Morelle that has all the dough—the Wellers just live like they do. When Brittany found out, her mom flew her home and nursed her back to Barbie health. She comes back on board, but pines for Bryant, who by this time is back home, and then throws herself at his feet—at least from what I hear."

"And ..." Chalise leaned forward.

"He didn't bite, if you know what I mean. Not for her trying, though."

Megan had to know, though she couldn't understand why. "So it's not over? I mean, is she still hoping for ..."

"I'm sure she's not," said Chalise. "Brittany's gorgeous, she could have any guy. And if Bryant said it was done, that's a pretty clear signal."

Jillian roughly scooped some rice. "Hah. Brittany is a fighter. Do not mess with her when it's something important—like a prime gig, or a prime guy, things like that."

"Brittany?" Chalise shook her head. "She's one of the nicest people I know. And seriously, she's hardly spoken to him since we got here."

Megan looked toward Chalise but at that moment saw beyond her shoulder into the distance—a blonde girl in a white camisole shift, leaning on one arm against a table, talking to someone with a mango-colored sleeve.

Yes, chummy indeed.

The dark-haired Chad sat next to Bryant, playing with an electronic device, but she saw him glance up at the girl with an annoyed expression.

Megan turned back to the conversation, slightly bothered by seeing Bryant and Brittany together.

Jillian picked up her glass. "Hello, Chalise, they *dance* together. Can you imagine how uncomfortable that would be?"

Chalise shook her head. "I've seen them today and you wouldn't even know there had been anything between them."

"That's why they're Premier Performers, *Leesy.*"

Megan looked down at her shrimp. She didn't even know why she cared, sitting there, gathering up every word about him as if they were falling pearls.

Good grief, what's wrong with me, she chided herself. Will I ever learn? He's a performer, he's a surfer, he's got baggage. Technically, there's no dating between cast members. And besides, I'm off men.

Finishing up, the girls left the buffet room. On the way out, Jillian found Derek who had been playing on some techie toy with the guys and had forgotten all about dinner with her. They had an intense conversation in the hall that Megan chose to avoid.

Chalise invited her to go dancing—"It's disco night, come on!"—but Megan begged off with a polite refusal. Maybe she was getting older, or fussier, or just plain boring. But she was sick of dancing, lights, and sound. By now all she sought was a silent refuge.

Searching on the higher decks—quieter by far, with everyone moving below into the clubs and casinos—Megan walked in a through-way and found the perfect spot. Moonlight framed a small nook between the ship's wall and a staff service station.

With her back against the cool metal of the ship, she pulled her knees to her chin and wrapped her arms around them. The tangy air engulfed her and she breathed deeply, in and out, letting the air pass through her lungs in cadence with the ship's tremendous pulsing engine. She could feel the day's agitation float away.

As soon as peace came, surprisingly so did thoughts of Bryant. Without invitation, flashes of him broke over her like waves—his staring at her on the dock, making her tingle in the hallway, talking to Brittany.

He was an enigma, a walking contradiction, and his expression unlike anyone she'd known—as if he were constantly figuring out a math problem. But then he'd break into a smile and it was sun on the water, Mr. California. Of course, he could be from Maine for all she knew.

His hair—she smiled in spite of herself. Perpetually mussed but it suited him. The kind of style that other guys could try to copy but wouldn't work—on him it was a natural wave. And clean cut but always a bit of stubble, with a random knick somewhere. He must hate shaving. She pictured him staring into her, his blue eyes with that thin concentric black circle encasing the iris— piercing, focused.

Megan shifted. She didn't want to think about Bryant, so why was she? Deep inside her something unexpected had opened in the hallway, touching him like that. The most random gesture and yet, it had cracked open a crevasse. But why? It had been simply a touch. Had she been so hands-off about romantic emotions, so raw from holding back that the first sensation of feeling made her woozy? Or was it something about him?

She closed her eyes, willing the subject away but like tentacles the thoughts continued. What had been between Bryant and Brittany? Was it still there? She wasn't exactly hard to look at. But then, neither was he.

Megan hugged her knees closer. Rehearsal tomorrow morning would tell her more.

Not that she cared.

CHAPTER THREE

Megan dressed in her typical white workout shirt and capris pants. But surprisingly, she felt to put on some lip gloss. Before walking out the door, she pointed to herself in the mirror.

Stay focused.

Today, she would not mess up. She would not be nervous. She would be her Bold Self. And she would not think about anyone in particular. This was business. This was the New Megan.

Okay. Good.

A few minutes later she stood on the stage in the Coral Theater while Clint tried to elicit interest from twenty sleepy performers and crew members at the early hour. His urgent voice echoed through the empty theater.

"Let's wake up people. I know you haven't had your beauty sleep. Wait till you're our age—you don't need any." He winked at his wife, who gave him the usual, "Go on" look, and went back to putting a tape measure up against one of the girls.

Megan waited in formation for the "Unsinkable Molly Brown" number opposite of Jillian but near Bryant. Though she felt his presence, she steadily ignored him. Everyone stood ready for the number which happened to involve him and Brittany—and her big solo—but she hadn't arrived yet.

"Brittany Shay still not here?" Clint glanced at the main auditorium door and back to the cast—he narrowed his eyebrows. "Hmm. All right, let's go ahead since this needs lighting work. Megan, why don't you just stand in for now." Clint motioned to the designated spot but Megan stood speechless and pointed to herself. "Yes, you dear, just stand in for now, Bryant knows what to do." He hollered directions to the lighting crew watching from the booth through a small open window.

Megan felt her face flush and moved as slowly as she could get away with. So much for staying in the background.

"Morning," Bryant said, wearing that bemused expression that almost bordered on arrogance, as if he knew of her discomfort.

Was he mocking her? Megan wore an overly cheerful expression, determined to show he did not affect her. "Top o' the mornin' to you."

He looked down. "I have a cousin who's Irish."

"Bully for you."

"That's British."

Exasperated, she looked up at him. "What, are you the international committee?"

He shrugged and grinned.

That smile. Megan ignored him, and the desire to smile back.

Clint clapped his hands. "Okay, take your positions—we're going to do the first main poses but no performance energy, just blocking. Find your first marks."

Bryant took up her hand and Megan felt a quiver of something, whether it was nerves or from him, she wasn't sure. But either way she'd never let him know it. In a quick movement he put his hand in the small of her back and led her to the first mark, at the center of the stage.

Low and quiet he said, "I'm going to lean you back." With her panicked reaction, he added, "Bend your left knee. Kick out your right leg and rest your heel on the stage. It's easier."

On Clint's cue, he went down on one knee and dipped her backwards as she obeyed his instructions.

Bryant balanced her back on his thigh and stared straight ahead while Clint commented on the solitary shaft of light now focused on them and what color it should be. Megan wrapped her right hand around Bryant's arm to steady herself. Not pumped up muscles but solid, like a working man. Very nice. No, not nice, nothing, it was nothing at all. She stared at the black lighting tray above her, trying to focus on Clint's directions.

For balance, she continued to hold onto his arm but not too tight—she didn't want to give him any ideas. He held her firm and confident. Somewhere inside she knew he wouldn't drop her, even if they stayed that way until dinnertime. And he smelled good, like getting back from a day at the beach then taking a fresh shower. Megan stole a glance to the side—the shaving knick was along his upper neck today. Such a small thing, but so frustratingly appealing. Still—she reminded herself—with his tanned face and surfer hair he was way too All-American Boy.

He glanced down at her. "Yes?"

Had she been staring at him? "Nothing, you just look like someone I think I know." It was an awkward response, but she didn't know how to justify looking at him.

He took it in stride. "You look like Gidget."

"I get that all the time, especially from the old timers."

"Are you saying I'm elderly?"

"No, but I can't believe you know who that is." She was conscious of his strong arm still around her shoulders, her lower back resting on his knee.

He stared ahead again. "My family is into the oldies channel—*I Love Lucy*, the Mayberry show, all those."

Megan nodded, her mom was too. How many nights had they sat munching pretzels and watching the black and white reruns, one of their few ways to connect.

"They're all right," Bryant continued, "but after a while I can't take one more, 'Gee that sounds swell.'"

Megan laughed in spite of herself, and he looked down, eyes clear and open. Why was he so disarming? One minute he looked maddeningly arrogant, the next like her new best friend.

Clint clapped them back to reality. "Okay, to the bridge of the song," and he sang a few lines, "hit the transition marks. Bryant—you and Megan hold the next position for a minute there while we get the right color gel."

Bryant helped her stand upright then took her hand as naturally as if they'd partnered for years, walking her to top of the stage. Megan focused on not stumbling.

Speaking quietly, he said "Face the seats, raise both hands to the sky, feet straddled," then he moved to stand behind her. She did as he directed, once again aware of how tall he was. He placed his hands on her waist—lightly at first, as if hesitating for the briefest moment, then holding her firmly.

Nice, solid hands. Megan fought to ignore the pleasant sensation.

Clint shouted directions to lighting when the auditorium door slammed shut. "Brittany Shay, you grace us with your presence," he joked, but an undercurrent of seriousness laced his comment.

Brittany gracefully moved down the aisle giving the two of them a piercing look. It wasn't disapproval, but more of a cool assessment. Megan instinctively pulled down her hands. She didn't want to appear like she was taking over Brittany's spot. Or former guy.

Bryant kept his hands on her waist.

Brittany walked straight to Clint. Bedecked in black leggings and silver tank, her hair, skin, and smile pulsed "flawless." As she spoke with him, he nodded, seeming to approve of what she said, and motioned to the stage. When Megan moved slightly to his side, Bryant dropped his hands. Brittany glanced once more at the duo—all smiles and charm again—but Megan wondered about the look. Was it seeing Bryant with someone else, or that someone was in the star performer position?

"Okay everyone, Brittany Shay has been hobnobbing with the *board members* at breakfast while we've been working," said Clint. A series of "ooh-ahs" popped from the cast. "Let's get back to work."

Brittany walked onto the stage, hips slightly swaying. "Sorry, Bry," she said, looking at him with an unreadable expression, then turned to Megan with a smile. "Thanks for stepping in—the board didn't think we'd be that long."

"No problem. Thankfully, they didn't have me do much," Megan said, and with a half-look at Bryant, returned to where she thought her current position was. Brittany exchanged a few more words with Bryant, who responded and then took his position.

Megan wondered at the sudden unease within her. She hadn't been doing anything wrong, Clint had asked her to stand in. So why the nervousness? It couldn't be jealousy, she hardly knew either of them. Looking at Bryant and

Brittany take their position, taking her hand, holding her close, she shook her head. Stop it.

Not. Going. There. It's too soon, too obvious, too ludicrous.

The rehearsal progressed through the next few hours to Clint's satisfaction and just as Megan felt fairly decent with the result, he called for the salsa number again. "We're still having a few troubles with this one. I know the music is fast, so let's try it again."

Everyone groaned, ready to break for lunch. And while he didn't say her name, Megan felt sure it was because of her. Of all the numbers this was the hardest one.

The music started and Megan paired up with Garrett, who smiled briefly and took her across the stage. As she attempted to twist her hips and turn in formation with the rapid music she stumbled into another dancer—thankfully, not Tag. After the third and finally barely successful try, Clint called out, "Okay, that's good work. Let's break for lunch."

A round of relieved groans went around the room. Clint smiled but scratched his head and surveyed the stage again.

The group moved towards their water bottles and bags. Jillian approached Megan. "Hey, after lunch we're hitting the special cast showing at the cinema. Gonna come?"

"Um, I'm not sure ..." After the morning's rehearsal Megan had decided on other plans but wasn't about to divulge them.

"Megs, *come on*. Two words for you—Be. Social. Can you say it with me?"

"No, it's nothing like that. I've just got a few things to do."

Jillian gave her a doubtful look. "Trim your toenails?"

Megan sighed. Jillian was only trying to help, she knew that, and would likely keep "trying to help" unless she caved on something. "Okay, what time's the movie?"

"Two o'clock. Be. There."

"Two words for you—May. Be."

Megan smiled as Jillian shook her head and pointed at her. "I'll see you there." Then hurried off to Derek.

Clint talked earnestly with Bryant at the front of the stage while Megan noticed Marvy trying to scoot some prop boxes to the side, her hand discreetly rubbing her back.

Megan walked towards her. "Here, let me get some of those big ones," she said, to which Marvy smiled appreciatively. Within a few minutes the boxes were tucked away as Marvy wanted and with a genuine thank you, she left with the last few stragglers, one of them being Bryant.

Megan looked around. Good. The less people who saw her, the better. Just to be sure, she slipped out the side door and entered the restroom. After waiting a few minutes she exited, reentering the now empty theater, and scanned for signs of life.

No one. She breathed normally.

After dropping her bag at the top of the stage, she took her first mark for the salsa dance and began counting in her head. She twisted briskly across the stage, switching from a meringue to a salsa to a mambo step, pretending she had a partner. The tricky part came when switching from the 1-2 count of the salsa to the 4-1 count of the mambo. Twice she stumbled, and at the same place—usually where Tag stood.

Back to the starting point, Megan focused on her counting, crossing in a grapevine step while twisting her hips, arms raised in front as if led by a partner, until she slammed into a body.

"What in the—" She fell back while Bryant caught her.

"You've got too much twist on the wrong beat," said Bryant, with his condescending surfer smile. "And you're watching your feet."

Megan stood facing him, humiliated and not knowing how to take his advice. Why was he really here? Was he worried about her messing up the show? "So, you sideline as a 'Dancing with the Stars' coach?"

"That's right. I'm just here working on my tan." He didn't move. "Want some help?"

She noticed another knick she hadn't seen on his neck. "Do you teach like you shave?"

"Do you dance like you talk? Come here." He took her hand and pulled her over to the middle of the stage. Megan felt a familiar heat rising in her face.

34

He grasped her right hip with one hand, took her other hand in his, and pushed her forward in the right direction, then pulled her back. After a few moments he switched the count, directing her to cross sideways, both of them moving slowly in the grapevine, then to the salsa through the change-up of the mambo. Briefly but accurately he directed her with short commands—"Wait, cross. Not yet. Go with me"—his eyebrows were slightly bent in concentration.

At first she tried not to look up, out of embarrassment, and confusion. In her soul, she didn't want his help. Or to be this close to him. Or to feel his hands on her hips. But his direct manner felt strong and reassuring. What was it about him that was so immediately disarming?

Thoughts dueled inside her head: I am here to dance, not to date. I don't even want to date. And we can't date anyway. He's a performer, so he's a player. He's the wrong type. It's the wrong time. It's all wrong, wrong, wrong.

Wow, he smells good.

After the fourth pass, they were up to speed and Megan had successfully and easily crossed without one stumble. They repeated the pattern a few more times. Relief, lovely relief stole through her—she could do this. For the first time she felt a small excitement about performing tomorrow.

"You're actually quite good," she said, forgetting to dislike him. "I mean, not like Fred Astaire good."

"Okay. I appreciate that." They stopped in the middle of the stage, letting go of one another.

"No, I mean, you're more like a Gene Kelly. Very athletic when you dance, not so much the flair thing. More manly."

Oops.

"Manly?"

"Um, yes." Megan escaped toward the top of the stage for her water bottle. Bryant followed her.

Why was he following her? Why were her hands shaking?

Stop it. I can handle this. Just a little friendly chitchat with a cast member—a very normal, social thing to do, right? And Jillian would be happy, and leave her be for five minutes.

"So, a little curious, how does a basketball star get into dancing?" she said, trying to sound casual.

He raised his eyebrows. "Basketball star—who's been listening to gossip?"

"It's not exactly a secret." Bryant eyed her water bottle, and Megan paused, then wiped it on the bottom of her T-shirt before handing it to him.

"Girl's germs?" he said in a mocking tone, taking a swig. "It started with Mom. She heard ballet was good for football—that was before basketball. Then the teacher said that I was good—not *Fred Astaire* good—"

Megan made a mocking face.

"—and she needed more guys for the recital. We just had to lift and turn in a circle, not so bad. One thing led to another, and I found out I could get a scholarship if I tried out for some Young Stage Stars group. Badaboom, I'm dancing and singing in the rain. Surprising what you'll do for money."

Megan used her towel to dab her face and neck. "And what else would that include?"

He thought for a moment. "A summer at a theme park as a Wiggle—"

"—ouch—"

"—and being demoted to Dorothy the Dinosaur when a co-worker got heat stroke—I think on purpose."

"You danced around in a dino costume?"

"And sang. To children who pelted me with French fries and cried when I waved at them." He handed back the bottle. "In 103 degree heat, in a costume with one ventilation flap, for minimum wage."

"Mmm. And how was that?"

"My definition of hell."

"And so now," she said, "do you *like* dancing?"

"What does that mean? You think I wear tights on the off-hours or something? Of course I'd rather be playing ball. I just can't make the same money—no offers."

They were basic questions, really, but underneath his relaxed countenance there was an undercurrent of frustration, a tightening of his face. Had she said something wrong?

"No, I'm just saying, you just don't seem like a dancer," said Megan, speaking more candidly than she desired. "The cruise ship—for some reason, it doesn't seem like your kind of gig."

"Oh, this," said Bryant, shaking his head. "It's for my family who thinks this is my last chance to . . . well, connect with 'good Christian up and coming young people.'" There it was again—a lightness but edged with anger. "So what's your story?"

Her story. Where did she start? Did she even want to? "Favor to a friend," she finally said. It was a safe answer. He cocked his head, with an expression that made her feel like he'd x-rayed her soul, like he knew more than he opted to say.

"And that friend with the favor—is that Jillian, of the Jillian and Derek duo?" he asked.

"The same."

"Looks like you'll be solo mio, doing a lot of buffet lines, watching a lot of basketball. At least I would be."

"Only if it's the Knicks."

"The Knicks?" He shook his head. "Maybe thirty years ago. The only game in town—in any town—is the Lakers, baby."

Megan looked incredulous. "The Lakers? Half their players run the court in a walker."

He folded his arms over his chest. "Seventeen-time NBA champs versus what, two-time wannabes?"

"Their team is deep this year, and with the new drafts, they're poised to win and you know it." She stepped closer to him, hands on her hips.

"Too early to tell. It's all predictions until prescason."

"But high expectations—and they'll deliver," said Megan. He looked down at her, eyes almost laughing again.

Brittany walked into the theater, toting a costume piece, and Megan instinctively stepped back. That same nervousness washed over her. Quickly, she bent down to grab her things.

"Well, I better go." Megan moved, leaving him standing alone. "Promised I'd be somewhere. Thanks for everything." She crossed the stage with a quick "Hi," to Brittany who wore a pleasant but familiar piercing expression. After opening the theater door Megan glanced back at Bryant, still standing on the stage watching her, arms folded with that half-smiling arrogant expression on his face. She'd seen that expression before—that knowing look, that sureness. Someone else had smiled at her that way—like he knew her, and how to reach her, and would eventually reach her in the end.

And that someone had hurt her. A lot.

Megan slammed the theater door shut and strode down the hallway.

She would not fall. Not again. Not ever.

CHAPTER FOUR

Megan pursed her lips in frustration—railroaded by Jillian again. She had planned to arrive right at two o'clock to a dark cinema room but Jillian had found her intentionally hiding out at the small cafeteria rather than the crowded buffet line, and had shepherded her to the movie a half hour early.

That was meddling Jillian, who didn't understand that this was a new Megan. It was too soon for her to fraternize with the enemy—way too soon. She would not—repeat not—get anywhere close to caring, especially for one of these Premier Performer types. She'd learned her lesson and things were different now. Much better to spend her time on safe pursuits, like not falling on stage, rather than falling for some guy.

Entering the small gray room, Megan saw about 30 theater-style seats with over half of them full. Most of the cast and crew—and some others she didn't recognize—were seated in three and four rows, laughing and talking. Megan looked for a seat farthest from the fray. Jillian tugged her towards Chalise, who was sitting by Brittany and several others on one side, with open seats on the other.

Thinking of an excuse, Megan allowed herself to be momentarily led. As they closed in on the row, she said, "Um, I'll just see about popcorn." A perfect time to bolt.

"Oh, Bryant went to get some, don't worry," said Chalise, pointing to the empty seat next to her, and the rest of the row. It was then Megan saw a man's jacket.

Bryant? Megan remembered her feelings slamming the theater door.

It's all right. Be cool, be distant. Hostile if necessary.

Jillian nudged her towards Chalise. "I'm sitting with my handsome man, I just wanted to drop her by." She pulled a face—"Megan's being *social* today."

Megan sat down hard. Awkward conversation for the next 30 minutes between Bryant, Brittany *Shay*, and Chalise—lovely.

Just as Megan finished small talk hellos with the girls and settled back, Bryant walked in balancing complimentary bags of popcorn and large soda cups. Chad came to his rescue and took some for the row behind them—he was sitting with someone she recognized from the sound crew.

When Bryant approached their row, he paused, then continued, stepping around Megan as she stood to make room.

"Sorry, let me lean back here," she said, scooting back as far as she could. He faced her, side stepping, looking down only inches from her face, squeezing popcorn and soda between them. As he divided the spoils, Megan could have sworn she saw Brittany looking over every few minutes, though it could have been to talk to Chalise, which she did frequently.

Settling in, Bryant passed Megan popcorn.

Feeling his body close to her, warm and solid, she decided to jump straight to hostile.

"I don't like popcorn," she said.

He gave her a look. "You're American, aren't you?"

She returned the look.

"Fine, take this," he said, handing her a soda cup.

She took the soda cup, wiped the straw tip with her finger and took a quick sip, trying to ignore his sun on skin smell.

Why did he affect her so much, make her feel so ready to let down? Megan tried to sort through her own confusion. She kept trying to compare him to Jackson, but he didn't seem so much like that. Instead, he was so familiar to her in another way ...

Sam. That's right, he reminded her of Sam. Megan's eyebrows lifted. That's all it was. A yearning for home. But she'd never yearned for home, not even at college. She frowned. This didn't make sense. Well, it didn't have to, because it wasn't going to be anything. Like a mantra she repeated to herself: Be cool. Be distant. Nothing personal.

Bryant leaned over to Chalise and Brittany, then turned back to her. She tensed.

"So, heard anything about the movie?"

"Yes, it has subtitles, so you should be okay," she said. The sarcasm hung in the air. Megan swallowed. She was not handling this well. Couldn't the movie start already? Couldn't he smell like something other than ocean surf? Couldn't he be ugly?

Bryant stared steadily at her, eyes crinkling at the corners. He moved the soda straw toward himself, briefly touching her fingers in the exchange, then obviously wiped the top and sipped. It was a mimicking gesture. She got it and couldn't help a small grin. His laughing eyes knew she got it, which only irritated her more. They'd barely talked and now they were sharing private silent jokes?

Not going to happen, she reminded herself. Refusing to give him any other satisfaction, she stared defiantly at the blank movie screen.

Chad leaned forward in his seat. "I think it's a movie about these two people who like each other but can't get along, so they move farther and farther away, only to end up at the same place."

"It's a knock-off," said Megan. "Sounds like *The Great Divorce*."

"The what?" said Chad. "I haven't seen that one."

"It's not a movie," said Bryant, "it's a book. C.S. Lewis. The bus scene, right?" He turned to Megan.

She tried not to look impressed. "Did you read that on SparkNotes?"

"Actually, I read it all the way through, sounding out the big words."

A laugh escaped her, she couldn't help it. He just smiled as she took a few kernels of popcorn to cover her momentary lapse.

Leaning in closely, he half-whispered, "So, what's with the hostilities?"

His breath tickled her neck. She fought to ignore it. "Hostilities? I don't know what you're talking about. This is basic conversation."

He shook his head. "No, this is enemy territory. It's like talking with the Berlin Wall."

"The Berlin Wall? You *do* know it came down a few years ago?"

"Yeah, somehow you didn't get the memo." He offered the popcorn bag.

Yes, definitely like Sam. Pressing her lips to stifle another laugh, she reached over and scooped more kernels as a distraction. Their fingers touched momentarily again and she instinctively moved them away.

Be cool. He's just a cast member, Megan told herself. Talk normally. "Okay, I have a non-hostile question for you," she said.

"Shoot."

"Why the letter 't' at the end?"

"Of what?"

"Your name. Why not stick with Bryan?" She seriously wanted to know.

He paused, chewing and thinking. "Actually, in all my 27 years, no one has ever asked me that."

Twenty-seven? He was *27 years old?* What was he still doing singing on a cruise ship? Loud warning sounds blared in the back of her mind. Not your type. Be distant. *Run.*

"And exactly who do you hang out with?" she said.

"College jocks. Community Ed rejects. Power tripping construction workers."

"Well, that explains it. What did you major in, He-Man Welding?"

"No, Berlin—Mechanical Engineering. With a minor in Rec Management."

She shook her head. "I'm sorry, that's not a real minor. That's for people who can't do fractions, who live to river run until they die—I mean literally raft until they keel over into the river."

"That's the first I've heard it described that way." He settled farther down into the seat, his round muscular shoulder pressing against her smaller one. "So, Madame Curie, what's your major—Nuclear Physics?"

"Psychology," she said. What was she *doing?* Way too personal. Keep it distant. Rude. Sarcastic. Fight!

"And that is a *real* major?" he said. "It's the quickest degree you can get."

"It wasn't my first choice, but some of us have to put ourselves through school."

"I know how that goes," he said.

42

Surprised, Megan took that in. Beautiful surfer boy had to work to go to school? Softened momentarily by what it implied, she added, "I'd actually thought to go into law. But I don't like the industry. Then I considered counseling, but I work at a temp agency, which is a lot like counseling. You get tired of hearing people whine. You just want to tell them to suck it up and go to work."

"You're right. Counseling is not for you." He shook the bag for her. "And now, what are your plans?"

"I don't know," she said quietly.

Warning! Warning! Too close!

"Hypocrite. Here you seem all put together and you're not."

"So sue me." She looked at him. Putting a popcorn piece to her mouth, she stopped. Crackling. His blue eyes conducted an actual energy she could feel, sparking like a bright blue fire.

From her peripheral view, Megan saw Brittany lean forward—ostensibly to get something from her purse—and glance their way. Reflexively, Megan stuffed the entire handful of popcorn in her mouth then shoved both hands in her lap. She did *not* want anyone getting the wrong idea.

Someone asked Bryant a question from the row in front and he leaned forward. She tried not to notice the details; the ripple of his Polo shirt when he moved; the broadness of his shoulders, the profile of his forehead down to his jaw.

The room went dark and the opening trailer began. "Man, these bags are small. More popcorn, anyone?" said Bryant as he stood up.

Turning, his foot caught in Megan's purse loop and he almost went down, saving himself by putting both hands on either side of Megan's seat, but with the rest of his popcorn landing squarely in her lap.

"Oh, sorry about that—" but he was trying not to laugh as he said it, his face only inches from hers in the movie light. Trying to move, he stepped on her open toes.

"Ouch!" said Megan, trying to move and only getting closer to his face.

The row behind him called out—"Yo, get down," and, "Get a room, this is the good part."

"It's the credits, give me a break," said Bryant. In the dark he whispered, "Sorry, Megan."

Hearing him speak her name—unreasonably, a string of goose bumps flashed up her spine. She shook her head to clear her mind, which he took differently and apologized again, finally extricating himself from the situation.

Foregoing the extra popcorn, he sat down and let it be, although she heard him chuckle a few minutes later, which seemed to have nothing to do with the movie.

Round One Bryant. Megan set her lips in a tight line. This was not how things were to go. She was here to work, to focus, to heal. Not to think about blond men with laughing, sparking blue eyes. That was it. Rein it in. Refocus.

Round Two would be hers.

In the early morning sunlight, Megan glanced from side to side, double checked she was alone, and opened the metal pool house door. A smile stole across her face. She had outwitted him.

Since the Cinema Fiasco yesterday, she had purposely made herself scarce. Or tried to, except that Bryant seemed to be everywhere.

After rehearsal she had hurried off to nowhere in particular, ending up at a gift shop and admiring a beautiful swimsuit. Funny that she'd even noticed it, she hadn't bought something new in a while. The colors had drawn her—a mix of soft peach, hot pink, and fresh white—and the cut was modest but pretty, like something she used to wear. A long time ago.

As Megan had held it, debating the ridiculous price but duty-free benefit, Bryant materialized on the other side of the rack. For some reason she had turned a bright pink and quickly headed to the cash register without looking back. Was it just a coincidence he was there? But if it wasn't, why would he be seeking her out? It wasn't like she was encouraging him. Because she *didn't want* to encourage him.

Right?

Megan had spent the rest of the afternoon trying not to look for him, when she realized she was doing it again. Falling into the same trap, leaping before she looked, just because someone seemed *so* nice. No, the safe thing to do was to stay distant, disconnected, not opening any emotional door in the slightest.

Then yesterday evening while the rest of the cast enjoyed a pool party, she'd opted to jog on the indoor treadmills. Engrossed in her book, she hadn't even noticed who was running on the machine next to her until she smelled an ocean and sand scent and looked up. There he was, smiling that smile—confident, almost arrogant. Like he knew her, knew her feelings, her struggle to act one way but that she felt another. For just a moment looking at him and his sharp blue eyes, she had felt raw, exposed. How did he do that? Afraid he had seen too much, she punched the stop button, grabbed her book and towel, and walked away.

Megan had run Emergency Exit stairs to work off the frustration. How did he know her like that when she tried so hard to stay detached? Why wouldn't he let her be—let her curl up and be alone? Yet at the same time something inside her yearned for him, his solidness, his openness. Then just as real came the fear, the out of control feeling that she would lose herself again. Her heart had already begun the Yo-Yo cycle of interested/not interested.

Without warning, Jackson's smiling face flashed through her mind. She'd felt the same way at the start, that compulsive pull toward him. And it had begun innocently enough, too. He'd pursued her but not in a pushy way. All along he'd made it easy and before she knew what was happening they were a couple, and her mom was hinting wedding bells at the Tuesday ladies' lunch.

Megan frowned. Jackson had made her believe it was love. But it had been like getting the measles when you were older, and it had hit her hard. The game had been so natural to him, one that he played well, and enjoyed. She, on the other hand, had to fight for every bit of understanding her emotions, avoiding them since her parents' divorce. And now she was paying the price.

But this time, she was smarter, right? She did have more control. And she would not be pulled in to another possible Jackson.

This morning, she had decided to change it up altogether, to be her bold self and swim. But early. Opening night was tonight and she was anxious to be well-rested for it. And she would avoid Bryant, especially in swimwear.

Jillian had said, "You're on a cruise ship. He's going to see you in a swimsuit. Though honestly, I have no idea why you care, as you'd look gorgeous in a paper bag."

Megan couldn't explain the truth—the swimsuit rating scale, the way Jackson had looked at her sometimes when she wore one.

She fought down a burst of humiliation. Men.

Well, she wasn't going to give up being herself and the swimming she loved, but she would do it on her own terms. Alone. Quickly resurveying the empty echo-sounding pool room, Megan took off her cover up just as the door banged open.

"Top o' the mornin'," Bryant said, walking straight to where she stood.

Not possible!

Furious, Megan stared in open anger at his face, trying to ignore his taught bare chest as he put down his key and took off the towel from around his neck.

He looked up at her. Megan flushed involuntarily, feeling practically naked. With his arrogant smile he said, "About that swimsuit—"

That's it. Megan felt something lash out from inside. She didn't care what she said, that knowing smirk was going to get wiped off his face.

"All right, surfer boy, let's get this straight, right off. I'm not Talia, okay, or Mahalia, or Brittany, or even Betty Boop. This is what a real woman's body looks like, it's got some curves to it, and it's not drug-addict thin. It's strong, and supple, and healthy, and about mid-day it gets a little poof right here around the middle no matter how many sit ups you do. So just to be clear—I will never have a bimbo body and I'm sick of hearing and feeling like I need to. And if you think you can sit in judgment like one of those bachelorette shows, let me tell you, buddy, you are—you are wronger than wrong."

"Wronger than wrong?"

46

"That's right, and I don't care how bad the grammar is. So long as we understand each other. And whatever little comment you were about to make, you can just swallow it, right along with your whale-size ego."

Megan's chest rose and fell but he just stood there. Then he picked up his towel. "I was just going to say that your price tag is still on." He took his key and walked out.

Megan looked down and sure enough on her shoulder strap was a price tag for $69.99. She wanted to crawl under the ship.

Megan walked cautiously toward the Green Room, checking her watch. She was a good forty-five minutes early, giving her time to dress and think of a sincere apology for Bryant, but without making her sound too vulnerable, or interested, but appropriately remorseful. She was sorry and embarrassed but she dreaded talking with him face to face. How could she even begin to explain her behavior?

Gurgles sounded in her tummy—she couldn't tell if it was from nerves for the evening or from her thoughts. Opening the door she stopped short—Bryant turned in the folding chair, holding a letter, his expression was as shocked as hers.

"What are you doing here?" said Megan, unable to withhold it. Of course she wanted to apologize, but first to figure out what to say.

"Do I need a reservation?"

"No, but for heaven's sakes, you don't need a lot of—" she was about to say makeup but it sounded strange—"costume changing."

"I wanted to think, some peace and quiet." With his foot he pushed out a chair for her to sit on.

Megan debated—each interaction so far had been way too close despite her best attempts to stay distant. Cold and distant was not her usual way. Pretending to be was even harder. Especially with him. For months she'd been able to stiff arm any feelings she didn't want to feel but he had a way of softening her, without her permission. Then, remembering her need to apologize for the Swimsuit Incident, she instantly felt contrite. But then, wasn't she supposed to be winning Round Two? Sarcasm and fight?

Okay, contrite was good. But with an edge of sarcasm. Right after she apologized. Megan sighed inwardly. Before she could confuse herself further, she strode to the chair. She'd just have to wing this. "Peace and quiet? And you can't find that in a four-person bunk room?"

"Exactly."

"Who's the letter from—one of your many adoring fans?"

"All over sixty." He looked at the letter. "Just my family." Again, the bitterness.

"And they still write actual letters? It has to be from your mother." His expression remained pensive so she stopped being light. "Is it bad news?"

He folded up the letter and stuffed it back in the envelope. "No, it's not bad, not for them at least. It's about my post-cruise life."

"So after the summer dancing extravaganza, you go back to a real job like the rest of us?"

"Why, is your temp agency hiring?"

"No, I mean cruise singing is great and all that, but don't you want to graduate from the Mickey Mouse Club?"

Too sarcastic. She knew as soon as she said it. He just looked at her.

"Sorry." And she meant it. What was it about him that made her defenses go on alert? She took an imperceptible breath. It was now or never.

"Bryant, about earlier . . ." For a moment the thought came to her that she liked saying his name. "About the swimsuit diatribe . . ."

His mouth upturned slightly.

"I don't know how to explain this, but, it had nothing to do with you. As if you couldn't tell."

"Yeah, I think I got that message."

Megan smiled deprecatingly. "For some reason, I don't know, well, I kind of do, but it's hard to explain, that I feel sometimes, let's say the tiniest bit hostile toward you." She could feel her face reddening, which made her speak faster. "Which is very odd because that's not my nature, really. And I find myself saying or doing very unusual things, that don't make sense to you, I'm sure, and most of the time not even to me." She blew out a small breath, watching his confused face. "There's just so much that I wish I could explain that would make sense why I said what I did. But I just can't." Megan wanted to add *not yet* but simply shook her head. "You're . . . a really nice guy." She felt the redness spread to her ears. "And I am sorry for being rude. And treating you like a disease. And making you feel like you're always doing something wrong." Megan paused. "Did I miss anything?"

"No, I think you've hit them pretty much on the head." He leaned forward. "I don't want anything from you, Megan. Just a chance to get to know you. So if we can call a truce, I'm all for it."

"A truce, yes. Getting to know me, I'm not so sure." It had been said with a lightness but she could see his expression. He knew a five-minute conversation wouldn't lower her guard that much. "Anyway, I wanted to assure you, I'm working on eliminating all hostile responses. Truce officially signed." She held out her hand.

He took it and held it a moment longer than needed. Megan could feel his warmth and that flutter something went through her again. Immediately, she let go. Eyes on the letter in his other hand, she switched tracks.

"You were telling me about your fan club?"

Bryant leaned his elbows on his knees, a darker expression on his face. "Ah, the family. They have plans for me. And they're anxious for me to get back to them."

"Plans like 'American Idol'?"

He smiled, but it was thin. "My family owns a lumber yard in northern California, *very* exciting career. And every letter they talk about two things: one of them being, when I will come home and take over the yard."

"I knew you were from California. So you surf?"

"*Northern* California. By Mount Shasta. And I've never surfed in my life."

"Are you serious? But you look so, so surfer guy."

"I'll be sure to hang ten on the stage."

Megan crossed one leg over the other. "But isn't that a good deal, having a built-in job waiting for you?"

"It's a dead-end—no future. If I step one serious foot in the door, I'll never get out. Then I'll be just like my dad."

Megan wasn't sure how to take that. "Is that a bad thing?"

He stared at the letter. "Not bad, just stuck in lumber. That's his dream, not mine. Well, not that you'd call it a dream."

Sensing a hot button, Megan switched topics. "So, what's the second thing they talk about in the letter?"

Bryant turned his head, staring at her in a "Hello?" way.

"Oh. The M-word." Megan tried not to act awkward. "Well, it sounds like your family cares a lot about you—securing a job, marriage. And you're being a dutiful son."

He spoke woodenly. "Forced respect. I got this job through my mom's friend, she's also big on the job and marriage combo." Megan felt the bitter current running through his voice. "They both think it's a great plan, and are pretty much vocal about it whenever they can be."

"That can be tough when two women are maneuvering you."

"Mom and Mrs. Weller are not just two women, they're national governments. The term movers and shakers doesn't even come close."

She looked at him sharply. "Weller?"

He nodded, a wry look on his face. "Brittany's mother."

"Got it." Megan didn't know where to look. Brittany's mother was involved? Talk about complex. This little soap opera had Train Wreck written all over it. "So, Dad wants you at the yard, Mom wants you at the altar. What do you want?"

He shrugged. "Don't know. Trying to figure it out."

She stiffened. Red warning signals flashed all over her head. Twenty-seven years old and still singing on a cruise ship. Peter Pan Syndrome. Can't commit.

"You seem a little old to be undecided."

He looked up, his face darkening again. "Am I on a schedule?"

"No, but I'd think you'd want to be. Unless your income is supplemented." She had tried to be funny, but it hung in the air like frozen icicles.

Bryant narrowed his eyes, his voice suddenly strong and bullish. "I told you, I'm here to please my parents. My mom sends me here," he glanced around "to find a wife, like it's an option on the buffet line. She thinks marriage will settle me down. My sister tells me. My brother tells me." Bryant rapped the letter, his eyes hard. "They all think this little show place is great for me. And once I've settled down, it gets even better—I get to take over the lumber yard full-time. Wow, what a life. I hate it but it makes them happy, so for the duration, I'm here and making the best of it."

Instinctively, Megan knew the outburst had nothing to do with her. But she'd seen that same face and heard that same tone from a hundred temp workers. She sat up facing him squarely. "I don't know about your life, Bryant, and I'm sure you have your reasons. But where I come from, there are a lot of people without a job. And in fact, if they had a job, or even an entire lumber yard for the asking, they wouldn't be so quick to thumb their nose at it."

"What are you saying, I'm spoiled?" He leaned in toward her.

"No, but it sounds like you have a good family who want what's best for you. And honestly, I'm racking my brain trying to figure out why you don't jump at the chance. You're of age, and it seems like a sweet deal that's ready made for you."

"Because maybe you don't see the big picture." He shook his head in disgust. "Just like my parents."

She paused, then stood up to leave, afraid she was too far into Temp Agency mode. "I'm sorry, Bryant, I'm sure I've misunderstood."

"No, you have something to say, say it."

Megan had seen this attitude before, a hundred times, and it grated on her nerves. Privileged guy, easy money, ready-made job and still whining about the injustices of life. She'd seen plenty of real injustices, of families scraping to feed their kids. But she didn't want to get sucked into this conversation, not when she'd just apologized to make everything right. "It's just, that must be it," she said lightly. "Everybody else sees it wrong."

He rose too, all chest and shoulders in front of her, not content to let her walk, like he wanted to explain. "It's not as simple as it seems. You think I haven't thought these things through, like I'm some idiot with a microphone who doesn't think ahead to next week? I *know* the reality of what they're asking. And once I commit, the rest of my life is history, as well as my choices. I've seen my dad on that road and where it goes. No thanks."

Standing this close, Megan could feel his body heat but ignored it as she gave into Temp Agency assistant. "Bryant, all I'm saying is grown-ups do grown-up things, like move on purposefully with their lives, without a guarantee of fulfillment. You've obviously got some great options. Of course it would make someone wonder why you're not taking them. But blaming others for not moving forward, or that they'll pigeon-hole you for life doesn't sound fair. Or mature."

Bryant's blue eyes sparked, partly in anger but almost energized by her challenge. He searched her face for an instant before replying. "Wise words. But they don't sound like they're just for me, do they? What about you? Are you really here for the sun and stardom, or is there something you're blaming for not moving forward? Or don't want to face?"

Stunned, Megan flushed with the reality of it and for a moment, couldn't say anything. His words sounded too much like what she'd heard from Jillian. Had he been talking to her? Not likely. Awed and angered by his awareness, she wanted to scream—leave me alone!

"What do you even know of me?" she shot back fiercely.

"I'm guessing a lot more than you'll let me." He took her in—eyes, mouth, soul—making her feel wide open and shy at the same time. She rebelled at the connection between them, at the precise moment she yearned for it.

No, thought Megan desperately. Fight! "Look, I'm not trying to be rude but—"

"No need to try." He wore a wry smile. "I asked for your opinion and you gave it." Without breaking his steady gaze, he stepped into her. "Megan—"

Her name—that warm liquid honey spread through her and she felt herself losing. "Don't. Don't say my name—like that." She had to stop him, it was too close, too raw. This conversation was all over the place, moving too fast on too many levels. Megan scrambled to understand what was happening, feeling herself falling into something she promised herself not to. Any second now she would throw her arms around his neck and kiss him and hold him and tell him everything. What was *wrong* with her? FIGHT, Megan.

"Bryant, I don't—"

The door opened. One of the cast girls entered then stopped. "Um, sorry. Am I bugging you guys here?"

Suddenly Megan felt acutely aware of how close they stood together, breath rising and falling, energy intense and electric. How had she gotten here, standing with him, talking like this?

Megan turned, her face hot. "No, I was just leaving." She nodded at Bryant, who looked as if he wanted to say something then thought better of it.

In the restroom, Megan splashed cool water on her burning face. What had just happened? Her heart continued to beat irregularly, and she drew a few calming breaths to settle herself down. Replaying the conversation in her mind, she couldn't understand how quickly it had escalated. More than that, how close she felt to Bryant, how natural it felt to talk that way together, as if they'd known each other for years.

Thoughts blazed in her mind of his intense face and solid body, pulsing and pulling her in, an astonishing electric current between them. That connection—how did he do that, his way of being with her, knowing her.

Megan splashed more water on her face.

Apology? Now she had bigger things to worry about.

CHAPTER FIVE

Bryant brought down the barbell to his chest, then pushed up again, hard and fast, holding for four counts before returning it to the rack above him. It felt good to work out the frustration, at least of the encounter with Megan. He still couldn't ease the confusing thoughts.

He had spent that afternoon performance between trying to forget their heated conversation and ignore feeling drawn to her. What was up with him? Why did he care? She didn't even show interest. No, not even a lack of interest. An intense hostile dislike, she had said so herself.

Until today.

Standing in the Green Room, he could still see her flushed cheeks and serious brown eyes as she read him the riot act of Get on With Your Life. And she had been right. Actually, she had sounded and looked just like his sister. But different. He definitely did not view her as a sister.

From the beginning he'd been drawn to her, but not in the typical way. Obviously, she was pretty—that was a given—but not in the Premier Performer style. In his mind he saw her straight chestnut hair, glossy in the sun, framing her face usually devoid of makeup. He liked it. It was fresh and real, not like what he was usually around. She had talent, yes, but not real star potential. And had a way about her that was soft, when she wasn't aware he was watching. Talking in the hall with Rosa, helping Marvy with boxes, practicing the salsa with him. When she let down her guard, she was the real Megan, he could feel it.

The salsa. He smiled, thinking about the way she'd fought him at first, then relaxed, then given in. The feel of her waist, her moving with him, the way she'd upturned her face and made the Fred Astaire comment before thinking.

Bryant lifted the barbell and did another set of repetitions. Without guile. That's how he really saw her, even though she did her best to show him a colder side. Strange that he remembered the phrase from the Bible. Stranger still that this girl who tortured him daily made him think of it. But at times, he could feel it, had felt it from the moment he saw her on the dock. Bryant shook his head, replacing the barbell again. She was a study in contradictions, most of the time like she was almost afraid. But that didn't make sense as he knew she had spunk, and plenty of it. So what was she afraid of? And why was she here on a cruise ship? His comment in the Green Room about blaming something, or someone, had definitely hit a nerve. This trip was more than a favor to a friend. It had to be something about a guy, or maybe her family, but what? Whatever it was kept her at arm's length, at least with him.

Sitting up, Bryant towel dried his face, pensive and bugged. It was still there, that gnawing confusion about her and the need to know, to find out the truth. Why he felt so driven, he had no idea. But he cared about her, that was for sure, more than he'd felt before and in a different way than other girls. They all seemed the same—giggling, over-pleasing, and without their own thoughts. Something beyond his understanding was definitely there with Megan—almost compulsive between them—despite her outward rejection of him. It bugged him and attracted him at the same time, a challenge and an aggravation. And yet he had to be careful. Too strong too soon and that would be it.

Bryant blew out a breath of frustration. All he knew was that until he got the real Megan, he couldn't leave it alone.

A few hours later, several of the cast stood on the side stage peeking through the velvet burgundy curtains at the evening audience. Nervous energy vibrated through the cast, many of them standing in twos and threes, chatting excitedly, touching up makeup, or adjusting their costumes. Mrs. Van De Morelle had been rumored to attend, but it hadn't been confirmed.

"People, people, this is so unprofessional," said Marvy, shooing them away, then turned and peeked through the slit in the side curtain.

Megan approached stage right, hesitating, trying to act natural. Automatically, she scanned for Bryant but was relieved not to find him. Since the Green Room Incident, she had vaguely seen him twice, both times acting as if she hadn't. It was utterly juvenile, of course, but her insides jumped like fighting cats. She couldn't focus on being mature. A dangerously close connection lay open between them, like cut live wires lying close to each other. It didn't take much to make a spark and she would have to be so very careful. Several times random moments from their encounter had replayed in her mind. The rawness of it, the sharing of such personal things so freely and unrestrained. And the feelings. It unnerved her that they could connect so quickly so deeply, but she couldn't stop to think about why. Right now she needed to get through the performance without a mistake. Clint had announced tonight they would do the salsa: apparently, he was feeling more confidence in Megan. More than she felt at any rate.

Jillian hurried to Megan, fixing a hair piece. "Can you believe we have a full house opening night? That never happens. Usually everyone is too enamored with sightseeing to bother with us." She put in another bobby pin. "In a few days they'll be full on both time slots, mostly snoring in the back, but, oh well. It's an audience. You look great by the way."

Megan touched her skirt self-consciously. The white and silver form-fitting dress had slits up the side to just above the knee—this was, after all, a family-friendly tour. But still, she felt partially dressed. Jillian had done Megan's chestnut hair in an updo and dramatic makeup, and despite feeling part streetwalker, part supermodel, she had to admit Jillian had done an amazing job. The cast energy began to touch her, and Megan looked forward to being part of something big. At least it would help her move beyond what was, to start creating memories of a new life, and to push the old Megan far, far away.

Walking gingerly in her dance shoes so as not to make a sound, she carefully made her way to the first song position. En route, she saw Bryant enter from the opposite side heading in her direction. He was carrying a few costume head dresses alongside Brittany, who chattered on about something, and put them down on the stage where she pointed. After exchanging a few more words, he stood up and scanned the stage for something. Or someone?

His eyes rested on Megan and moved on, then immediately came back. Surprise, but a pleasant one, showed on his face, enough that Brittany stopped talking and looked in the same direction.

Megan continued walking to her spot near them. "Break a leg, guys," she said, in a voice more confident than she felt. The outfit had made her bold. Even as she took her mark and heard Marvy tell everyone quietly to get into position, she could feel two pairs of eyes staring at her: Bryant's and Brittany's.

A loud drum roll and the first bars of the opening sequence played on the minus track as the heavy velvet curtain opened. Megan was shocked to see and hear 150 people clapping just for them—she had forgotten how this felt. The sharp beat started and they began. The first two numbers went almost flawlessly, and by the last three she had finally felt her rhythm and begun enjoying it. But in the back of her mind there remained a silent dread about the salsa number. Only two more to go.

Bryant and Brittany's big number came next. Watching them in performance mode surprised her. Always there had been a practiced quality about what they did, even in the dress rehearsal, as if they'd been holding back. Now, with his hands on her hips, moving her from spot to spot, leaning into her, turning and swooping, Megan felt uncomfortable, though she knew it was silly. Only that she immediately thought of Bryant and her doing the salsa on stage, alone, with his hands on her hips.

When he started singing his solo directly to Brittany, his warm baritone voice clear and compelling, a pang of jealousy pierced sharp between her breast bone. Annoyed she could react to it at all, Megan reminded herself it was his job and focused on a piece of back scenery for the rest of their number.

Salsa beats brought her back to the present and everyone began taking their positions. Megan breathed deeply—if she could get through this, it would set the tone for the tour.

The music came on, the loud Latin beat pulsating in the room. Everyone began moving in synchronicity and Bryant caught Megan's eye just before she passed him. For a millisecond she froze, but unbelievably he winked, his expression saying, "You can do this." It wasn't like nothing had happened earlier—it was like he was enlivened by it in some bizarre way. Megan pushed it out of her mind and attended to the moment. The dance, the number. This was vital.

Building up to the X-crossing, she almost held her breath but unwittingly thought back to how Bryant had led her—his directions, his clarity. Out of necessity, she pretended he was her partner as Garrett took her and together twisted and turned across the stage, gloriously making it through without a hitch.

Relief!

The rest of the song was a happy blur. Turning once again, she saw Bryant and without thinking, winked back at him. For a moment they shared a suspended look—an understood feeling of secret success—then moved to their positions.

A bird-like feeling swept through her, light and happy. The connection between Bryant and her was, for the moment, normal. She hadn't blown the performance. The applause was consistent and genuine. Just the finale to go.

They all lined up in position. Megan saw Brittany turn and check her costume hem, glancing back at her as she did so.

The music began and they all moved into positions, singing and weaving in formation in two lines. Brittany and Bryant shared the center stage with two other performers, and moved in and out of circles as they sang a 1920's Broadway belter.

Like a slow-motion nightmare, it happened.

In mid-turn Megan inexplicably tripped over a girl's shoe, stumbling over the person beside her. They went down hard, colliding with Tag who spun and took Brittany and one other girl down with him. The remaining cast on stage stood paralyzed, not sure what to do. The minus track still played.

Bryant moved quickly and did an emphatic Charlie Chaplin gesture of shock and surprise. Overacting, he flung out an arm down to the pile. Megan caught on and jumped up, one hand taking his, the other expressively slapped over her mouth in an "Oh!" expression, her leg playfully kicked out behind her. The other members played along and swung back into places to the

1920's music. A hesitant, then stronger applause followed. The audience believed it to be part of the act.

Now dancing, Bryant and Megan exchanged concerned looks. He spun her off to a side position and took up Brittany to finish the number on time. Breathing heavily, with a panic only cast and crew would recognize, everyone took their bows for an enthusiastic crowd.

Post-performance backstage, a dull roar of conversation filled the Green Room. When Marvy and Clint entered with painful smiles—his toupee sliding from the sweat ring on his forehead—the group quieted down. Then Bryant followed in behind. The place erupted in applause: "Nice," and "Sweet save, Bryant," popped around the room. Megan retreated to the back corner, confused at what had happened but applauding too. He truly had saved the performance.

"C'mon, kudos to everyone"—he shook his head—"especially Megan. Where is she?" All eyes rubber-necked the room. Bryant walked straight to her and put an arm around her shoulders, his expression approving and kind. "This little lady knows how to improv. Give it up for Megan."

Flushing what she knew to be a brilliant red, she nevertheless felt warmed by his praise, especially after their earlier encounter. Until she saw Brittany's face. There was the sentinel smile but her eyes didn't match it. As if a cold front passed through her lungs.

Brittany.

A flash of memory came to her—a peroxide blonde had turned into her on the dance floor. Megan could see it in her mind, like a slow movie reel— Brittany glancing back at Megan; then in formation, then in front of Megan, *but she wasn't supposed to be there.* Megan's mouth opened. It was Brittany's shoe—she had moved into the wrong position, right in front of Megan. But why? Had it been an accident or to trip her up? Could she actually *do* something like that? No, that didn't make sense. Brittany was a nice girl. And what threat was Megan to her? Megan could barely sing a note and hardly dance as well as the worst of them. It had to be an accident.

As soon as she thought it, Megan considered Bryant's affectionate grip and matched it with Brittany's steely gaze.

Trouble. She could feel it to her toes.

Megan frowned as she slipped into the tangerine colored mermaid style dress. Why did she care what she looked like? Already she had spent an unheard of thirty minutes on makeup and hair, never mind the time on choosing a dress and jewelry. Thankfully, Jillian had come to the rescue on all fronts.

Putting on the silver evening shoes, Megan felt ridiculous. It was just a Cast Meet & Greet. In the middle of the afternoon, no less. But, when duty called . . . She tried not to think about who would be there—the Knockout and the Nemesis. She still wasn't sure the role Brittany had played in the performance fiasco a few nights before, or the scuttlebutt between her and Bryant. But something didn't feel right, that much was sure. And before the week was out, she was going to find out what it was.

Jillian put on a white slip. "You go on ahead of me, I'm meeting Derek," she said, then grinned. "You look fantastic, Megs. I'm guessing all this work isn't just for the passengers."

"Marvy said we needed to look our best—'showy' was her exact word." Megan put lipstick and mints in the small evening purse, trying not to blush. "Besides, the passengers expect something special."

"So does somebody else." Jillian smiled mischievously.

How much did Jillian know? Megan considered telling her about the Green Room encounter but shook her head, cursing Jillian's continual sixth sense about her and men. Of course she had noticed something, Jillian noticed everything. "Will you ixnay the matchmaking, all right? I'm honestly not interested."

"Sure, uh huh." Jillian wriggled into her dress, ignoring Megan's tone. "In fact, aside from your tan, I'd say you were practically glowing. Any particular reason?"

"I don't glow." She gave Jillian a look and headed out the door. Walking through the hallways, Megan hoped the party would be uneventful. For her and Bryant it had been a few days of studied avoidance. And she wanted to keep it that way.

Entering the fluorescent-lit concierge room, Megan searched for familiar faces. Rumors flew that Mrs. Van De Morelle was to attend, but as usual, no one knew for sure. Megan's eyes stopped near a beautifully arranged seating area set off by clusters of silk palm trees. Brittany stood in a stunning baby blue strapless dress set off against her tanned flawless skin and platinum blonde hair. She shimmered like a Barbie doll, so unreal it was mesmerizing, surrounded by three eager young men already.

Megan reflexively touched her hair and began wondering if she should have worn the lavender dress.

The room practically swam in food, surprising Megan with the effort made for the cast. Elegant plates and tea stands teemed with food—petite four sandwiches, chocolates shaped like elaborate seashells, and fruit cut into complex sculptures. Glass pitchers of brightly colored lemonades stood in rows, all with condensation running down the sides.

Most of the cast and crew had already arrived, standing in a roughly formed half-crescent between banquet tables. Many were already in conversation with early passengers—loud touristy types and hefty couples from the Midwest—all coming to say thank you, and, she guessed, for the midday delectable. The next buffet didn't start for another hour.

Megan walked toward them feeling self-conscious in her form-fitting dress and wondered if others would think she'd dressed for a particular someone. But it was too late now.

"Is this new?" Bryant's voice came over her shoulder, giving her unexpected and unwelcome goose bumps. She steeled herself and turned to him.

"It's required dress." Megan tried to be aloof but could feel her face warm with his appreciative look.

He stared at her. "You look amazing."

"Who knew?"

"I always knew," he said, but turned to look at someone calling him. "It's about time you showed it."

Though he moved away, she kept that comment, and took it out in turns all evening.

"I always knew," he had said. Knew what? That she looked amazing—that's what he had said. And that he had always known it, despite her dressing and acting completely to the contrary. This unwitting transparency bothered her. How many other things did he know about her that she tried to hide?

Chalise approached Megan, who stood at the outer rim of cast members, eyeing her gorgeous dress and updo hair. "You look especially phenomenal. Anything going on?"

Before Megan could respond, she was aware of Jillian by her side, slightly breathless from obviously hurrying to be on time. "She's hoping to attract a certain person's attention."

"*I am not*," said Megan.

Jillian rolled her eyes as Chalise asked, "Who?"

"Hottie Bryant Boy," said Jillian, "the man with the golden six-pack abs and voice that could melt butter."

Talia had entered the conversation, drawn to what the buzz was about. "Bryant? Man oh man, he is a catch. But I thought he and Brittany were on."

"Not a chance," said Chalise, glancing over at Bryant. "That's all over with. At least I'm almost positive. He's a catch all right—but nothing next to Garrett of course—and half the cast is after him, from what I understand. But he doesn't give them much encouragement that way. Must have someone back home."

Jillian ignored Megan's insistent warning looks. "No encouragement except to our Megs, to whom he seems *particularly* attentive."

Chalise and Talia looked with new interest at Megan, who shook her head vehemently and said, "You know that is absolute gossip, cruise talking—"

"—actually, I think you're right." Chalise turned to Jillian, staring thoughtfully. "He sure does seem friendly to her, now that I think about it."

"He's friendly with everyone," said Megan automatically. "Besides, we're not allowed to date cast members."

Almost as one, the three of them laughed. Talia said, "Fifteen marriages and counting. And don't think for a minute that isn't part of Clint and Marvy's hidden agenda."

"Although none of that after-hours nonsense," said Chalise seriously. "They don't put up with that at all."

62

Talia picked up the thread. "But you're right, Megan, Bryant is a friendly guy, with pretty much everyone."

"Not as friendly as Garrett, of course," said Chalise, moving to the line while Megan followed slowly behind. She tried maneuvering for a spot as far away from Bryant as possible but landed five people from him.

Throughout the afternoon, she tried not to notice Bryant's professional but warm demeanor as adoring passengers swarmed him. She was impressed, despite not wanting to be. He had a kind manner, and was infinitely patient with the older ladies, like the one speaking loudly with him now, who seemed to eat him up like butter mints. Megan leaned slightly closer on the pretense of talking with others.

"I hate bingo," the lady was saying, "and all this rich food. It's not good for my figure." She beamed at Bryant. "I used to dance, you know. I was a New Jersey Nets Senior Sensation and all that."

"Is that right?" said Bryant.

"Hired me at seventy-two they did, when I could still do the splits. And I still can too, but just not every halftime." She patted her gray, tightly curled hair. "It served its purpose—got me out of bed when Reggie died, to be sure. Now my daughter sends me on these cruises. It's supposed to be an Under 75-Over 65 Swinging Singles cruise, did you know that?" Bryant shook his head. "Oh yes," she leaned closer, "but I think some people are lying about their age. You can't tell me some of these men are under 75." Bryant laughed outright.

Brittany—who stood four or more people beyond him—turned in Bryant's direction, catching Megan's eyes in the same glance.

A gentleman interrupted Megan. "Are you the lovely little lady who dances in the follies show?" Megan automatically nodded and shook his hand. A spry gray-haired man, he wore a bright yellow bowtie and fitted Italian suit. He must have been close to eighty.

"I'm glad you enjoyed the show, thanks for coming," said Megan. She experienced that watched feeling again and glanced in its direction. From down the way Bryant stared at her over the tops of heads as the woman dug in her purse for a moment.

Megan turned back to the gentleman. Something seemed familiar. "Do I know—wait a minute, do you use the treadmills?"

He broke into a toothy smile that had to be the best dentures money could buy. "That's me. Thirty minutes every day. Arthritis and two hip replacements can't stop me. Used to ballroom dance too"—he swiveled his hips—"but you just can't find a good partner these days. All the women are too tired." He raised his eyebrows in a flirtatious gesture.

Megan laughed and chatted for a few more minutes until he moved down the informal lineup. Watching him leave she caught Bryant's eye again. He was talking but looked at her, then *looked* at her, and turned back to his conversation. Megan shivered from the top of her spine to her toes. That look would be the death of her—focused, packed with some kind of energy. But what did it mean? She saw past his shoulder to Brittany's face who then turned back to the line.

As the loud woman moved on, Bryant made as if to walk over to Megan. She panicked for no convincing reason and slipped to the lemonade table on the pretense of getting a drink. Thankfully, Bryant was intercepted by another adoring fan.

Pouring herself a drink of raspberry something, Megan half-listened to the conversations around her, thinking through her confusing reactions to Bryant. One moment a shiver, the next pure panic.

Why couldn't she figure out these emotions? And why did she feel so comfortable around him, so ready to let down when only her white knuckle vigilance kept her from doing so? He was so easy to be with. But that was friendly Bryant, wasn't it? He was a Premier Performer, this is how they behaved, why they were successful. It was acting, or playing games—they were on a cruise ship, after all.

But being around him didn't feel like an act. It just felt . . . good, like a best friend. Like Sam. At least, when she wasn't being hostile. But that was her only protection. And yet, it wasn't working. It only seemed to provoke more annoying attention.

Megan sighed and sipped her drink. An acquaintance. Yes, that was the best way to respond to him. Chad was an acquaintance, and thoroughly pleasant while hardly saying two words. That would work, Megan nodded to herself. Okay, no more hostility. Her best defense was Courteous Acquaintance. Bryant was merely a distant, casual co-worker. Who just happened to be an easygoing, enjoyable person to talk to, when she wasn't being rude and annoying. And a caramel blond, six-pack ab-sporting, butter-melting male.

Stop it. You are not interested in anyone or anything right now, except peace, rest, and getting your life back after this tour.

Resolved, Megan glanced over the cast in line, resting finally on Brittany. Brittany Shay Weller, star Premier Performer, and seemingly nice person. Possibly. How serious had it really been between her and Bryant? Jillian said that Brittany had been making wedding plans. That was pretty serious. A fingerling of nausea crept through her stomach. She knew wedding plans could be a universe away from actually getting married. But what had he felt? And still felt? Sometimes he and Brittany seemed so professional, without any feeling at all. At others, the way Brittany looked at him, gazed at him, made Megan wonder.

Of course, it could just be Brittany's competitiveness to be on the Intrepid. Or it could be Megan's imagination.

At that moment, Brittany crossed over to Bryant, both of them shaking hands with a familiar passenger standing with Marvy, all laughing at some shared information. Megan stared for a moment at the happy comfortable trio, all bedecked and sparkling.

Sudden and heavy, a sinking truth hit the bottom of her stomach. Megan breathed in to soften it. Who was she kidding? She could play dress up but the reality was, she didn't fit in. Beautiful people like them shone in this cruise world—she didn't. She belonged with a tennis racket, or a book. Or real and familiar friends.

With the scene like a snapshot in her mind, Megan put down the drink as a hard place in her throat started to form. Abruptly, she turned to leave and bumped into a corpulent woman draped in expensive jewelry standing by the door. She gave Megan a peculiar smile.

"I'm so sorry," Megan said.

"No harm done, I'd have done the same, trying to be coy with a catch like him." She glanced at Bryant.

"A catch—no, I'm—I was just thirsty, that's all," said Megan but she stopped, feeling the woman's candid expression. These nosy, elderly women.

"Bryant is a catch, and good as gold," she said, folding reading glasses.

"Oh, do you know him?" said Megan, not knowing what else to say.

"Oh yes, we go back a few years. But you're new. You're the girl who fell in the show last night."

Megan gaped. "How did you know that?" She really did not like this woman.

"Oh, don't take it personally, we notice everything. Especially the fact that Bryant's been watching you for about thirty minutes, wherever you are in the room. Did you know that?"

"No—I mean, how did you—" Of all the tactless . . .

"—he's got loads of girls after him, I'm sure. Most particularly one, I would imagine."

"That's absolutely fine with me. Birds of a feather," said Megan, feeling heated. She was done with Nosy Woman. "Superficial lavish environments draw a certain type, don't you think? If you'll excuse me—" She wanted to leave, right now, before the threatening tears came to the front.

The woman only chuckled and adjusted her diamond encrusted necklace, making no room for Megan to pass. "Take my unasked-for advice, don't waste a minute. He's got a good eye."

The woman shrewdly surveyed the room then stared hard at Megan. "When he finally figures it out, poor lamb, he does know what he wants. And is willing to wait for it." With a smile and a touch on Megan's arm, she added, "But don't make him wait too long." She moved across the room, being stopped midway by Tag for an enthusiastic hand-pump.

Just as Megan considered what to do—find out the woman's name or leave immediately—she saw Bryant, his head naturally above the rest, staring unapologetically at her with that half-smile.

I'm a Courteous Acquaintance, Megan wanted to shout. Men. So confusing, and not worth the energy to figure them out. Exasperated, she turned toward the door, this time intercepted by a bubbling Chalise.

"What did she say? I can't believe you talked with her. Did you find out what they've decided?"

Megan stepped back. "What are you talking about? Who—that lady?"

"That lady?" Chalise was between incredulity and confusion. "That was *the* Mrs. Dolores Van De Morelle, didn't you know?"

Megan shot a glance through the room and saw Mrs. Van De Morelle approach Bryant and say something, to which he laughed and bent down to give her a kiss on the cheek. She turned to the cast members on either side and received a polite hug from them.

Megan groaned. The woman with the money, power, and now obvious adoration for Bryant. And Megan had practically dissed her, him, and the cruise ship.

Would she *ever* get it right?

Heading back to her room, Megan met Rosa in the hallway, folding and stacking towels on her cleaning cart, looking more tired than usual.

"Como esta, Rosa?"

"Bery good, Megan McCormick. Your Spanish get bery good."

Megan smiled at the obvious exaggeration. "You tired? Como se dice 'tired'?"

"Cansado. And yees," Rosa stopped and leaned on the overloaded cart. "Yees, I tired."

Megan smiled sympathetically, then had an idea. "Rosa, if you had your dream, what would you do instead?"

Rosa's eyes moved slightly in thought. "I go to America and start cleaning, how you say, business? And I 'ave many peoples to hire, and we teach each other bery well, do good work, for bery good price. I clean long time back for big houses, but..." a darkness passed over her face. "Dey were, how you say, big drug people."

"You mean, like a drug cartel?" Megan wondered again just what this girl had seen pre-cruise life.

"Yees, but bery nice to me. But I no stay. Bery young. So I tell them I go work on a ship, and they say okay. I sign papers. Now, I make not so much money. But I know lots things in cleanings, good ideas. I make myself cleaners, no? Lemon juice, bake soda, vinegar, dees all bery good. No hurt de tile." She shrugged.

Megan felt a mix of surprise and irony. Rosa obviously had imagined her life, and was not able to live it. Megan could hardly envision her life anymore, but had every chance of achieving it.

Looking at Rosa, Megan smiled, feeling a deep respect and appreciation for her. "Rosa, you are a good lady. Como se dice 'good lady'?"

She smiled. "Megan McCormick."

Megan laughed, gave her a quick side hug, and headed back to her room feeling a warmth about the sweet girl. Rosa only needed a boost, something to help her catapult from here to America, and her dream. Megan thought about it as she dressed in her pajamas, lying awake for a half hour before she had something of a plan.

CHAPTER SIX

Sweaty from her early morning run, Megan entered the girl's cabin surprised to see Jillian still there. She had run longer on purpose, sure her roommates would be at breakfast by now. The last thing she wanted was more ridiculous speculation on her and Bryant, especially when there was nothing there, right?

Besides, she had wanted time to think of more important things. After a few days of ruminating and talking with Rosa, she had just about finalized a plan, for Rosa anyway. The other issue—How to Behave as a Courteous Acquaintance—was still a bit hazy. She'd simply kept her distance from That Person, both of them silently respecting an ignore-each-other truce. Although a few times she *had* seen him look at her with that intense math problem stare, right before she clearly turned away. And, it was true she'd noticed the outline of his chest muscles beneath the flimsy renaissance white shirt for the pirates' number. But then, what girl wouldn't? No, she was safe in her self-promise. No men, no worries.

Jillian was tying her sneakers. "Ah, she returns."

Megan made a face as she grabbed a hand towel. "Gotta question for you—who would I talk to about helping an employee on the cruise line get another job?"

Jillian stopped mid-tying. "Why, are you quitting?"

"No, no—not me. There's a Latino girl that works here and I think she could make something better of herself, with the right help."

Jillian continued tying. "Meddling, are we? The real decision-maker is Mrs. Van De Morelle. She's the king, queen, and House of Commons."

"But how do I get to her? She's like this invisible icon."

Jillian laughed, then laughed again, hurrying to put on earrings. "This is actually a beautiful thing." She turned to Megan with a triumphant smile. "She and Bryant are pretty close from what I hear. Very mother and adopted son-ish, at least out at sea."

Megan frowned. "Just exactly why are you looking at me like that, and saying 'Bryant' in that tone?"

"Don't play coy with me, Megs. I'm your dear old pal and college roommate, remember? I'm the one who bailed you out of the Eric Granger date disaster without you having to say a word. One look at your face, I knew exactly what was going on. It's the same with B-boy. You're into him."

"What—into—are you out of your mind?"

"Skip it, I know you like him. And he obviously digs you, despite the horrible wardrobe. So what's the hold up?" She aggressively brushed her long blonde hair.

Megan was about to deny it again, but stopped at Jillian's insistent expression and walked to her bunk instead. She sat down hard. Right here is what made Jillian so annoying—she cut to the chase and made you own up to yourself, like it or not.

Megan took a deep breath and stared at Jillian.

"All right, I can't like him," she said. "It's just not right to like someone on a cruise ship. In a show. That's a blond, 6' 2" *dancer,* who's also a former basketball star. It's so utterly cliché, it's disgusting. This is a fairy-tale setting, the most unreal setting you can get, except for maybe being stranded on a tropical island, and I don't rule that out at this point."

"So"—Jillian sat down across from her on the opposite bunk, brush in hand—"you won't allow yourself to like him because it's too fairy-tale good?"

"No, because it's just too fairy-tale, period. You know how these performer types can be, excepting Derek of course. I mean, he works weird hours and it's not even a real job. And when he gets back to the mainland the family business is waiting for him but he doesn't want it, but can't commit to something else. At *twenty-seven*! Talk about an unsafe bet. The only thing that's remotely appealing about him is the way he looks like he's figuring out the tip on a receipt all the time. And the way he helps—okay, I'll give you that, always carrying things for Marvy and helping the girls with the costume tubs.

Bringing Clint some orange juice for his hypoglycemia. And yes, he's like an Adonis but in a next-door-guy way, but like that matters to me. Sure he's easy to talk to when there's not this—this tension between us, which, okay, I admit is mostly because of me. But there's still something that's not quite right about him, which I can't figure out. And I get that he's fun to be with, when he's not got that annoying smirk on his face, which actually reminds me of Sam. But other than that, I ask you, rationally, what's there to really fall for here?"

Jillian stared at Megan for a moment then shook her head. "Wow. You've got it bad." With a consoling look she patted Megan's knee. "The good news is that I'm here and you will not get away with hiding from Abs Man, nor ruining your chance for something good. Big Sister Jillian's got your back."

"Oh, no you don't. Remember your promise," said Megan, starting to worry. She'd just opened up with her unspoken feelings and now they would be used against her?

Jillian walked to the door, dropping her brush on the vanity counter.

"Campaign promises, my Megs. Oh, and I have a *message* for you from a certain someone." She stood with a sly smile.

Megan was about to reply when she realized what Jillian had said. She dabbed her forehead with the towel feigning boredom, though her insides felt a small swirl.

"Someone asked specifically to have breakfast with you."

"I'm not hungry." This was suddenly true.

She paused dramatically. "It was Brittany Shay Weller—don't forget the Shay—and she *personally* requested you meet her at the Starboard Dining Room. At nine thirty." She added a Princess Wave.

"You are evil," said Megan, as Jillian closed the door behind her.

What in the world would Brittany want to talk to her about?

Thirty minutes later Megan entered the almost empty Starboard Dining Room. She felt slightly nauseous, praying in conversation she wouldn't betray any supposed interest in Bryant, while at the same time not seeming unnaturally uninterested. Maybe Brittany wanted to tell her mitts off, he was still hers. Or maybe that she stunk doing salsa. Or tips on how to do a Princess Wave.

Brittany caught Megan's eye and motioned her over.

"You got my message, terrific. I hope this is okay for you?" She smiled openly, completely disarming. In an odd flash, Megan remembered visiting a tiger exhibit in the zoo as a child. That part had been the most intriguing to her. Beautiful, tropical surroundings. Soft, thick fur.

Big teeth.

Sitting down, Megan dismissed the image knowing the unfair judgment came only because Brittany was a former flame of Bryant's. And, that she was gorgeous. And nice.

Grrr.

A waiter approached. Everyone usually did the buffet but Brittany preferred a waiter.

"Eduardo, do you have freshly squeezed orange juice?" The enamel sentinels stood at charming attention.

"Si." Eduardo smoothed his hair.

"How long ago was it squeezed?"

"Half an hour."

"Can you have them squeeze some fresh?"

"Si, Senorita Brittany."

"And bring the two American specials," she inquired at Megan. "I ordered ahead and had them kept warm, is that all right?" Megan nodded. Brittany turned back to Eduardo, smiling again, who bowed and with a lingering deferential look, made for the kitchen.

Megan played with her water glass.

Brittany shifted in her seat. "Listen, I haven't had a chance before now to really talk. It's been a bit crazy with the board and their constant networking needs, with all they're trying to change up. Seeing as my mother has an ad-hoc seat, I get roped into a lot of things."

Megan couldn't figure out for the life of her where this was going. Brittany ran a finger through her sweeping white-blonde bangs.

"What I wanted to say was—well, to apologize for opening night." Brittany stared straight at Megan without flinching. "It was my fault, all mine. I already spoke to Clint about it."

Megan opened her mouth slightly. "Really? I—"

"I've had a lot on my mind. Some things, wonderful things, are happening and I did not have my head in the game. It wasn't like me. Well, not usually on opening night." She shrugged. Disarmingly sweet and genuine. Bummer.

"Thanks, I appreciate that," said Megan, cautiously. "I was fairly sure it was me. Likely still was, in some form, anyway."

"Well, I wanted to clear the air. About a few things." She paused, tipping her head to one side slightly, as if thinking how to approach her next thought. "I understand—I'm aware of some conversation, and, well, let's just say, in case people are wondering, Bryant and I are"—she paused for the right words—"not an item. Not in any sense, not for a long time now."

Conversation? Ah, the girl chat at the Meet & Greet.

Megan hoped her face didn't bely panic, and immediately wondered how much Brittany knew. Thankfully, Eduardo arrived with the fresh juice and breakfast plates, then excused himself with a low bow. Megan busied herself with the food. *Not an item. Not for a long time.*

Brittany opened a salt substitute packet, easily continuing the conversation. "It actually helps us better now. You know men, when you've had an emotional connection it helps when you dance. Makes it seem more real. Like the way he holds me, or looks at me, like he's really looking. But that's just performing. It helps for others to know it doesn't mean anything in particular." Brittany looked at Megan purposefully.

At that moment, Brittany's words felt true. At least, Megan wanted them to be true. She remembered the way he had looked at Brittany during the dance—close, caring, romantic. But as soon as they were done, he broke apart, like they'd been studying calculus. She felt momentary solace.

But then, what did that mean for the way he had been with her in the Green Room, winking at her on stage, talking with her in the cinema? Was that just performing? Did it not mean anything?

"So did you two date a long time?" Megan ventured as far as was wise. She focused on cutting her eggs.

"Oh, you know how it goes, especially in the performance business." Brittany carefully scooted out ham chunks from her egg whites and pushed them to the side. "We met at Three Pines College and hit it off right away. He was more gung-ho than I was, but, that's Bryant. When he sees what he wants, he's kind of laser beam about it." She laughed lightly. "And it was okay, I went with it, because he really is a great guy. But then this intensity, it kept going, and turned more serious and before I knew it, he wanted to get married. It was so fast, and too stressful. He can be so intense, almost demanding, at least then.

"And suddenly, he was gone. A lot. But like I said, when he sees what he wants ..." She sipped her orange juice. "He was already onto the next thing. Doesn't know what he wants one minute then suddenly does the next."

"You mean, he left the cruise ship?"

"No, we were done with the tour. He worked with a house-building program and decided to stay on, without a lot of input as they say. Bryant's just like that." She shrugged, looking past Megan's shoulder and smiling at someone, then the Princess Wave. "I mean, he was okay about it. But, seeing as we had been seriously dating for several months, I guess I would have liked more say in the matter."

Megan tried not to show confusion. From Brittany's version, Bryant wasn't looking too good in real life. Trying to jive this version with Jillian's didn't quite add up, at least in the way she wanted it to. But then, Jillian had told her she wasn't exactly omnipresent during that phase of her life.

"Is that what made it break up?" said Megan. It came out before she could think. A hard expression fleetingly crossed Brittany's face. Then the sentinels.

"Oh, you know those things are always complicated. I had some needs— you know women. We crave connection, not just for the first two weeks. He

74

was more focused on the thing of the moment, unable to ultimately commit. To anything long-term, really. And I could feel it. A woman wants to know it's a done deal. So someone else offered to fill those needs, and be there. But then, I could have been more grown up. It was a learning lesson, for both of us."

Brittany pushed her plate gently away. "I'm sure he's more mature now. Time does that, changes people." She looked at Megan, "And things. He's likely in a better place."

That's what she said, but an undercurrent passed from her, clear and unmistakable—"Bryant is this way and will always be this way." Like a friendly warning. But why would Brittany want to warn her? And about what exactly?

She said Bryant was unable to commit. That he wanted what he wanted and focused until he got it. That she had felt pushed. Megan wanted to disregard it, but was it so false?

She had seen that he was unable to commit in his life, bouncing from college to cruise ship to lumber yard—or the avoidance of it. And intense, demanding? Yes, she'd seen that to. On the dance floor, just the two of them— "Do you dance like you talk? Come here." He had that forcefulness, to be sure. And she had liked it. But isn't that how it always started? You liked the thing you came to hate.

Unsettled, Megan was about to ask a delicate question when Chalise approached the table, almost bouncing in her enthusiasm.

"Finally, we get an excursion today, can you believe it? Everyone's going ashore, you gonna join us? It's a can't-miss."

"Is that the excursion or Garrett?" said Megan.

She shrugged. "Does it matter? Either way it will be exciting." She winked. "Bryant will be there. Coming?"

Brittany looked directly at Megan, who flushed involuntarily. "Tenzanio's has the best shopping—Fossil bags and Prada for practically nothing. And the beaches are gorgeous, like crushed white shells."

"Sounds great," said Megan, though inside she'd rather do a tax audit. Something passed through her soul, making her uncomfortable that Brittany encouraged her to go knowing Bryant would too. Megan wanted to say no, right then and there, but somehow couldn't verbalize it.

"Okay, we'll catch you at the landing dockside." Chalise smiled exuberantly and hustled off, presumably to get ready for Garrett.

Megan stood. "Well, I better go. I've got a few things to do. Thanks for breakfast, and, for telling me your thoughts. It's very private, and I'll keep it that way."

"I know you will," said Brittany, with a peculiar expression.

As Megan walked away, that expression stayed with her, but why, she didn't know. One thing she knew. When that shuttle left, she would not be on it. Not until she figured out who Bryant really was—is—and got her bearings again. She would not be duped like before. If he conned her, she'd have learned nothing. But the stories were so different—from Jillian, from Brittany. It was time to get some facts about Bryant, and she knew exactly who to get them from.

Megan approached the gangway leading to the dock, ready for some new sights and sounds. It was only after Jillian confirmed that Bryant wasn't going on the excursion that she had agreed to join them. More time away from him, like the past few days, that's what she needed. After divulging her private thoughts to Jillian, Megan felt that familiar warning. It was too close and too fast with him and these emotions, and she didn't know what to make of it. All she could feel were bits of puzzle pieces—his behaviors, their conversations—and she needed to know, had to know, what the picture made before she let herself be pulled in. Not that she planned to anyway.

Megan breathed in deeply. It felt good to get out.

Five minutes later, Megan regretted ever befriending Jillian. On the dock, surrounded by five or so adoring females, stood Bryant.

Tugging Jillian's arm, Megan spoke in a tense whisper. "You said Bryant wasn't going."

"I know. I lied." Jillian looked around for Derek.

"Lied? Just like that? What kind of a friend are you?"

"The kind that gets my friend over herself, *and* hooks her up with a gorgeous singing basketball star." She shook her head. "That every girl had such a friend."

"No, I mean it, Jillian. Stop the matchmaking, you don't know what you're doing." Megan panicked. She had decided not to tell Jillian what had happened in the Green Room, and now, this would only make it worse. "I'm not kidding."

Jillian smirked with a complete disregard for her most urgent plea.

Megan gestured with both hands open, beyond frustrated. Was she the only sane person left on the tour? How in the world was she going to act around Bryant? They hadn't spoken in days. What would she say? Well, that was easy, she'd play mute. There would be no need to talk because she wouldn't go near him.

About 12 of them squeezed into the small, obviously worn shuttle. The driver wound through the streets like a back roads bus on a Peruvian mountain highway, all the while singing loudly to a South American song. Squished next to others, Brittany and a cast girl sat on one side of the bus, Megan and Chalise sat on the opposite side and adjacent to them sat Chad and Bryant talking about Tesla coils and engineering components.

Megan hugged her beach bag and set her face in a bored expression. Occasionally, she felt him looking at her, but for whatever reason, he left her alone. Good. Maybe that tense Green Room conversation had been just the ticket and he'd leave her be.

They arrived at the shuttle drop-off feeling slightly shaken but alive. The driver made a long announcement in a thick accent that most of them didn't understand, except to be back by five o'clock or they would miss the shuttle to the boat. And that taxis would take them anywhere they wanted to go, for cheap. Even Megan knew that was not true but they smiled anyway.

After he finished, the group began breaking into clusters following the buddy system. Whatever happened, Megan didn't want to be with the main crowd, and most definitely not with Bryant.

Jillian came to Chalise and Megan, the others standing close by deciding their destinations.

"Hey, where do you guys want to go? Derek has to help one of the lighting crew find some special bulbs that burnt out, but he didn't want me to miss the shopping. Anybody game?" She included the girls standing nearby. Bryant, Chad, and some others stood within listening distance.

The girls added a happy yes, and one of the crew said there was an incredible restaurant by the main strip of stores which got a response from the guys.

"I think I'll just hit the beach," she said quietly to Jillian.

"Can't," she shot back, "have to stay in the buddy system. Anybody want to hit the beach after shopping?" Several were in agreement. "Okay, if we have time that sounds perfect. I think we can all share taxis," and she began divvying people into groups.

Megan opened her mouth to speak but closed it as soon as she saw she was outmaneuvered. That was Jillian for you.

Ultimately, Bryant, Chad, Brittany, and Jasmine ended up in one taxi, while Jillian and Megan shared another with two crew guys. It was a tight squeeze but with comfortable chatter. Both groups merged at the main strip loaded with badly dressed—and hardly dressed—tourists. Brightly bedecked locals called out to them from the shop fronts in broken English and encouraging gestures, inviting them into their stores with a frantic wave or a shock-white smile.

The group mingled and talked throughout the few hours with Megan careful to keep her distance from Bryant. The success made her careless so that when they entered the restaurant, she was looking at the décor before she knew the seating arrangements.

"Over here, they can seat us now," said Jillian, pointing the way for Megan, Jasmine, Bryant, and Chad.

Megan looked stricken, but Jillian was having none of it.

"Hello, didn't you hear? They can seat us but only at two tables. You guys take the outside." She leaned into Megan. "Brittany doesn't want more sun on her skin and Chalise wants to talk to me about Garrett. Not exactly guy conversation, if you know what I mean." She added with a certain smile, "And be nice to Bryant today."

Megan gave her a look.

The waitress led them informally to a table poorly shaded by an obviously fake thatched roof umbrella. Plastic silverware lay strewn on the white plastic table.

"Trust me, the food is better than the decor," said Jasmine, pulling out her iPod earbuds. Her auburn hair was pulled back in a loose ponytail and she wore a sixties tie-dyed shirt over a flowing skirt.

"Nice skirt," said Megan. It looked cool and comfortable.

"They're the best air-conditioning around," she said, settling in a chair next to Chad, and took up a menu. "You should get one. They sell them at that corner store we just passed."

Megan gazed up the street at the store just as Bryant took the seat next to her. She ignored him and continued, "You've been here before?"

"Oh, yeah," said Jasmine. "The chimichanga is good, and safe. They deep fry it. You can get a lot of stomach bugs on these trips so be Indiana Jones—'Choose wisely.'"

The waitress took their order, smiling and wearing a red, yellow, and green colored blouse and skirt. All of them ordered chimichangas.

Jasmine and Chad struck up conversation, something about natural energy sources. Bryant turned to Megan.

"So, Berlin, feeling less hostile today?" His eyes crinkled in that almost laughing way.

She immediately appeared interested in the store fronts and noisy tourists. "Don't know what you're talking about."

"You did good this week, dance wise." He leaned back in the chair. "Got the salsa solid, anyway. You stopped looking at your feet."

A sarcastic remark was on her tongue but she saw his earnestness and simply said, "Thanks."

Both of them sat for a while in silence, gazing at the passersby. Megan felt her face flush with the awareness of his tanned arm close to hers, his strong legs almost touching her knee. What was the matter with her?

Remember, Casual Acquaintance. Be polite. She added, "I never really thanked you properly for your help."

"Lunch would work." He squinted at her, smiling. She ignored the familiar tingle in her tummy.

"I thought Dancing with the Stars coaching was included." She went to take a drink of water.

"I wouldn't do that," he said. "Only do bottled at these places."

"Oh. Thanks. Again."

"That's included." He smiled at her, relaxed. She tried to look indifferent but those eyes, that energy, like he could read her real thoughts. She could smell his ocean scent and felt the pull of his easy, inviting smile. Without the fight, she could feel herself slipping into that comfortable realm with him, letting down her guard. Truly, it was too exhausting to keep it up. But what else could she do to stay emotionally safe? She needed a new strategy.

A Buddy. That was it, like she had been with Sam's friends. A light-hearted go-to pal. Someone to talk sports with and shoot hoops, none of this emotional garbage. Just keep it light, fun, devil-may-care. Yes, that would work. Because Casual Acquaintance definitely wasn't working. They practically had sparks coming out of their faces already.

"You know," she said, "I finally figured out what's wrong with your face."

"Oh, here we go."

"No, I mean, there's something different that I couldn't put a finger on. But it just came to me. It's your nose."

He nodded, understanding. "I broke it."

"Football injury? Star QB makes the game-winning play, cool victory dance at the end?"

"Not even close."

"Hockey injury?"

"In northern California?" He cocked his head. "It was a fight."

She was shocked, he didn't seem the aggressive type. "Any bars involved?"

"No, just my brother." The waitress arrived with the food on large platters—a sea of refried beans, Mexican rice, and sizzling chimichanga bars loaded with toppings. They each dug into the offerings.

After a few minutes, Megan started again. "So, this fight, what was it about? Two brothers fighting over the same woman kind of thing?"

He spread the toppings then sliced a big chunk. "It was a cow," he said and popped the piece into his mouth.

"Oh, that's rich." She cut into her meal. "Come on, details."

He shrugged and swallowed. "I was supposed to sell her. I'd raised her—well, my brother, Mitch, and I. But he'd lost interest after a month, and said so. I'd done all the work. And I'd already talked to Wendell about the sale—when she'd be ready and all that. And you better believe I had every penny of that $1400 planned out."

"You actually raised a cow, surfer boy? Do they even have cows in California?"

"Yeah, they come down for the wine festivals." He cut another bite.

"So I'll say, just to be a sport, that you actually did raise a cow. Did you have a farm?"

"No, it was an experiment of my dad's, trying to teach us suburban white trash some good old-fashioned values."

"Did it work?"

"I raised the cow, didn't I? Man, this is good." Stuffing more food in his mouth, his apathy only fueled the fire. She really wanted to know.

"So then you wanted to sell it. For?"

He paused. "A GTO."

She stared. "I'm guessing that's a car?"

His turned his head sharply. "Guessing? A '69 GTO? That's the best muscle car there was, at least for sale, and restoration. And Mitch bought it right out from under me, and gave the guy the promise of my share of Zippy, if you can believe that." He banged his fork on the plate as he cut another bite.

Jasmine looked up from her meal, earbuds hanging out, as Chad looked up from his electronic game; they returned to both.

"Zippy? Is that a real name for a cow?" Megan bit into her chimichanga. "And obviously you've come to terms with this experience, your anger and all that. What happened?"

"Dad said for us to go work it out."

"So?"

"Do you only speak in monosyllables?" he said.

"Wow, that was a big word, and you didn't even sound it out." She chewed slowly, a half-smile with closed lips.

"Yeah, we worked it out. On each other's faces."

"Sounds helpful. How did he look?"

"Busted jaw and 13 stitches." He tried but could not repress the smile while Megan shook her head in disgust. "Come on. It's a big deal to be fourteen and take down your older brother."

"How much older?"

"Twenty-two months."

"Hail the conquering hero."

He passed her tabasco sauce which she ixnayed.

"At the time he was a wannabe body builder, so a little more to it than that." With a few more bites he finished the rest of his chimichanga. "I couldn't use my hand for a week, but it was okay."

"So, you're good friends then, you and your brother Mitch?"

"Yeah, the best."

"That sounds about right." She smiled at the irony, finishing another bite.

He glanced sideways at her. "You got brothers?" The sunlight caught the waves in his hair. With his white shirt, khaki shorts, and easy repose, Megan found herself thinking how nice sitting together on the beach would be.

Be. A. Buddy.

"Yep, three older brothers and pretty much the same. Fighting, wrestling, plotting revenge, that kind of thing. They'd do small stuff at the beginning, Vaseline on the toilet seats, tape the kitchen sink sprayer and whatnot. But it was usually Mom who got the brunt of it. Then, they got older and it got more intense."

"Explosives," he said, a slight glimmer in his eye.

"Apparently you know the drill," she said. "They were always making something out of household whatever. But when they blew up the shed that was it."

"What'd they use?"

She shot him a glance. "Renegade."

"You have to admit, it's kind of cool they knew how."

"Right up until Dad jumped off the porch, took their heads, and literally cracked them together. That was worth seeing." She sat back and crossed her legs, thinking back to those days. "I don't think he really blamed them though, I didn't either. They basically grew themselves up at that point."

"Why's that?"

Megan reined up. How had she gotten so personal so quickly? Where was the Buddy? Next, she'd be telling him everything.

Turning her wrist, she noted the time. "I think we had better head back if we're to make the shuttle in time."

"Was that an obvious detour in the conversation?" He waited.

She paused, deciding.

"We don't want to be late." She gazed steadily at him.

He shrugged. "You're the boss." He grabbed the ticket lying on the table before she had a chance. Megan gave him a look but he ignored her.

They stood up and Jasmine and Chad came to life. As Megan looked out at the street, she stopped cold. Coming out of a small side souvenir shop much farther down was Derek, but he was with a girl that was not Jillian. They were laughing about something. He handed her a shopping bag and she hugged him, beaming. He held on, finally separating but talking close. Megan squinted and stared harder. But Derek was supposed to be buying lightbulbs with the guys on the other side of town. And yet, that was him. And that was most obviously not Jillian.

What in the world?

"You coming?" Bryant stood next to her, looking in the same direction, then stiffened.

"Un-be-lievable. That can't be right," said Megan, wondering whether to call out to him but unsure he could even hear over the noisy street sounds. The guilty pair had glanced warily from side to side then split up. Derek was now walking down the street, looking at nothing but with a huge smile breaking over his face. Megan felt sick.

"That two-timing jerk." Megan felt an overwhelming anger surge through her. "I'm calling him on it."

"Wait," Bryant put his hand on her arm. She looked down at it. "Take a minute and think this through." He glanced at Jasmine and Chad walking up to the cashier stand.

"Think what through? He's a cheat," she said, yanking her arm free.

"Megan, you don't know what it was." The way he said her name, it did something to her. Warm, reassuring, it was like butter syrup. She ignored it and came back to the moment.

"Are you telling me that I didn't see what I saw?"

"No," he said. "But there could be a hundred reasons for what it was. Don't say anything until you know more. Maybe it could cause problems that aren't yours to cause."

Megan was shocked. His look was strange, his manner insistent. And then she got it.

"It's just a great big boys' club, isn't it?" Megan spoke low and disgusted. "Smile and all's well when Jillian's around. But when she's gone, the true colors come out and everybody's in on it. I thought you had character. But it's just the silent oath, isn't it?"

Standing close to him, she saw his eyes widen then his jaw shut tight, but she turned and walked out, not looking behind her.

The shuttle ride back was painstakingly quiet. Megan had chosen a seat as far from Bryant as possible and observed that Brittany sat close by him, although to be fair, it was one of the last open seats. They chatted off and on during the ride home, but Megan wasn't interested.

She can have him, Megan thought, a sick feeling in her stomach. She had tried to think of other reasons why Derek would have been there, would have lied, would have been hugging the girl so close then looking around to see if anyone saw. Derek had seemed like such a good guy but it was a Jackson kind of move all over again. And the kicker had been Bryant insistently defending him. Typical guy.

Jillian and Derek sat in the back, behind her. Megan forced herself not to look, or say anything, at least not yet. Staring out the window at the passing exotic landscape she sifted through disturbing questions. What would she tell Jillian? How much? And more importantly, when?

CHAPTER SEVEN

Throughout the next day, Megan tried several times to catch Jillian alone but someone or something seemed to continually get in the way. Perhaps it was fueled by the fact that Megan still had no real plan of how to break the news. Each time she thought of it, a burning anger welled within her. The situation was bad enough, but to be forced into it, for her to have break her friend's heart because *they* couldn't man up, made her furious. For some reason mostly at Bryant.

By the evening show, Megan hadn't seen Jillian and studiously avoided eye contact with Bryant. After the routine performance, she hurried off stage as soon as it was over but only to be detained by Marvy on a costume issue. On her way to change, Megan saw Derek in the hall. He said a bright hello and she returned a terse nod.

The nerve of the male species, she thought, and opened the dressing room door.

Jillian jumped up from her chair. "Derek wants to hang out so can I take a rain check on girl chat tonight?" She had already changed and was finishing her hair.

Megan opened her mouth, on the verge of blurting it out, but an unseen something held her back. Bryant's warning flashed annoyingly in her mind—*might cause problems that aren't yours to cause.* She wished to swat it away like a summer fly.

"No worries, Jillian. I just hope that—" she faltered. What should she say? Be aware, guys are creeps? Don't trust them as far as you can background check them? She settled for, "Just be careful. Guys can be, well ..."

Jillian pinned up her hair. "Oh, not another one of those talks." She grabbed her big purse and side hugged Megan. "I won't be late." She winked and headed out the door.

Watching her leave, Megan felt nauseous. Should she stop her, tell her? Tell Derek? She bit the corner of her lip, wondering the best thing to do, which ultimately, for now, was nothing.

Slowly heading back to the room, she entered a narrow hallway and saw petite Rosa with her large cart, topped with unfolded towels.

"Buenos dias, Rosa."

Rosa broke into a big smile, like a teenager. "Es buenos noches, Senorita Megan. It ees bery late evening, but close morning."

"Right, thanks—I mean, gracias. Still working?"

"Yees, always working, Senorita Megan," she said, but smiled. "Do good show tonight?"

"Si," said Megan, picking up the towels that were still warm. "Can I help? How do you say ...?"

"¿Cómo puedo ayudarle? No, I fine."

Megan took up a towel and folded it anyway. "Rosa, do you have a—how do you say, como se dice love, boyfriend—"

"Mi novio? Si." She smiled again, also taking a towel and folding it. "Enrique. Good man. Works in de kitchen."

"How long have you, um, dated, been in love ...?"

"Bery short, only three month. But he a good man and we bery happy." She stacked towel upon towel. "You not happy, Senorita Megan."

"Me? No, I'm good, very good." Megan had thought to ask her advice but she couldn't even begin to phrase the question.

"No—you no so good. Can I question? Why you always dress like boy?"

Her question was completely unexpected, and innocently asked. It stopped Megan short. She thought of her sweat pants, unfitted T-shirt, and makeup free face. True, she had just finished a show and had dressed down. But even as she wanted to refute the question, Megan's distance, her clothes, her prickly manner, everything ticker-taped through her mind and she knew what Rosa had said was true.

"You bery pretty. Wear skirt, do hair like dis." She mimicked curls. "You bery pretty girl. Dere be amor for you." She nodded, childlike.

"I—I think." Megan slowly finished her towel. Was it safe to return to some old ways? Maybe. In order to be herself again, perhaps it wasn't a bad thing to allow a few feminine touches.

"Maybe I'll try, Rosa. Muchas gracias," said Megan, and spontaneously kissed her on the cheek.

Rosa reached down and gave her a good-sized decorative bag filled with the caramel chocolates she loved. Megan laughed as Rosa nodded and pushed her cart. "Gracias por ayudarme a doblar las toallas."

"Gracias por avyu—," said Megan, trying to repeat but gave up as she headed to her cabin thinking about what Rosa said. No, she wouldn't dress for guys, especially not now. What was the point? She wasn't interested in romance, and all they wanted was a trophy girlfriend. When they finished with her they'd go onto the next one, just a bit of pretty fluff on their arm. But Rosa's comment, so genuinely said, hit a chord. In her quest to be the New Megan, she had let go of everything Old Megan. But that wasn't necessary, was it? Some things could be kept, to still be her. Like a butterfly near the end of its cocooning, she felt the strict constraints she had put on herself over the past few months beginning to feel tight. They didn't seem to fit anymore.

She wished she could say the same for Jillian. Megan frowned, thinking of what needed to be said. Her cocooning would be just beginning.

Opening the door to the cabin, Megan stopped short. Jillian sat on the floor, crying.

"Jillian, what—what's wrong? What happened?" And then she knew. Men. So predictable. And women—when would we learn?

Dropping the chocolate bag Megan hurried and knelt by her, saying, "I'm so sorry, I knew it, I knew—"

"Can you believe it?" Jillian looked up, her face shining as she held up and flashed her ring finger. A modest but unmistakable engagement ring sparkled. "I keep putting it on, taking it off, looking at it in the box—isn't it gorgeous?"

"Jillian, my goodness, when?" Megan's head swirled. If there was a time to say something about Derek, it was now, absolutely now.

"Just a few minutes ago! He had wanted to do it earlier, but then he had to meet with Clint and Marvy to spill the beans, but before curfew, and we were late enough as it was—"

"—Jillian, I have to tell you—"

"Derek just bought it today!" Jillian couldn't tell it fast enough, wiping the tears still fresh on her face. "Chalise and her man-chat about Garrett, it was all fake! Not that she doesn't think he's amazing. She and Bryant were sworn to secrecy but told to keep everyone busy."

Bryant?

"Derek said he hit the store supposedly getting those *bulbs*—oh man, I had given him such a hard time over that, too. Talk about humble pie. I had no clue. He did it while we were sightseeing, isn't that romantic? Lindsey helped pick it out. She knew exactly what I wanted, which makes at least four of you. I wanted to be sure he got the right thing, you know." She gazed back and forth from Megan to the ring.

Lindsey. Derek. The store. That's why she had hugged him, why they looked so happy.

An anchor dropped through her stomach. It was legit. Derek loved Jillian, was trying to surprise her. And Megan had almost ruined it.

It was me. All me. Me and my twisted, warped, hurt little mind.

"I'm—I'm so happy for you, Jillian, truly," Megan gave her a strong hug. "He's really a solid, solid, great guy." Tears were coming and she fought them back. How could she have been so narrow-minded?

Bryant. The things she'd said. The bite of her words came back, sharp and painful. *I thought you had character.* The anchor in her stomach dropped to her feet. What did she do now?

"What? No annoying guy lecture tonight?" Jillian laughed, nothing bothered her now. "I came back to tell you guys but Chalise already knows. I saw her on the way here. Can you believe it?"

The door opened hard and Brittany hurried in. "Is it true? Chalise just told me that—Jillian, are you serious?" She hurried over and knelt down, turning Jillian's hand to see the ring. "Yep, he's a keeper, Jills." She looked at it in the light. "That's a real marquis, can you see the bow-tie facet it makes in the light?" She fingered the diamond with a wistful then too cheerful expression. "Congrats, sweetie, that's such fantastic news. You'll have to tell Marvy and Clint."

"Already did. They're letting us make a ship-to-shore call in—wow, like right now." She jumped up. "I gotta go. Mom already knows. Derek says he asked for my hand before on another call, remember when he was supposedly playing video games? Isn't he amazing! I had told my mom something like this might happen, but you never know." Abruptly, she looked at Megan with an expression of sudden awareness.

"It's all good, truly, don't even think about it." Megan smiled with the complete reassurance that she felt.

"You're the best, Megs," and gave her a quick squeeze before running out the door.

Brittany turned to Megan. "Well, that's real news," and the enamel sentinels flashed brightly. Immediately, Megan had two feelings—to get out of this conversation with Brittany, and to go make amends with Bryant. But it was already curfew, did she dare risk it? And how would she leave with Brittany here?

"Well, at least the shower's free," said Brittany. Obviously, she felt the same awkwardness. Megan changed into pajamas and her worn cotton bathrobe as if to ready for bed. Opening a book, she tried not to look at the clock. Every minute meant she'd be in more trouble, and less likely to catch him awake. Brittany took her time gathering shower items but finally entered the bathroom.

Quickly, before she second-guessed herself, Megan got up, grabbed the bag of chocolates and stole into the hall, heading to Bryant's room.

Walking quickly through the hallway, Megan felt a lightness and a plummeting at the same time. How could she have misjudged him so completely, again? And made a fool of herself, again. Thinking back to her words, her feelings—so spiteful and mean—remorse filled her until she felt overflowing in apology.

Megan stopped short with a realization: she didn't know Bryant's room number.

Great. Megan thought back to the first day. Rosa had been standing close by when she'd pointed out the way, and she remembered seeing Chad coming from a door at the end of the "D" hallway. She only guessed that he roomed with Bryant, but there was no way to know if this were true and berated herself for not listening more closely. Quietly, she stole through the corridors knowing that if Clint caught her, she would be toast.

Surprisingly, a small giggle escaped her. She felt 16 again; curfew, sneaking out, chocolates in hand. It was ridiculous. In fact, as she stood before what could be his door, the idea seemed less and less realistic. But she deserved the humiliation, it was her penance. She looked from side to side, blowing out a breath. Hesitantly, she knocked softly, twice. As she listened for movement, she looked down. Her bathrobe? Faded, with a homemade patch done back in high school, it was a sight. She'd completely forgotten. Panicked, Megan turned to go as the door opened. Bryant squinted at the corridor light, his caramel blond hair askew.

Wow, he still looked good.

"Oh, sorry to wake you. Did I wake you?" said Megan.

"No. I was practicing my salsa."

She bit back a laugh. This was serious, at least it had been half an hour ago. Now it was just ridiculous.

He ran his fingers through his hair as he stepped into the hallway and closed the door behind him. "Taking breakfast orders?"

"No, just"—she said, remembering Jillian's words—"just an order of humble pie." He looked puzzled. "Listen Bryant, I barely found out, minutes ago actually, about their engagement, Jillian and Derek. And, well," she paused, waiting for him to make a smug remark. But he just watched her.

"And I know sorry, at this point, is a bit trite. So I brought an equally trite peace offering." She raised the bag.

"Concierge chocolates?"

"It's the best I could do on short notice."

He hefted the bag, appearing thoughtful. "Well, they are pretty good," he said, and pointing to the floor they sat down, side by side. He passed her a chocolate and they both unwrapped and helped themselves.

"She's sky high, you know," said Megan. "When I saw the ring and heard that Lindsey helped, I finally got it."

"You catch on fast."

"I really apologize. Again." She paused, trying to find what to say, and how much to share. Curse this cruise, and Jillian, and engagements, and misunderstandings. And sitting in the hallway, touching elbows and feeling the heat of his closeness.

Focus.

"I guess it touched a nerve in me, a very raw nerve. I was just scared for Jillian because ..." How she wanted to tell him everything! The need, the yearning to help him understand rushed through her so powerfully she squeezed her right hand painfully to distract her impulse. "Bryant, I know it's not good enough, and I wish I could explain more, but I *am* sorry, for—for what I said. And how I said it."

His face clouded and suddenly it felt stiff between them.

Megan wanted to make a joke, something, but knew she couldn't take back the anger, the meanness of it. She wanted to tell him that hadn't really been her, that she never spoke to people that way, that she couldn't fully understand why she was so nasty to him. But, unable to begin, Megan just sat on the hallway floor, awkward, in her bathrobe, praying he understood anyway.

They ate in silence.

"It hit a nerve with me too," he said finally, and popped another chocolate in his mouth, a melancholy expression on his face. "My dad. That's how he used to talk to me—disappointed, and like I'd never measure up. Most of the time he didn't have the facts, or care about asking for them. He'd just speak and we obeyed." He scrunched the wrapper.

Megan felt twice stung, though she knew that wasn't his intent. Then a warmth began, small and sweet, at the realization that even with all that had passed between them, he was opening up to her. "Are you and your dad close now?"

He shrugged. "Yes and no. Close as he can be, I guess, but through work mostly. He works hard, the business is hard. But now he's in and out of the lumber yard, not as controlling as before. I think that's more from traveling and the yard changing than changing who he is. It's who his dad was. I guess it's the nature of the Johnsons." He stretched back, kicking his legs out and trying to appear casual, but Megan saw the pull at the corner of his mouth.

"That was a tough generation. They weren't able to talk like men can now."

"Yeah, different days I guess." They let the silence sit.

He leaned his head back against the wall and half-smiled. "Once he had me and Mitch drive the tractor, I think I was nine or something. We were bringing him wood. Dad was on the roof fixing something, yelling down directions to Mitch, and I'm sitting on top of the wood, barely able to hold it down on the trailer. I thought Mitch would throw up from being scared because he didn't know how to drive the dang thing. So he was trying but didn't know how to stop it and rammed a tree. Put the fan in the radiator."

"Were you guys okay?"

"At first, yeah. He got thrown over the top but rolled off. I got thrown clear and banged up, but that was all. Dad hustled down that ladder like a monkey and hit Mitch with a 2 x 4 on his back, yelling and swearing."

Megan turned and looked at Bryant's profile. "Effective discipline technique."

He shook his head. "Old school. We didn't know they had zero money, none to fix a tractor anyway."

"I thought you didn't live on a farm."

"We didn't, not really. It was an experiment, to make some 'extra money,' you know how that goes. He tried to raise table grapes for a little while, and it was brutal—some years good, some not."

"*The Grapes of Wrath.*"

"John Steinbeck." He half-turned to her and smiled. Even at this early morning hour he looked heart-hammering attractive. "Anyway, that was before he turned to lumber, trying to help out a neighbor."

She took the chocolate he proffered and tried to lighten the mood. "So your parents are a little on the tough side?"

"Just Dad. Mom was always the sugar." He shifted his position. "Except at ball games."

"Seriously?"

"Oh, she was bad. She watched the Big Four with me one time and threw her sandwich at the TV screen when the refs missed a key foul. She jumped up and down, yelled. My friends love it. She got thrown out of one of my high school basketball games."

"You're kidding me."

"No, and she's a little thing, about 5'3", but takes her sports *very* seriously. To be fair, the refs were terrible that game, especially to me."

"What did your dad do?"

"Oh, the whole town knows and gets it. The ref said, 'Shirley, you best sit down now or I'm gonna put you in the locker.' And she said, 'You and what army, Bill?' So he marched up to the stands and carried her down in a fireman hold. The crowd was laughing—Mom was still talking smack to him. But Sunday she was in her dress and holding the ladies' tea and all that."

Megan laughed. "Sounds like a great family."

"What about yours?" He handed her another chocolate. "Probably tight-knit and quilting bees, that kind of thing?"

Megan shook her head, thinking for a minute. "My parents divorced when I was 10. It was messy." She fingered the wrapper. "We all reacted differently. My brothers got into a lot of trouble, mainly because that was my dad's streak, and I think they sensed this could be a time to play it up."

He nodded, as if he understood.

Megan paused, wondering how much to share, and why she even wanted to. "My sister and I are . . . let's say she's more of the Rodeo Drive type, and I'm just the rodeo type. I'd rather play football with the guys than cheer them in a skirt." Her voice tightened slightly. "Kara's big on appearances—matching shoes, purse, toenails, the whole nine yards, and that's just to go to the bank. Not really my personality. But, there you are."

94

He looked over at her. "Pretty different strokes." Then he added, "That must have been tough, seeing your folks split up."

Megan half nodded. "Yes and no. It's never that clear cut. He had some issues, and she did too, with not dealing with his issues. Hence the counseling and law interest for a while, trying to solve it I think. Or at least prosecute it."

"And the psych major now is to what, understand it?"

She looked over at him. This was what she couldn't fight. His warmth, his genuineness. A part of her wanted to lean into him and never leave. But still, that gray fear kept her back. What did she really know of him, the mainland Bryant versus cruise line performer?

"You've got chocolate on your chin," she said, and reached up to wipe it with her finger. The touch of his skin surprised her—it looked rugged but was soft, even with the stubble. He gently held her wrist as she pulled away. A shiver tickled her spine. He stared at her with that clear, knowing look, like he'd known her a very long time. A part of her, deep and scared, didn't like it, not one bit. She wasn't ready to for him to know her that deeply. That's always how it began, slipping into comfortable togetherness, where you can see yourself with that person, until you can't see yourself without them. A flash of nausea went through her—she'd been there before.

Abruptly, she let go of his hand and stood up, gathering her faded cotton robe about her. "It's late, Clint will have my head. Anyway, I hope you can get past today, with no hard feelings?"

That's it, keep it official. Keep it impersonal.

Bryant stared at her for a minute—his eyebrow raised—then stood up close to her. Megan felt her ankles start to tremble. Gently touching her shoulder Bryant fixed her robe collar to sit flat. Then he caressed her face. Frantically, she tried to think of something to say or do, her heart thumping loud and hard.

No, no, no. I will not fall.

She stepped back. "This feels right out of 'The Love Boat.' Any minute I'm going to hear Captain Stubing wish us good night."

"I'm sorry, I wasn't trying to make you feel uncomfortable."

"Too late."

He gave her the puzzled math look.

"I mean," she backpedaled, "it's just really cliché. And you're—perfect, amazing. A really good . . . person."

"Person?"

"Guy. Man," she said, rambling. "Hunk. Heartthrob. Whatever. It's just, there's this lineup wherever you go, and that's not my style. I'm not going to beat down hairdos to get to someone. No offense."

Bryant shifted his weight, completely baffled.

"I—it's curfew. I'll see you tomorrow." Quickly, she turned and hurried down the hall before he could ask questions. There was no possible way to explain.

Moving to her cabin, Megan's emotions bounced between wanting to cry and laugh at the same time. *It's curfew?* She rested her forehead on the door, bonked it once intentionally, then turned the handle and entered the dark cabin.

It stops tonight, she promised herself. Back to normal. Back to safe.

In his room, Bryant lay on the bunk, arm behind his head, staring at the frayed mattress tag above him.

What was the matter with him? He had almost tried to kiss her. What happened to taking it slow and not scaring her into flying away? Idiot. But it had been her tonight, that real Megan he wanted. She had been soft and open, almost fragile. He'd wanted to hold her, right there in the hallway, even fall asleep like that.

"So what happened?" said Chad sleepily, from the opposite lower bunk.

Bryant rolled to his side, arm still under his head. Recalling the conversation, he opened his mouth to speak. But then considered his reason for trying, and failing, to kiss her, and he felt confused. Thinking of her rejection, he scowled and closed his mouth. He shrugged.

"I seriously have no idea."

CHAPTER EIGHT

Megan raised her hand to knock on the door, dropped it, then raised and knocked three times, trying to push down the nervousness. For heaven sakes, it wasn't like she was meeting with the president of the United States.

With more performances routinely going well and Mrs. V. having attended a few more of them, Megan felt slightly more confident in talking with her. Slightly.

A uniformed Jamaican man with white gloves opened the cabin door. "May I help you, mum?" His smooth, lyrical voice soothed her.

"Yes, I have an appointment with Mrs. Van De Morelle. Bryant Johnson recommended me?" It came out as a question.

"Dis way, mum." He led her into the lushly decorated salon room that reminded her of a 19th century Rockefeller home but with modern touches. She saw a set of closed double doors that presumably led to the inner sanctum of Dolores Van De Morelle, wealthy heiress and tireless philanthropist.

Sitting on the Victorian-style dais, Megan observed that the overly decorated room was devoid of personal items. Everything looked exquisitely expensive—silver and ceramic pieces, ornate frames on thickly painted art—but no photos or personal touches.

"Hello dear, I must apologize as I have a meeting in 15 minutes." As the older woman entered, Megan was immediately struck by her energy. Though physically she had merely walked into the room, Mrs. Van De Morelle was a *presence.* Bedecked in a regal full-length burgundy gown fit more for a dinner party, Megan had the feeling she slept and awoke in the exact same state. She *was* the dress, incarnate, and all that that embodied.

"Thank you, Mrs. Van De Morelle, I really appreciate your time." Megan had automatically stood with the matriarch's entrance.

"Tush, sit down. And it's Dolores, none of that pomp and circumstance." She spoke with a mixed accent—British with a hint of New England—and settled her full body into a majestic wingback chair. She rang a small silver bell. The butler entered from another white door that led off to another room.

"Keenan, a very quick gnosh if you don't mind. Just the small silver tray and some lemonade."

"Yes, mum." And he quietly left the room.

"Keenan is a treasure, been with me for 25 years. Believe it or not, it's hard to find good domestic help. No one wants to stay in one place for long, or to value it." She fingered a set of reading glasses that hung by two miniature pearl strands upon her ample bosom. "My grandmother was in service over in England and I can tell you, it was an honor to help at the big houses. We've lost the value in taking care of people, I think."

Megan nodded, struck by the direct but warm manner of the woman. "My grandfather was actually a tradesman, a home builder. Even after doing very well, he used to say that staying close to the ground kept his feet there too."

"Sounds like a sensible man. I like that." She paused, taking it in for a moment. "All right then, to business. I dispense with all that preliminary nonsense, if you don't mind. You have a question and I have 15 minutes. So let's get down to cases." Her tone was factual but a smile played at the corner of her eyes. Megan couldn't think why.

"As Bryant may have told you, there is a young girl in the employ of the cruise ship, a cabin maid. I know there are many, but there's something about her that's different." She saw a fleeting look go over Dolores' face. Megan realized she was likely in a long line of people with their hand out.

"I'm sure you hear this a lot, but, in my interactions I've seen and felt that if she could have a chance to do something with her life, she could not only shine but help a lot of people in the process. She has a plan for her future and how to give back."

Dolores tapped her glasses, the warmth still there but a shrewdness about her face. "Tell me about her plan."

From Rosa's conversations, Megan recounted in greater detail her idea to create a cleaning company, preferably in a bigger city such as Los Angeles where she had some distant cousins. Rosa had shown surprising knowledge of cleaning permits, taxes, and payroll. But there was more. She had outlined a plan, with the help of Miguel, her friend who spoke better English, to provide rotating daycare for the cleaning shifts. Rosa had shared stories of women who left their children in the car in parking lots while cleaning on night shifts at commercial buildings.

Dolores listened carefully, occasionally tapping her glasses on her chest. After Megan had finished, she nodded slowly and said, "Well, my dear. You give me something to think about. How much start up cash do you think she wants?"

"I believe she would be the best one to talk to about that. But I understand she is hoping for a modest loan that can be repaid with a decent interest rate and time frame."

Dolores's eyes went up. "She's not looking for a cash gift?"

"No," said Megan. "Rosa doesn't want a hand out. She specifically said she wants to earn her way and to pay it back."

Tap, tap, tap went the reading glasses.

"Thank you, dear. Give me a few days to think and talk with my bean counters. This is when I miss Harold the most, you know." She sighed. "Everyone comes with their hand out—not your type, dear—but it's so tiring. My Harold used to take care of it all, and enjoyed the money side to no end. But it just *exhausts* me."

Megan didn't think Dolores could be exhausted about anything.

The butler knocked and entered the room with a silver tray of a few delectable-looking cookies and a pitcher of cold lemonade.

"Thank you, Keenan."

"Mum, your meeting is in five minutes."

"Yes, thank you. We're just wrapping up." After offering lemonade, which Megan took, he bowed and exited through the same door.

"Now, dear Megan. Why don't you ask what you really want to know?" Dolores sat back in her chair, that same merry quality around her eyes again.

Megan sat in stunned silence. What she really wanted to know? But she'd said everything that Rosa had told her, hadn't she?

"Come now, Megan, I may be old, but I'm not dead, at least not yet. I told you Bryant is a catch, and he's had occasion to share how highly he thinks of you."

Bryant had said something to Mrs. V.? Megan thought back on her attendance at the performances and occasional backstage pop-ins.

"But something keeps you at bay, doesn't it? What are you worried about?" Mrs. V. had tipped her head slightly sideways.

"I—I'm really not sure what to say." Megan debated between baring her soul and getting up to leave. This woman had some nerve. And yet, she had to admit it fit Mrs. Van De Morelle. She was a combination of Grandma and nosy talk show host.

"Well then, my dear, let me share with you a few things and perhaps in the mix of it all you might find some help."

Momentarily, Megan wondered how she should respond to this whole conversation.

"For one thing, Bryant comes from a stern father, and he has that in him too. But I've seen him for almost five years, in one way or another. Took to him right away, there's just something about him, very son-like. But I've been careful. Cast and crew don't take lightly to favorites." She smiled then resettled herself in the chair.

"He's been lost at sea, as it were. Pulled between home and lumber yard, and feeling constrained."

"Like he doesn't want to settle down?"

"Ah, the commitment worry. No, it's not that. More"— she lightly stroked the arm of the chair —"Bryant is the type of man who will take time figuring what he wants. But he's not lost. He's weighing the options, going deep, deeper than one would guess face front. He's processing, all the time."

Megan thought of his expression—continually figuring out a math problem.

100

"And very intelligent. But his biggest flaw is personal communication. Over the years I've seen him work with the company, the passengers, the bigwigs"—she nodded deprecatingly —"and he started off so strong and, frankly, overbearing. But he learned quickly that it got him nowhere. That's Bryant. He's an observer, and a quick learner, when he wants to be. And he made small changes. Helped someone with packages. Remembered someone's name. Brought a passenger down to dance on stage, on impulse. Now it's a plus, he's really very good. But it took a while for him to see it and get there."

Megan couldn't deny it. Part of her recoiled at this conversation, but the other part thirsted like a dying man in the desert for every word. Beyond her worry of showing interest, she craved the truth.

Mrs. Van De Morelle brought her glasses to the edge of her mouth. "Mind you, he needs someone with enough spitfire that he won't trample them. On the other hand, he needs an innocence, a pureness to trust. That's the way he is. He's not one for shopping around. When he gives his heart, he does it fully and completely, no turning back."

Did she mean he'd given his heart fully to Brittany, no turning back, or did she mean he was ready to do that with her? Megan had to know. This was key, absolutely crucial. Tossing pride aside, she could feel the sweat bead on her forehead as she worked up to ask that very question.

A knock and then Keenan entered the salon. "Ms. Van De Morelle, dey are waiting for you."

She sighed. "Well, my dear, I'm called." Mrs. Van De Morelle rose and guided Megan to the door, all the while Megan thinking furiously how she could still get an answer. But the butler remained, asking a few logistical questions.

Dolores turned to her. "Now, do yourself a favor, and take what I've said with a grain of salt." She tapped her with the glasses. "The best thing you can do for yourself is to find out, *for yourself.*" She ushered Megan to the door. "And remember on the fourth number to smile more. You look like you're getting a root canal." With her trademark grin, she limply shook Megan's hand, then turned and stepped back into her main salon.

Meandering back to her cabin, Megan replayed the revelatory conversation, chastising herself for not being more bold and asking her question. And why had Mrs. Van De Morelle been so open with her about Bryant anyway? She had shared unbelievably intimate information, even though Megan hardly knew the woman, although that was certainly the style of Mrs. V.

Megan unwittingly pieced together a picture of Bryant from what she now knew, confusing as it was. Phrases ran through her head like a ticker tape: Lost at sea. Weighing options. Stern father—he has that in him too. Biggest flaw is personal communication. Overbearing. Brittany's words tacked onto the end: He wants what he wants. Focuses like a laser beam. Loses interest. Just performing, it doesn't mean anything. Megan frowned. So far the picture of Bryant wasn't pleasant. Those traits alone should make her cautious, if not run.

Passing through main ship entertainment areas, the carnival-like sounds surrounded but did not touch her. She thought of how it felt to be with him. It didn't feel like a performance. Something deep within her said some things shared were a true likeness, and some were not. And even so, he was a real person, with flaws and imperfections to be smoothed and ironed out. He had done some smoothing already, *was* doing that still.

And he was good. Megan could feel that to her core. She realized it was what instinctively attracted her to him. A sort of intangible tangible feeling of security and trust enveloped her when she was with him. That's why she constantly felt able to let down and had to work so hard to keep her distance.

Obviously, Mrs. Van De Morelle adored him, and she was shrewd. And had generously shared plenty of positives. Quick learner. Small changes. Helped people. When he gives his heart, he does it fully, no turning back.

No turning back. Was he still in love with Brittany? Was he just being friendly to Megan, her own sensitive, starved-for-love mind and soul playing tricks?

If only she knew how he felt. More importantly, how she felt about him, truly. Was he just a rebound interest, a safe place for her desperate need to trust? That wasn't fair to him. Maybe that's what held her back.

Entering her cabin, she breathed with open relief. Empty. Flopping down on her bunk, Megan's thoughts crowded her mind like minnows. Clear moments returned to her—wiping chocolate from Bryant's face. Him touching her wrist. Looking down at her in the hall, puzzled, almost hurt. So open and trusting. She swallowed. It had been too real, too raw, no performance about it. His eyes, that electricity and warmth, it filled her up in places she didn't know were empty.

Instinctively, she tried to push those thoughts away, to be rational, or at least draw up some sort of hostility and dislike. But she couldn't.

Megan was slipping into a realm she didn't want to go, wasn't ready to face, and grasping for handholds to stop her. Enemy. That hadn't worked. Acquaintance. Buddy. None of it had worked. Falling, falling, with no other safety hold to stop her, the truth waiting at the end of the fall.

It didn't make sense, and it defied all that she wanted right now. But there it was. She cared for him. Deeply. On his own merit. In allowing the admission, a loving rush of feeling like wave and foam washed over her, confirming it.

Heaven help me, she thought, I can't fall, not yet, and she emotionally grasped for a hold. It was insane, they hardly knew one another. But still, it was clear. And yet just as clear, that she was not ready for this.

Megan checked her watch. Only two hours until she would see him again. How long could she hold this back?

CHAPTER NINE

Sitting at the makeup mirror with round globe lights emitting soft bright light, Megan finished her makeup feeling a curious uneasiness. It was twenty minutes until curtain, and the special July 4th celebration show. But she'd yet to see anyone in the Green Room. Already a full house awaited them, including in the third row a regal Mrs. Dolores Van De Morelle who was surrounded by a great show of tuxedos and expensive gowns.

Megan dusted her face with finishing matte powder, wondering how to behave around Bryant. After pushing aside her previous thoughts from the afternoon, the only thing that came to mind was, be yourself. As if she could trust what that was.

A knock on the door made her jump. "Come in!" she said, surprised someone would knock, looking through the reflection in the mirror rather than turning around. Expecting to see one of the girls, her mouth opened at seeing Bryant instead. The soft bulb lights from the mirror reflected around his image.

"How'd things go with Mrs. V?" he said, about to enter but hesitated.

"Good," she said, soft but unsure what more to say. He watched her, waiting for more. Still gazing at him through the mirror, she put down her brush.

Quietly, she said, "Actually, really well. Thanks for—" She searched and rejected how to say *I'm sorry, I've been horrible, I care for you but can't let myself, I'm still scared but I don't know what to do about it.* So she settled for a generic but earnest "—thanks for everything you've done."

She hoped he understood.

Bryant stared for a moment, as if taking in her face, her manner, her message. "You bet," he said, a slow smile spreading. "Anytime."

He held her gaze. A feeling passed between them, though she couldn't say what.

With a thud, a solid-looking African-American cast girl pushed past Bryant through the door. "You will not believe, will *not* believe this. Clint wants to see you, Bryant, right now." She waved her muscular arms towards Megan. "Everyone is sick."

Bryant turned to her. "Maya, what do you mean everyone? Brittany?"

Megan shot him a look. *Why did he mention her?*

"Not just Brittany, we're talkin' half the cast." She jabbed an earring into her earlobe but couldn't find the right spot. "They went on this excursion thing for some kind of fish and two hours later, they're heaving their guts. They are knocked out"—her arms cut in a referee slide motion—"food poisoning and that's it, baby. And now it's you, you, and me"— she pointed—"and about five people to do the whole show, and twenty minutes until curtain."

"On the Fourth of July show? Mrs. V. is supposed to be out there," said Bryant.

"Not supposed to*, is.*" She shook her head, taking a hair band from her arm and wrapping her black springy curls into a bushy ponytail. "Marvy is talkin' crazy, worried about funding, and Clint looks like he's about to keel over with panic. Get your butt over there and figure out a solution, buddy. Because I can tell you this, I cannot be dipped."

Megan hurried to finish her makeup while Bryant left to talk with Clint. A thousand thoughts fired through her: who would do Brittany's numbers and how would they change the show so last minute? Her hands trembled as she layered mascara. Of course Mrs. V. had to be out there, the Woman with the Golden Purse.

Word had obviously gotten around as the remaining healthy cast and crew members entered the Green Room with expressions ranging from panic to terror.

"How's the rest of the cast?" said Megan.

"They're pretty bad off," said Becca. "I saw them, all white and pasty looking. So nasty."

Another girl nodded. "I know, Tag cannot be consoled. This was his big chance." They both tried to suppress momentary smiles.

Bryant opened the door and strode in. She could sense the energy about him, that take-charge, point-and-shoot she had seen before. Trying to seem unaffected, she ignored the swooping in her stomach.

"New game plan guys, gather round. Marvy's gone to check on the sick people and Clint is doing the sound booth, so we're on our own. I'm gonna stage manage so bear with me. We've eliminated the young Disney sequence, and two of Brittany's numbers. Becca, you're doing the blues segment and the 'Wicked' number, you have the best belt." Becca looked pleased, obviously a dream moment.

"Ron and Sienna, you're doing the Zorro number—just repeat the tango sequence at the end. Patrick you're partnered with Lisa tonight for the last two. And Megan—" he turned to her with what seemed like a slight crinkle at the corner of his eyes. "You're taking Brittany's spot in the salute to Broadway numbers."

Megan's face fell. "You're joking."

"No, I'm not. Clint suggested that would be the best plan as your style is better for the 1950s. And last minute saves." There was a definite merriment in his expression that she couldn't help but return with a glare.

"I can maybe do the Millie song," she said, "but that's it. And you'll have to pitch it down unless you want birds dropping dead."

"We'll see." He turned to the cast, pointing to a paper. "Here's a quick list, I'll post it by the stage. Curtain is in ten. Review your steps with your partner. *And don't eat anything*, that's an order from Mr. C. himself. Good luck and *do not* break a leg, not tonight."

Immediately, they broke into controlled but barely restrained panic. Rapid, animated conversations broke out while people simultaneously adjusted costumes and practiced dance steps.

Megan turned to Sienna. "What if we forget what we're doing?"

She fixed the toe of her nylons. "That's called 'freestyle.' And if you forget words to the song, just mouth 'watermelon' but turn your head and do a spin at the same time. They'll think it's just hard to hear."

Megan nodded somewhat dumbly.

"And smile," said Sienna. "Whatever happens, *smile!*"

As soon as she could, Megan surreptitiously stole up to Bryant and pulled him aside. "Bryant, I can't do this. It's not humility, it's reality. I'm not a star performer. Why not have one of the other girls do that medley? Anyone is better than me."

She flapped her arms like a bird. Bryant eyed her suspiciously.

"Sweat patches, I'm trying to stay dry," she said. How could he stay so calm?

He grinned, completely un-phased. "Megan, don't underestimate yourself."

A shiver went through her. "Megan" he had said, in that tone.

Focus.

Bryant connected eye to eye. "Imagine it's the temp agency and you're selling the job to that ornery worker." She looked dubious. "It's the best I can do on short notice. Just get on stage, own it, and sell it." He stepped into her and took both her hands. They shook. "Get a soda, the sugar helps. You can do this. I've watched you dance, and I've heard you sing."

"Oh, really?" She smiled but it was limp.

"Yes." He stared into her. She felt that sureness from him, his eyes, his being, calming her mind. The fluttering reduced to a small, hollow space below her navel and she felt a sense of self-control return. Borrowing his confidence, she felt bolder.

He winked. "Twist an ankle." Megan slugged him on the arm as she moved to the doorway.

Ten minutes later the curtain opened to a packed audience. It seemed everyone wanted to be where the celebration was tonight. Megan swallowed down the nausea in her stomach, but Bryant looked almost revitalized by the emergency. How could he seem so carefree when clearly they would have to fill time from the eliminated dances?

The opening numbers felt a bit shaky but not noticeably so. On the fourth number, Bryant forgot his lines on the "Fiddler on the Roof" but instead turned to the audience and said, "You know this one, sing along with us." Moment to moment he continued to save the performance. After the initial shock, Megan began enjoying it, even ad-libbing with Bryant during one of the sequences. With the adrenaline of the unknown, an unusual devil-may-care attitude prevailed in the dancers, creating a real and pulsing energy on stage. Megan could tell the audience felt it too by their unusually rapt attention.

Near the end of the seventh number, Megan remembered they were missing the two after it. A nervous wave went through her. She didn't want to provide any on-call duets. What exactly what was Bryant going to do?

As if in answer, Bryant let the last of the music fade out, then stepped out of rank and took the microphone, asking the dancers line up around the semi-circle of the stage and sit in a waiting position.

"How are you all doing tonight?" he said, walking down the middle of the stage like Wayne Newton in a Vegas show. "You may not know this, but we have some stars right here in our audience this evening. Mrs. Van De Morelle and our distinguished Board of Directors. Translation, the Money People." A ripple of laughter went through the audience and polite applause as Mrs. Van De Morelle stood and waved, then gestured to the people on her right and left.

"And for an unexpected treat, we boast a star dancer in her own right. Yes, we have a former Net Senior Sensation with us, who has wowed audiences at halftimes for the New Jersey Nets. But she's not just any dancer. She is seventy-five years young and still going strong. Ina, come on down for just a minute and let us salute you and your shining career."

Megan's jaw dropped as a slightly round-shouldered figure with a dazzling yellow wig stood up and moved down the aisle, waving to the rows as she passed. She smiled particularly at a gray-haired man with a bowtie—Megan remembered him from the Meet & Greet—who alighted to lead her down to the stage. They chatted as they climbed the stairs.

Megan was standing somewhat close to Bryant, who had moved to stage left. "What are you doing?" she spoke quietly from the side of her mouth.

"Killing time, babe."

Stepping up on stage, Ina drew Bryant to her and whispered something in his ear. "Is that right? I do believe we have a request." He gestured to sound booth. "Clint, do we have Glenn Miller's 'In the Mood' in that jazz medley?" A pause and then a thumbs-up. "Ina, this is your lucky night, and ours."

Ina and the bow-tie gentleman smiled and took a dancing position as the minus-track began to play. Bryant stepped off stage to watch. Megan caught his eye and he winked again, holding her gaze. She smiled, small at first, then full of their shared, connected feeling that she couldn't articulate but that electrified her.

For the next few minutes, Ina and Bow-tie Man delighted the audience with a Fred Astaire-Ginger Rogers style of dance, culminated by Ina going down in the splits in her evening pant suit.

The crowd erupted in applause.

Collectively, the cast approached the final number with a buzzing anticipation—just minutes to the finish line. The crew had prepared some pyrotechnics, a nod to Fourth of July fireworks that went with the closing scene, and adding jitters about whether or not they would work.

Megan played down her own share of nerves. The last sequence was the Broadway medley, the one he usually danced with Brittany. It was a romantic 50's story in song and dance of three girls on a trip to see the world who all end up in love. Megan was petrified at seeming too into it, or not enough.

A few minutes later as the brilliant spotlight funneled on the two of them, Bryant had Megan in a low dip holding onto her back, just as he had done on her first rehearsal. Two other couples were frozen in different positions, as if dancing at a small French café. The curtains were ready and this was it, do or die. Megan breathed irregularly, both from the awkward position and from her rising fear.

Just before the curtains opened, Bryant looked down at her, taking in her face, suddenly serious. He looked as if to say something important. Then said, "Don't watch your feet."

Megan laughed, short and spontaneous. Immediately, she relaxed and turned her face toward the crowd.

The music started, a jazzy American sound awakening the couples as the girls showed the Parisian men their native style of dancing. Turning and moving with upbeat steps, Megan beamed at the audience, but prayed the performance would hurry up and end.

After completing the humorous part, the music for Bryant's solo, "Love Surprised Me," started slow and soft with a single clarinet. The Parisian jazz café dimmed and a single light focused on Megan while the other dancers stole away from the stage. The smoky jazz sounds, the romantic eclectic colors, it reminded her of an old Cyd Charisse movie her mother used to watch.

Megan stood beside a café chair with her suitcase, dramatically showing angst as she glanced from the door to her watch. Her beloved was late and she was leaving to return to America. After a short dance solo, ridiculously simplified, she picked up her suitcase to go, when Bryant hurried in, disheveled and obviously something amiss. Together they began a coy dance, not knowing what, but wanting to say something to make the other stay.

As she thought ahead of the dance, Megan felt curiously detached and began to think this wouldn't be so bad after all. Not much was required on her part—she'd seen them perform it for weeks—mostly sitting, turning, and acting while he tried to explain why he was late, and his feelings for her. Turn, stop, sit on the chair, look pouty and pained. No, it wasn't so bad after all.

Then he started singing.

She'd heard him sing before, but not to her. He took her hand, just the fingertips, then pulled her gently into a turn close to him. Every movement, he was completely focused, staring into her, looking through her. Megan was confused. Was he acting? Was this real? Her face warmed from neck to forehead—it felt uncomfortably real.

Never knew, never knew until you let me.
All adrift, without a certain shore.

He sang, sure and clear to her. The lights made her dizzy, and she felt a closing in feeling but couldn't understand the source. His hands guided her smoothly and gently—her arms, her waist—then leaning into each other in a sort of waltz around the café. It was all tender and fluid and connected. At first she tried not to look directly into his eyes, but he compelled her to. He wasn't acting, not at all.

Never go, never go, unless we go together.
Until today, I didn't know what for.

No, she thought, that can't be for her. It's too soon, he doesn't even know me. He's acting, surely he's acting. But the sound of his voice had dropped, a warm, husky tone. His eyes didn't move from hers throughout the sequence, all the time serious and inquiring.

For now I know,
now I know,
I'm home.

As the music slowed to the finale, Bryant gently turned her and leaned her back as the closing notes of the single clarinet soulfully drifted into the air. His face was inches from hers and she knew she should do something, but what? Turn, turn her head, that was what she'd seen Brittany do.

But his face was before her, his mouth a breath away. He stared through her eyes and into her heart and she felt a tangible, pulsing current pass between them. The sometimes playful thread that usually wove through the dance was gone. It was deep and open and soulful. The music, the moment, it all had swelled to this point, as if waiting for a capstone ending.

Without warning or thought, he leaned in and kissed her softly on the lips, just once, as the last note sounded and faded. The softness of it, the feel of his skin to hers, and the shimmering tingle made her feel removed. She wasn't on a stage, she was somewhere, floating.

Boom! The small tubes of fireworks lit brightly behind them while the crowd clapped appreciatively. Megan couldn't tell if it was the heated lights or the kiss, but she felt warm and fuzzy. She could hear clapping and knew the curtains were closing but it registered slow and muffled. He still stared at her, she stared back. The current held between them as the last firework ended.

Once the curtains dropped, he lifted her up, gently, then turned professionally to the front as the curtain opened again. The obligatory bow—smiling, bobbing—hurled Megan back to the present. Had it been real, or was it for the show?

She had no time to solve it as the cast immediately barged in between them, chuckling and making comments, "Nice ending, dude. Can I do that number next time?" and "Hey, no PDA, this is a family tour."

Feeling her face hot and pink, Megan refused to look at Bryant and hurried back to the girls' dressing room to change, all the while wondering what it meant.

But arriving at the Green Room, already a few of the semi-recovered cast members had joined them to congratulate their performance. Megan tried to unobtrusively steal into a corner but the remaining cast entered—sweaty, elated, and ready to party.

"We totally rock, people!" said Sienna, who turned to Maya and gave her a high five. "Who's for The Cove?" Loud assents were all around, just as Bryant entered. After finishing talking to and thanking the others, the cast nixed changing and immediately moved out to celebrate.

With just Bryant and her left in the room, Megan sensed the awkwardness of the moment but he walked to her. "Come on, I know a place that's got great food."

Trying to smile at his joke, she was unsure. Was he playing with her? "Aren't you exhausted?"

"Exhausted but starved," he said, taking her hand and leading her toward the door. "I don't care if it's got e-coli, I need sustenance."

"Gee, now I've got an appetite."

Trying to go with the moment, Megan followed him but still fought the question of the kiss. Walking down hallways together, still in costume, they were stopped by various people who, on recognizing their dress, engaged in well-wishes and conversation so that by the time they made it to the buffet lounge, it was closed.

"Seriously?" Bryant stood in disbelief. "This can't be. A cruise ship and no food?" He turned to Megan. "Water, water everywhere ..."

". . . nor any drop to drink," she finished automatically. "*Rhyme of the Ancient Mariner*. Bryant, I don't know what to tell you. Maybe we could—"

A sound from near the doorway on the right made them both turn. A sweet-looking fair-haired girl gestured to them. "You singers, yes?" She sounded Russian.

Megan nodded.

"Oh-kay." She stared at their costumes. "I can get you food. Wait here."

Together they slumped into nearby chairs, the post-adrenaline from the show wearing off. In a few minutes the girl returned with round china plates piled high with chicken, pulled pork, a medley of vegetables and roasted potatoes, and soft buttery rolls balanced on top. She handed them over carefully, as well as two bottled sodas.

Expressing sincere thanks, they made their way to her favorite starboard area of the Atrium deck and put their plates on the empty chess board. Neither of them spoke for the first few minutes, both giving into the physical need for fuel. It had to be close to 2:00 a.m., but curfew worries were forgotten tonight. The aroma from the plate made her salivate. Savory sauces and juicy meats—the tastes were divine and they ate ravenously. In between bites both of them recounted the evening's successes, keeping the conversation on a safe level.

"My particular favorite being your impromptu variety show," said Megan, grinning as she put down her fork. "And the Senior Sensation? How do you remember these things?"

"Ah, the art of a true showman," he said, swallowing a huge bite of chicken. "And a kiss-up. I've learned for the past five years a little bit about making it work when you've got nothing in hand."

"Well, I think you sold Mrs. V.," said Megan, leaning back while crossing her legs. The strange evening and the late hour gave her a fuzzy, giddy feeling. The meal filled her with a peaceful contentment. She raised her soda bottle to Bryant. "To showmen."

He raised his. "To kissing up." Then he got a reflective look, and instantly she knew what he was thinking. She looked deep into her soda bottle for something to do. It struck her for the first time where they were—the deck devoid of people, and the ocean breeze surprisingly mild tonight, lifting both her hair and soft capri-length skirt in lilting motions. Everything in the environment overflowed with romance. She felt her mouth go sticky and took a drink.

He reached down for her feet which were close to him, and gently took off a shoe.

"I wouldn't do that if I were you," she said, light but tremulous.

"I've smelled worse."

"Thank you." He rubbed soft and slow, starting at the center of her foot then spreading out to the heel.

A dueling match went on in her soul, one that Bryant could hardly be aware of: her instinct was to pull away. Her in-the-moment feeling was to wait. Just wait. And let it play out for a few more minutes. She watched his expression as he focused on her foot—the math-solving eyebrows, the firm lips set in concentration. Too tired to fight it, Megan gave in to the sheer pleasure of the feeling as he kneaded out tension in the soft center of her arch. It almost made her sigh aloud, but she did not.

From below they could hear the drifting sounds of a Benny Goodman-type band playing on one of the open promenades.

After a few more minutes, Megan felt a touch on her hand. She didn't know her eyes had closed. Opening them, she saw Bryant standing before her. "Shall we?"

She returned a drowsy smile, heady with the air and the night and the massage. "Honestly, how can you want to dance?"

"It's not dancing. You're holding me up." He pulled her to him, and both shuffled in a tired but content circle waltz. She laid her head on his shoulder, allowing herself to lean into him. The ocean and man smell, the smoothness of the costume, the feel of his hand on her waist and the firmness beneath his shirt. For a few delicious minutes time was gloriously suspended.

Megan pulled back for a moment without interrupting the movement to look at him. She took in his startling blue eyes, the sure line of his jaw, and felt his firm hold on her.

Quietly she said, "Do you really want to dance?"

He looked down at her. "No, I just really want to hold you."

Together they turned in a close, relaxed circle, feeling the sweet normality of it.

CHAPTER TEN

Bryant glanced at the clock on the small nightstand again. Still 5:03 a.m. He could not get the evening out of his mind. And what had possessed him to kiss her, on stage? The picture came clearly to him: leaning back under the lights, her softly tanned skin with just a slight glow from exertion, her chestnut hair falling behind her. Those brown, soulful eyes. How could he help it? It was her, the feel of her, the way she moved with him, her essence. Her. Megan.

Agh, he rolled over, trying to find a comfortable position. She was a constant thread running through his life, ingratiatingly woven into him in some unintentional way. And now surely he'd blown it. Megan was not ready for public displays of anything, and he'd kissed her, *on stage*. Luckily, it seemed part of the performance so she was spared any real interrogation. He had no idea how she would respond this morning. Sure she had eaten on deck with him, even danced, but he could see she was humoring him, letting her guard down only for a moment. Even walking her to the cabin she had begun to shut down, return to her distant state. And now it was morning—almost—and she might be regretting she'd spent any time with him at all.

Not that that would stop him. But he had to get it together and move carefully with her. She was skittish, like an injured bird. Let her give the next clear signal. Allow her to be comfortable. Take it slow and let her give some direction, show her threshold.

Bryant let out an exasperated sigh. Too much work, that's what she was. And why for the five hundredth time did he care? In the dark quiet, with the sun barely lightening through the small porthole window, he listened for answers.

None came.

Megan lay in her bed, relishing the morning quiet of an empty room. Foregoing breakfast with the girls, she wanted the time to reflect on the night before and choose how to act today. According to Chalise, several of the cast members, including any who had recovered from the food poisoning, were gathering for the last excursion of the current voyage, this time to Jamaica.

Megan felt compelled to go. In general, she disliked touristy trips, but something told her Bryant might be there too. With his name came the mixed feeling of giddiness and fear. How should she be after last night? What exactly had happened?

He had walked her to her cabin afterwards. She had avoided a scene by being professional and slipping quickly into her room. Although she had tried to stay awake to savor the evening's events, surprisingly—in a state of complete contentment—sleep had come almost immediately.

But now in the peaceful morning she relived the sweetness of the performance kiss and the slow, tender dance on the deck. A warm, liquid feeling flowed through her, like drinking hot, creamy cocoa after a cold sledding day.

Unbidden, came the gray doubt, tainting the joy. But why?

Unwelcome thoughts about Bryant randomly floated through her mind. *A Premier Performer. Looks like it means something, but it doesn't. Just a friendly guy.* Could he be playing her? The cold grayness pushed out the warmth and she sat up. She'd been a sap before, that's right. She had had similar feelings, though not exactly the same, and had been wrong. Dead wrong.

And last night, nothing had really been said, or exchanged. He had kissed her—as part of the performance. They had eaten—they were starving. He had waltzed with her on the deck—well, turned in a circle. He'd wanted to hold her, but wasn't that men?

Nothing declared, You and I are a thing. And that's what she needed now. No, required. Some evidence or proof, actual words that said, "Yes, I like you and want to date you exclusively"—in writing would be even better. Yes, that's where she was and that's what she needed to feel safe. Forget this wondering and guessing and soaking in euphoria. If he wasn't going to state his intentions clearly, neither was she. Otherwise it was just a lot of stage lighting and giddy feelings, and she'd have learned nothing.

The gray doubt felt heavy in her mind. Shaking it off, Megan dressed for the trip but vowed no matter what, not to appear overly interested in Bryant. She would be wiser this time. He would need to state his clear intentions, not just for a night, but for a relationship.

After an uneventful shuttle ride through a few back streets of Jamaica—both she and Bryant had sat on opposite ends—the bus dropped all eight of them at the main gathering point. Bryant hadn't seemed particularly different—friendly to everyone, including her, but nothing distinct. That answered her question. It had been the performance, the headiness of the night. Fine.

Megan tried to behave the same as usual, ignoring the dull pain in her heart.

As the group made plans, everyone immediately opted for the beach, except Chad, who preferred to check out an electronics store. Clint had been clear about the buddy system, especially here. Megan watched the female cast members gaze openly at Bryant and Garrett. She pointed to Chad and said, "Buddy system, I'll go with him."

She couldn't be sure but from her periphery Bryant seemed to frown. Well, too bad for him. Megan still didn't know what last night meant to him and he wasn't saying.

As the girls excitedly chatted and clustered into taxis, Megan turned to ask Chad about the store location and, shockingly, found Bryant at her elbow.

"What's up?" she said.

"Chad is directionally challenged. I'd better make sure you guys can find the place." Another male crew member trotted up to them. "Taxi's full, can I ride with you guys? I need a cover for my phone."

Squeezing into the taxi, the two guys came in last, forcing Megan halfway onto Bryant's lap. He gently sat her square on his legs but kept his hand around her waist for balance. It felt good, she couldn't deny it. Those solid hands made her feel safe. But that bugged feeling came back, that feeling of falling but this time at the top of the rollercoaster, at the tipping point but fiercely holding back, knowing where this could go. But even as she thought it, Megan knew it was exhausting to try holding back. At some point, she would tire. Maybe that's what he was counting on.

Irritated, she purposefully looked toward the taxi front, wearing a neutral expression but involuntarily worrying she was too heavy for his lap.

Why did he have to stick his broken nose into things?

At the electronics store, the two other young men were in heaven. After thirty minutes and no signs of their surfacing, Bryant took Megan's arm and leaned in. "What do you say we make a break for it?"

"What about the buddy system?"

"And what am I?" He gave her a look. "Does it have to be nerds?"

"Then I guess you'll do." She tried to be light but before she could suggest they wait another half hour, Bryant was already exiting the store, pulling her with him.

Stepping into the Jamaican afternoon sunshine, he hailed a taxi.

"How's it goin'?" Bryant spoke to the driver who wore a brightly knitted cap. "Do you know where we can get a great dinner with some good local atmosphere?" Half-turning in his seat, the driver revealed blinding white teeth that set off his charcoal black skin.

"Call me Jahaman. And I know just da place," he said in a deep throaty voice, assessing the two of them and chuckling under his breath. Bryant and Megan exchanged looks—hers concerned, his adventurous. To avoid giving a wrong impression, she kept close to her window. A few times Bryant gave her a perplexed look but didn't say anything.

Megan felt her stomach gurgle. Why couldn't she just be? All this worrying and what should she do, how should she act. But he showed no signs of anything different. Well, it was a stage kiss. Get over it. This was life, the life of Premier Performers.

The driver took them down dirty strips of land that only denoted "roads" because of the generally consistent cut path through the people and hodgepodge construction. A variety of houses appeared on the sides—half-built cinder block foundations, wooden shacks, even cardboard boxes where brightly but barely dressed children stood in front, silently watching them drive by. It made Megan quiet and thoughtful.

"It's odd, isn't it, the disparity?" she said.

"Again with the big words." They had been mostly silent but it was comfortable when she let it be. He so reminded her of Sam. Her brother talked the same way, understood the same things. It was easy being with Sam. It was easy being with Bryant.

"But you're right, it is," he said. "It's the same thing on the cruise ship."

"All the opulence, and indulgence. You see that too?"

"Yeah, even us neanderthalic food hoarders."

"Sorry." She hadn't meant to infer he was clueless.

"I see them," he said. "Pot-bellied men staggering to the next buffet line, talking too loud, drinking too much. It makes me embarrassed to be American."

"You didn't include the ladies. That was gracious."

"Well, I've been warned about assault in Jamaica—" He grinned then looked out at the passing scenery.

Megan hesitated. "That's why I've wanted to help Rosa. She works hard, really hard, and wants more from life. I feel like she only needs the opportunity."

"Well, it's a good desire and I commend you on it. But"— he glanced out the window—"you have to watch out for the actual opportunists. I've been through that before."

She felt funny inside. In a way, it had been an attempt to connect as friends, to make things normal again, though she had no idea why since not ten minutes before she had been wishing he hadn't come. His realistic approach dampened her optimism. She sat quietly.

"I'm not trying to burst your helping bubble," he turned, aware of the silence.

"That's okay."

He faced her full on. "No, that's not what I meant to do." He looked down at his hands for a minute. "On one voyage I met a man, a Slavic gentleman who waited our cast table, back when we used to sit as a group for dinner. He was a good guy, diligent in his job. But there was, I don't know, a gloom and doom about him. He'd been an engineer in his country before the civil war, and he constantly bellyached that everything had gone south from there. 'No opportunities, nowhere,'" Bryant said in an accent, then sat back in his seat. "So, I got in my Ghandi mode and thought, I know a guy, friend of my mother's, who could possibly hire him. I made a ship-to-shore call, got the prelim done on it, then at dinner presented him with the idea, and the offer."

Bryant turned to Megan. "He looked at me kind of bored and said, 'How much?' I said, 'Excuse me?' and he repeated, 'How much does it pay, and how many hours do I work?' Then he rattled off a list of questions—how much vacation time, insurance, severance pay if he quit, stock options. I mean, seriously, he was looking for a better deal than my mom's friend. He said no. Didn't even thank me for the offer, not that I was looking for thanks. It was just very instructive. I thought I had to help this man to a better situation, but what I realized was"—he looked at her with his clear eyes—"this man was highly capable of doing it on his own."

Megan held his gaze, and understood. He wasn't downing her wanting to help. He was letting her know she wasn't the only solution. That was so him. His personality constantly seemed to strip away the strategic image she tried to pursue—yes, she wanted to help, and she could, but he was right. She didn't need to swoop in and save the day. So often being with him felt like that, always revealing herself to herself, even when she didn't want to know. But it was a good kind of knowledge, an awakening and a growing.

A rush of feeling, of several feelings, washed over her. Safe. Wise. Calm. Real. He was all of those. Why did being with him make her soft, that all her carefully laid protective bricks suddenly crumbled with no foundation to sustain them?

Inexplicably, she took his hand. It felt right. There was no other way to be, to express the rush of emotions seemingly unconnected with conversation about working immigrants. He caressed it for a moment, watching her, then sensing this was enough of a step, didn't push it and simply stared ahead, asking the driver how much farther.

A few minutes later they pulled up to a large pink plantation-looking building with beautifully manicured lawns. The driver put his arm over the seat rest and turned to them.

"You go dere, right troo dat entry, and tell them Jahaman sent you. Follow da path down to da beach. Dey have the best bahbaque in town, I'm tellin' you, man."

Bryant pressed some bills into his hand, patted his arm, then got out and turned back to help Megan out of the taxi. He took her hand and led them through the entry, past the uniformed man, and down the winding pathway that sloped to the shore, visible in patches through the lush green foliage.

Megan breathed in the salty air and the sound of surf that beckoned below. Near the bottom they reached a short boardwalk area that led to a private looking beach. Turquoise green water, so clear you could see to the sand, washed up with foamy white waves on the shore. Except for a handful of tanning patrons—some young, mostly older—the beach was fairly empty. Gleaming white lounge chairs dotted the sand in groups, and white-uniformed men and women expertly carried silver trays with a variety of drinks.

Bryant paused and surveyed the scene, then looked down at her like a little boy who has discovered a pirate's treasure. "Well?"

Megan smiled up at him, a swirling in her stomach. She let go just a little at the top of the rollercoaster.

After setting up a spot, they both grabbed some complimentary snorkel gear and swam in the clear aquamarine water. He showed her how to skin dive too, demonstrating how to take three or four deep breaths and blow it out slowly on ascending. After only two tries, she was able to hold her breath a good thirty seconds, and they explored the immediate reef. Myriad neon colored tropical fish darted from their presence. She recognized the Angel, Clown, and Dragon fish. At one point she and Bryant simply floated on the surface and watched the fish play undisturbed.

Dragging themselves from the surf a few hours later, they flopped onto the two large lounge chairs placed side by side, prepared with oversized towels, and watched the sky fade into early evening. They were close enough for arms to touch. He took her hand in his, kissed it and placed it on his chest. Megan let him, allowing herself to simply be in the moment.

They watched the beginning sunset that way, silently taking in the salmon pink and lemonade yellow sky, all gently sound-tracked by rolling surf on sand. Megan didn't know when, but they both fell asleep. She curled up next to his shoulder, their hands and arms still entwined.

When she awoke, he was looking down at her, that half-smile again. She sat up with a slight start, and felt a bit of drool at the corner of her mouth.

"You were KO'd, girl," he said.

"It's the sun, it does that to me."

"I thought it was my mesmerizing conversation."

She tried to straighten her hair but he shook his head. "It's a losing battle. Besides, it looks good that way."

She grimaced.

"I'm serious."

Megan looked out to the ocean, fingering her hair, feeling him watching her. Though the day had been wonderful—easy, friendly, warm—and she had felt relaxed against her will, now it was evening and in a short while they would need to return to the ship.

A few hours of evening togetherness—Megan's ribs tightened. For some indefinable but very tangible reason, she felt afraid. Not of Bryant, with him she felt absolutely safe. Too safe, she thought wryly. She had let herself go and enjoyed the day, and it had been lovely. Almost painfully lovely. She hadn't had these feelings in a long time, being with someone she trusted.

But now, what would he think about it? What would he want in return? She didn't know how to act, how to do this: to understand the signals and what her response should be.

Taking time fixing her hair, Megan tried to appear busy. She hated this, the never knowing, never being sure of herself. Were they friends, were they an item? He had kissed her hand. Friends didn't do that. But why couldn't they just be friends? Friendship was easier: it was clear, it was natural. Romance was confusing and complicated, and always with a hidden cost. It was sweet and wonderful, but then ... then came the surprises. Hurtful surprises. And she felt her heart go tight again.

Grabbing her towel, she stood abruptly. "What's that yummy smell?"

"It's 'da best bahbaque in town, man,'" mimicked Bryant. "The waiter told me it's expensive—an arm and a leg, and maybe an eye—but I think we should check it out." He looked between her and the dinner line already assembling. "I'm starving, how about you?"

She looked over at him, his legs straddling the lounger, leaning forward and relaxed like the happiest man on earth. Why couldn't she feel that way? And now that the afternoon focus on fun was over, she could feel the night.

After folding the towel, Megan put on a light swimsuit cover-up dress, grabbed her bag, and walked with him toward a red and white shack emitting sizzling bursts of spicy sweet barbecue. Strings of bulb lights hung between poles on a nearby wooden dance platform and makeshift bar. Ebony-skinned men with canary yellow and red outfits set up silver steel drums. More of a crowd had gathered on the beach, and a line had already formed in front of the shack with people of all shapes and sizes chatting, gazing at the surf, and toting overflowing plates of Jamaican Jerk chicken, cornbread, and exotic fruit to waiting white tables arranged on the beach.

"I'm starving. I hope this line moves quicker." In a natural motion, he put his arm around her shoulder and tugged her a little closer, gently massaging her left shoulder as they stood. "Man, you're tense. What's up with that, on a Jamaican beach?"

"Your other female fans are more relaxed in line?"

The rhythmic massage paused, then continued. "Okay, so you wake up slow. I'll keep that in mind."

Someone behind them spoke to Bryant, which started a social conversation so typical of him. He was good with people, even her. But something nagged at her—was he for real? Was this just his usual routine with women? Choose your target, connect emotionally, then what, no commitment? Is that what he did with Brittany? The thought of Miss America and their conversation flashed in her mind. Too serious too fast. Couldn't commit. Didn't mean anything. Megan stiffened.

"Hey, you all right?" He bent down to her ear.

That tickle of his breath went right through her cover up and down her spine. She mumbled something and looked for lip balm in her bag to release his touch from her shoulder.

Finally, they received their overloaded plates and Bryant led her to a smaller table near the outer edge. She didn't know how he knew that this would be preferable to the packed center and small talk with strangers—that wasn't her style. And yet, she didn't want to be alone with him. What was the matter with her? Why couldn't she just be? A mental picture of Brittany came to mind again. Surely it was not knowing where those two stood. And, not knowing where she and Bryant stood either. So they had spent the day swimming, and she had told herself to let go. But what did that mean? What did that mean to him?

"Man oh man, this looks incredible." He had pulled out her chair then sat down to eat. "Dig in, woman, this is a fine feast. And none of this, 'I'm on a diet' nonsense, or whatever you women are always on about." He picked up his chicken thigh, savoring the first bite.

Megan took a bite of cornbread, though she wasn't hungry. The soft crumbly bread melted in her mouth as she wondered how to ask, when to ask, what to say. The more relaxed he seemed the more nervous she became.

"I think we only have a few hours before we need to be back," she said out of nowhere.

Bryant glanced quickly at her, elbows bent and ready for another chicken bite. "Kill joy. Can't you just enjoy the moment? I mean, look at this plate."

"I'm just worried that we might miss the shuttle, that's all. We could get in a lot of trouble." She had no idea where this was coming from or where it was going. But inside she was shouting—*I need you tell me what we are and where it's going before I let go any further.*

He chewed, unconcerned. "We won't miss it, don't worry. Just enjoy the night."

Megan put down her fork, staring at him. Something clicked, something very deep down. That phrase, that attitude. She'd heard and felt that before, from Jackson. Sudden layers of feelings followed that thought.

"No," she said firmly. "I need to know when we're leaving to make it back in time."

Bryant paused, the chicken poised in front of him. "Okay." He wore that puzzled expression, but this time wary. He put down the chicken, roughly wiping his hands on the napkin. "Do you not want to be here?"

"No," she said, then quickly added. "I mean, no, that's not it." Her signals were confusing her, and surely him. "What I mean is, yes, I want to be here, I just don't want to be late." Desperately, she hoped he understood, her needing reassurance that what she said mattered. To know he could be trusted to keep his word.

He gazed at her in that way, like he knew something but what, she had no idea. She looked at her cornbread.

"Okay, good to know," he said, smiling, but with bowstring tension. "How about we do this. You choose a time that feels comfortable, and I will move heaven and earth, and Jamaican roads, to make sure we make that time. Deal?"

"Deal." Megan checked her watch. "What about eight thirty? The last shuttle is at nine."

"Done. Now, can we get back to eating before I gnaw on my arm?" He joked but his eyes didn't. The air had changed and it was more impersonal, two people eating a meal. In reality, that was exactly what she desired, to feel safe. But now, in a very small and private place, Megan felt hollow again. She was at the bottom of the rollercoaster, notching her way slowly, irrevocably to the next high point one more time.

The ping of the steel drums began, adding an energetic background to the chatter and surf and bulbed lights. They ate in semi-comfortable silence, Megan more relieved than happy, though still unable to understand her own behavior. A few older couples, obviously from a tour group, braved the wooden platform and began waltzing to the music, oddly American steps to the Jamaican beat. Within minutes, some younger couples joined them on the floor—laughing, hugging, talking—all the while moving to the music. The exuberant mood lifted her spirits as she ate and listened to several songs all with that light, carefree sound.

Bryant sat back and patted his taught stomach. "That was phenomenal," he said, smiling at her. "Time to work it off, lazy bones."

"What?"

He stood and took her hand. That same simple gesture, but it always took her by surprise, the feeling it caused. The naturalness, the easiness. That familiar feeling of home and love.

No, she wouldn't think that, not *that* word.

"Honestly, what is it with you and this incessant dancing?" she said. He only smiled and led her to the dance platform. They climbed it easily and he led her to the fringe.

"I don't know how to dance Jamaican," she said over the din.

"Neither do they," he said, glancing at the tour group. Taking her hands lightly, he started an easy shuffle step, once again surprising her with his ruggedness and build, how easily he moved to the music in an athletic, mannish way. How did he pull that off? She followed his lead, keeping an obvious social distance between them.

An older couple from the "cruise group" danced in waltz position nearby, so close that she bumped into Bryant.

"Oh goodness, I beg your pardon," she said, "I'm just not a dancer."

"Looks like you're doing fine," said Bryant. "Maybe it's your husband."

She blushed. "No, that's not my husband, it's my friend's husband." Seeing Bryant's confusion, she smiled shyly, obviously affected by his good looks. "I'm single. He's just doing me a favor."

"And what keeps you single on a night like this?" They all stayed slightly in motion.

"My Victor, God bless him."

"He passed on?"

"Oh yes," she said, with sweet frankness. "But he never liked to dance anyway. Pity."

"Well, if your dance card isn't full, maybe you can save one for me," said Bryant.

She giggled, though she had to be well over sixty. "Maybe just one, then."

He chuckled and turned back to Megan who watched him intently. "What?"

"Nothing," she said. Was he really, truly like that? All-American boy charm *and* genuine kindness. Did the two go together?

At the end of their dance, he nodded for Megan to sit on a nearby stool at the bar while he asked the older woman to dance. They did a fast and a slow, and from the woman's beaming countenance, Megan guessed it would be the highpoint of her vacation. After exchanging a few comments and returning her to the older gentleman, Bryant came back for Megan with an outstretched hand.

"Oh no, I'm good," she said, shaking her head. He tugged her off the stool anyway. The lively music made her laugh despite her inner battle. They shuffled and occasionally commented, but underlying it all escalated her need to clarify the situation.

A slow song came on. Megan felt the change of tempo and immediately her heart jackhammered. She didn't know where to put her hands.

Bryant stepped into her, pulling her waist gently to him, his other hand taking hers and raising it in a close waltz. Instinctively, Megan followed him, just like when they danced on the deck. But she kept a stiff distance, even though her face was inches from his shoulder, breathing his smell of ocean and sand. Her hand rested on his round, solid shoulder. Beneath her fingers she could feel his muscles move as he adjusted his hold. She tried to look anywhere but his face, so she stared straight ahead at his chest, barely visible through the opening of his white collared shirt. Grimacing, she looked up, to his Adam's apple, then to his jawline. Megan swallowed and stared across his shoulder.

"You must be a dancer or something," she said, trying to make light conversation.

"I hire out on the weekends."

Again, something about the phrasing hit her wrong, raising her guard again. Inexplicably, she pulled back slightly. "Is that how you met Brittany?"

Bryant stopped dancing momentarily, then resumed. "Brittany? What's she got to do with anything?"

"You looked pretty cozy on stage the other night."

"Was someone watching?"

"We were all watching," said Megan, purposely staring straight ahead. The music pulsed slow and rhythmic—Bryant's hand rested on her waist and she tried to ignore how nice it felt.

"What is this, Big Brother?"

"George Orwell, *1984.*"

He ignored her reference. "It's called performing."

"You guys are pretty seasoned *performers,* I guess."

Bryant pulled back gently to look at her. "What's on your mind, Berlin? Just say it straight out, because I'm not that good with guessing."

They continued to turn in a circle. Megan wanted to scream it—were you being with me just like you were with Brittany, with everyone?

"Doesn't it bother you, having felt so, so strongly for someone, and then, not? But still having to be ... together?"

"That's over with." His voice held a slight edge. "It's a closed door, and I just don't open it. Does that answer your question?"

No, it didn't. Megan wasn't sure if that meant he still had feelings and just didn't open them, or if it was a closed chapter.

"No temptation to open it, at all? I mean, she isn't exactly Phyllis Diller."

Bryant laughed out loud. "I seriously don't know how you remember these old timers. No, she's not a Phyllis Diller. And sure it was tough at first, but now, it's not a big deal. It's just performing."

Just performing. Like with Megan? "So, how long did it take, I mean for you to ... to get past it?"

"I don't know. It wasn't like we were getting married, okay?" That quick-flare temper skirted his tone. "At least on my end, it wasn't. I liked her, she's a good girl, and we dated a while and it was all good. But she got more serious than I did, lightning fast, so it was easier for me to leave. It was 'fly down to Daddy's cabin,' and 'you must go on our uncle's yacht,' and after a while I felt shown off like a prize turkey. We had only dated a month before she was already looking at wedding cakes."

Megan narrowed her eyes. Very different version than Brittany's. But, more the same as Jillian's.

"So you ended it because of presumptive wedding plans." She stared at the bulbed lights, turning and shuffling.

"Am I being interviewed on hidden camera here?"

She smiled but held her ground. He thought for a moment.

"I'm not much for shopping, and I'm big on loyalty. We dated and it got a bit serious but I wasn't sure. She played games to get me to make the big step, then jumped ship when I wouldn't. When the deal wasn't as sweet with someone else, she came to me as a backup guy. I'm not a backup guy." She could see his jaw harden. "Brittany was looking for a husband, I just happened to fit the bill."

Megan took that in. "And now you're looking for a wife."

Bryant looked sharply at her.

"Turnabout's fair play," she said.

He stopped dancing. "Whatever it is you wanna say, just say it, Megan. I've got nothing to hide and no agenda to push." His eyes bored into hers, their blueness set off by the clear black rings around them.

Her name. That feeling enveloped her, a whispered warmth, a sureness in hearing him say it. Suddenly it felt intimate and close with all pretense down, so Megan bored right back. "Do you still care for Brittany, that way? At all?"

"Why?"

"Because I'm big on loyalty too. And I don't let just anyone kiss me, even if it is on stage, on a cruise ship. Even if it is just one little kiss."

Then he smiled, that sun-on-water smile, like he finally understood something.

"No, I don't feel anything—that way—for Brittany, at all." He gently pulled her waist to him, steadily watching her. "And who said it was just one kiss?"

Leaning down, he softly, gently kissed her mouth, leaving her without thought or fight. She tentatively returned it, then yielded to him, reaching her hand to the back of his neck before remembering herself and pulling back.

Bryant took her in, calm and studying. "You don't need to, you know. I'm not here to hurt you. I've known it since I saw you on the pier, and I'm still here. You tell me if you're in."

She looked up at him—his earnest expression, his gentleness and security. "I don't know how to be," she whispered.

"Be what?"

"Be with you, as more than a friend. It doesn't come naturally."

"Yes it does. It has been." With a small grin he kissed her again, soft and sweet. Pulling away he said, "Just stop focusing on your feet."

In spite of the romantic moment, she laughed, free and spontaneous, remembering his mantra. It was the tipping point and she let go, down the rollercoaster with a whoosh. She hugged him closely, fiercely, and he pulled her in, holding her firm and tight as they danced and kissed in a circle to the Jamaican beat, oblivious to the world around them.

CHAPTER ELEVEN

Hiding behind the black stage curtain, Megan felt a childish nervousness. She remembered in third grade riding her brother's new bike and crashing it without anyone knowing. She had felt sick until confessing it to her mom. That's how it seemed now, as if she'd done something wrong and was about to get in trouble.

All morning Bryant had been kept busy on errands for Mrs. Van De Morelle so they hadn't connected since last night's Jamaican date. Scenes from the evening flashed continuously through her mind: touching his hand in the taxi. Getting back to the shuttle barely in time—she smiled—costing Bryant an extra $30 for the taxi to make it. Dancing on the platform under the white bulb lights. She instinctively touched her lips. He had asked if she was in, that he was here, but what did that mean? Why didn't anyone ever talk about this part? The movies all showed kisses and fade outs and ending credits. What about the now-I-like-you stage? She'd been burned and now she needed something more concrete.

Hearing sounds, Megan looked around the curtain to see cast members beginning to gather onstage. What should she say, or do, especially in front of them? Nothing. Cast members weren't supposed to show that kind of affection with each other, so there was nothing to worry about. Megan relaxed. And then she saw his caramel blond hair.

Bryant walked to the curtain and scooped her up in a crushing hug with a kiss on the cheek.

He smelled good. Again. But her nervous feeling remained. "I thought cast members weren't supposed to show physical affection."

He laughed outright. "Fifteen weddings and counting." She flushed—that wasn't what she had been driving at. "Just as long as couples don't 'flaunt' it, we're good."

Megan panicked, though she had no idea why. "Aren't you flaunting it by hugging me here?"

"We're behind a stage curtain. Besides, you haven't seen my best flaunting." He raised his eyebrows like Groucho Marx and loosely pulled her on stage, then kissed her hand and let go to get into position. Turning to her spot, she saw Jillian, her mouth hanging open, jerking a thumb toward an unaware Bryant. Megan shrugged and smiled, but blushed slightly. Jillian gave an enthusiastic but discreet two thumbs-up and started looking for someone, presumably Derek, to dish the news.

Once again, though it had been awhile, that sensation of being watched came to her. She quickly looked round, but only saw Brittany adjusting her heel strap and the others engaged in conversation.

Odd.

The performance was typical and went without a hitch, which was good, because Megan found herself fighting to stay focused. Dancing and singing, she reflexively searched for Bryant, and just as often caught him smiling at her. He seemed completely at ease. Megan alternated between euphoria and nausea. Something nagged at her, different than the doubting gray feeling—a warning, a foreshadowing of what she didn't want to know. Twice she could have sworn that Brittany was staring at her, but it was merely the position of the troupe.

After the last bow and the curtain closed, a cacophony of voices swelled in usual conversation—"Heading to the Mirage Deck?" and "We're catching a bite at The Cove, meet us there."

Megan stood at the back curtain, indecisive.

"What's a pretty thing like you doing alone backstage?" Bryant breathed it down her neck, like he had done at the beach. She smiled in spite of herself and turned upward to chide him but he leaned in to kiss her. Like a school girl she moved slightly away, checking for who might see.

Bryant ignored it. "Clint just told me he needs help carrying some damaged scenery backstage. But can I meet you in half an hour? Maybe at—"

"—the chess boards?"

"Took the words right out of my mouth. I got some contraband—oven-roasted turkey, rolls, and marbled fudge cake."

"How'd you get that?" He could have brought Spam and Megan would have been thrilled.

"I've made a blood oath not to tell." He stepped even closer. "But I *can* divulge it has to do with a woman in pearl eyeglasses."

"Who thinks you're the best thing since sliced bread."

"Or marbled fudge cake."

He leaned into her but she looked around again. Bryant mocked looking left and right like a spy, then planted one on her, shaking his head as he turned to go.

"And practice up on your ... chess."

"Ha."

She couldn't deny it, a helium-like sensation rose in her stomach. It was like happiness but different, a sort of freedom and that airy letting go. But still, an unseen weight stuck to the bottom, as if the feeling flew high and free, and then bam, caught on a branch, unable to go farther.

In the dressing room, Megan kept to the corner stall and changed into sweats as quickly as possible. Opening the stall curtain she gasped, almost walking into Jillian.

"What—are you stalking me?" Megan put her hand to chest. "You scared me to death."

Jillian moved into the stall and closed the curtain. "Okay, spill it. All of it. How long, how strong, and *why did you not tell me?*"

"I—what? It's—I don't know," said Megan, feeling claustrophobic. But Jillian put her hands on her hips, unmoved. "Okay but can I mention you've been busy with Derek, and sleeping when we got back last night, I might add."

"You couldn't wake me for this? Come on, details. When did this happen? Has he kissed you? I can't believe you haven't told me anything."

"Shh," said Megan, peeking out of the muslin curtain to check for listeners, then closed it, continuing in a whisper. "It's just, I don't know, it happened. But to be honest, I don't really know what we are. In fact," her face clouded, "we haven't had two seconds to talk today." She quickly relayed the experience in Jamaica the night before with Jillian responding enthusiastically.

"But now, I just think it's strange," said Megan. "And ridiculous, actually. I mean, where is this gonna go?" For the first time, she said aloud what had plagued her heart. The situation really was ridiculous. "And a kiss? Or a day in Jamaica together, what does that mean? At least to him. I'm not that way, Jillian, you know me. A kiss means something, and a few kisses even more than that. I'm not here to play around, and definitely not to—"

"Okay, you stop it." Jillian pointed a finger at her, whispering loudly. "You run with this. I'm telling you girl, he's the best thing going, well, except for Derek. If he wants to hold your hand, let him hold it. If he wants to smack your lips till they fall off, you say, 'Smack away.' If he says I love you, let go and tell him how you feel." She stepped closer to Megan, finger still pointing. "You jerk this guy around and he's going to get sick of it. Say what you think, ask him your questions, and talk to him like a real person. I don't know why you shut down like this, but it is time to stop sabotaging your own happiness."

Megan's eyes watered despite her willing them not to. Jillian grabbed her hands and squeezed, this time her expression soft.

"Megs, don't hold back. You can trust him, you really can. He's wonderful, inside and out, just like he seems. You're safe."

Megan nodded briefly. She could feel it in her soul—a holding back for so long for love and caring and wanting to trust, so full that the right word would make it spill over.

"Go see him, right now, don't wait. Well, maybe change into something nicer than old gray sweats, but then go see him. Wrap your arms around him and let yourself sink into this, okay?" Jillian gave her a quick hug, then exited the stall.

After storing her costume, Megan hurried back to her room to quickly change again. Only this time, she envisioned the capri skirt with white peasant blouse. She couldn't repress a smile. Checking her watch she frowned—only about 10 minutes until Bryant would be there.

Entering the hallway to reach her room, she saw Rosa leaning over her cart, stifling sobs.

"Rosa?" said Megan. "Rosa, what's the matter?"

Rosa looked up, surprised to see anyone at the late hour. Upon recognizing Megan, her face crumpled. Still, she withheld talking and only shook her head.

"It's me, Rosa, you can tell me. Did someone hurt you?" Megan looked her up and down for any signs of injury.

"No, no, yees, but not dat," and she let out a string of troubled Spanish and gesturing to the opposite hallway and the ceiling.

"Slow down and let me help you. Tell me in simple words."

Rosa took a deep breath. "Miguel, mi amor. We get paid, three days ago. We dock. I gave him check. My two checks. I no deposit last time, my shift no over." She hiccupped. "And he promise to cash. But no come back. He no come back!" She almost wailed but put a hand over her mouth. "He no come back, three days. He fired. The money, all gone. I send my family. I don't know what to do."

Megan was speechless. She put her arm around the puffy-eyed girl. "Rosa, I'm so sorry. Lo siento. I'm sure there's a good reason." But Megan spoke more positively than she felt. Bryant's words in the taxi came back to her—opportunist, manipulator, swindler.

Bryant. He would know what to do.

"Rosa? Listen to me, okay?" She took the girl's face gently in her hands. "It's going to be all right. I'm going to find the person who can help. No worry, okay? I will get help."

Rosa shook her head vehemently. "No, no. If someone find out, I in big trouble. No okay to give checks. I stupid. I be in big trouble."

"No you won't. This help is good. He'll know what to do and we'll figure it out, okay? Finish your job then meet me back here in thirty minutes, okay? Thirty minutes, entiendes?"

She smiled bleakly. "Entendio. Okay, I finish. But no make trouble."

"No trouble." Megan had said it confidently, yet inside, she had no clue what to do. But Bryant would. Or in her soul she hoped so.

Clint wiped his forehead. "Just one last piece backstage, if you don't mind, Bryant. Then I think we're done." He hefted three bulky loops of different colored electrical cords. "I'm gonna take these up to the sound booth."

Bryant felt a small sheen of sweat on his forehead. "No problem. I'll lock up." Clint nodded as he headed down the hallway in the opposite direction. Bryant lightly jogged down the hall and across the stage, but stopped still on the landing.

"Britt, what are you doing here? I thought everyone was gone?"

She had changed into hot pink leggings with a tank and low, loose dancer shirt, her hair pulled up with a few curls falling down her neck and shoulders. "Oh, I had to put away some of the costume tubs."

Bryant looked confused. "I thought the girls were helping with that."

"They were heading to The Cove so I said I'd do it, after I changed." Something in her voice, Bryant couldn't place it, but it urged him to finish quickly. Brittany lightly stepped over to a small tote next to a stack of three large tubs, obviously too big for her to carry. Bryant debated, checking his watch, but gave in to the gentleman breeding his mother had instilled in him.

"Can I help you with those?" he said.

"Well ..." She glanced between him and the stack. "Sure, that would be great. Thanks, Bry."

Picking up the small tote, Brittany followed Bryant who had lifted the three tubs in one load, and headed down the dimly lit hall. They stopped at the small stage closet, a 10 by 10 room crammed with props, costumes, DVDs, and boxes of paraphernalia.

Megan hurried along the hallways, into the now tomb-like auditorium, crossing over to stage left. She had supposed Bryant would be here but now with the low lighting, wondered if he had finished early after all.

Turning the corner Megan saw a light flooding eerily from the stage closet into the dim hallway. She wanted to cheer—he was here, he could tell Rosa what to do. It surprised her how automatically she had thought of him, relied on him, knew that she could turn to him. Just like Sam.

As she drew closer she heard voices—and frowned. One was definitely female. Confused, she walked closer to the room.

Scooting in the limited free space of the room, Brittany climbed the small ladder. "If you hand me one at a time, I can put them on the shelf."

Bryant paused. Again he felt something in his gut, unclear but insistent, though all he said was, "No, I can do it."

"Bry, I'm not a child. Hand me that first one." And she reached for the tub. "Show went good tonight, huh?" After securing it, she reached for the second.

He felt a sweat bead rivulet down the side of his face. Something wasn't right—her tone, her manner. "Yeah, it was a good show. It's been a pretty mellow run."

"But you've had some special excitement. And isn't that part of a good show?"

He didn't know what she meant.

She paused, looking down at him like Juliet in a turret. "I just want you to know, I'm happy for you, Bry. I am. But I think you should know ..." Her pink lips pouted as she took the third tub from him.

Just as she moved to place it in the cubby it shifted and dropped. Bryant reached for it and she stumbled from the ladder right into Bryant's outstretched arms.

With her against him, he fell back into a stack of cardboard boxes that gave with their weight. "Whoa," he said but she didn't let go of her arms around his neck as he flailed to get upright.

"Bry, I've never stopped caring about you, not once. I know this is crazy—so crazy—but," she was crying now, really crying. Bryant tried to take it in but it felt like slow motion video.

"I love you, Bry, I can't—how can I help you see it?" Sobbing and clinging she was millimeters from his face. "If you only knew ... understood ... I always have, and I'm ready now. One more chance, that's all I'm asking ..."

Still leaning back with her against him, he looked into her wet, fringed blue eyes—pleading and childlike—looked past them to see Megan standing in the doorway with an ashen expression. She uttered one sound, a wounded, soulful cry, then she turned and ran.

CHAPTER TWELVE

Bryant almost threw Brittany off of him. "What kind of a stunt was that? Are you insane?"

She leaned against a stack of boxes, wiping mascara that unwittingly smeared on her face. It struck him that she looked lined and tired, like an old woman who had been in show business too long. "I'm sorry, I had to . . . so you could choose, before ... before anything—"

"Get that out of your head right now, for good." His voice boomed in the closeness of the room. "There will never be anything between us again. And you can keep those kinds of shenanigans to yourself." She only nodded—broken, understanding—but still pleaded with her eyes. He turned and ran as fast as he could after Megan. Racing through the hallways and up the deck stairs, he breathed hard and angry. He knew where she would go.

Reaching the walk-through, he came to a sudden stop. This is where they usually met, it was their place. At one in the morning the chess boards were bare and the deck empty, as always.

He stood, chest rising and falling, listening. "Megan, I know you're here." Nothing.

Surveying the silent deck, he said. "I look like an idiot talking to myself." Then, realizing he needed a better tack than his own humiliation, he said, "I told Britt to knock it off. Just know, if she puts one toe out of line, I'll tell Clint and she'll be on another ship."

The chug, chug sound of the ship engines churning the water filled the silence.

"It wasn't anything you're thinking. You know what she's like. You *know* that." Bryant looked around, wondering for the first time if she was actually not there. "I told her, clear as day, there's nothing between us, never can be."

Bryant shook his head. "Listen, I can't do this. I care about you, Meg. I like you and I'm here, still here, even with all the grief you've given me from day one. There's a problem, so let's talk about it. But I'm not going to chase you down every time you get scared."

The waves churned against the side of the massive ship. Not a sound or a movement on the deck. Shaking his head, he turned and went back in the walk-through, down the steps.

Megan watched it all, crouched from behind the farthest chess table. As soon as he was gone, she grabbed her knees and sobbed silently.

It wasn't the shock of seeing Brittany and Bryant like that, not really. She could see it for what it was. It was that sickening, familiar feeling of betrayal. Brittany's blonde hair, her smacked up against him, the clandestine feeling, and Megan being the one that didn't know. Images of Jackson and his antics uncontrollably sped through her mind like a fast forward movie. That feeling of going along happily, thinking you could trust, but then a shock to that trust.

Rosa.

Suddenly the image of Rosa crying over her cart, her being betrayed by Miguel, trusting him with her money and him skipping town, came barreling back to her. And Megan had said she would help her!

She jumped to her feet, running back down through the hallways and finally finding her on the last rooms of her shift. Rosa exclaimed something in Spanish and began to cry again.

"Rosa, I'm so sorry, lo siento. I couldn't find the help, I mean, I tried but tomorrow—"

"¿Puedo ayudarle?" Megan froze at the sound of Bryant's voice.

She turned to see him approaching them, looking flushed as if he had been running too. He took in Megan's tear-stained face and squeezed her hand.

"We can talk about us in a minute. What's going on?" Bryant turned to Rosa. "¿Cuál es el problema?"

With utter relief, Rosa let out a flood of Spanish. Megan stared in amazement as Bryant conversed simply but fairly fluently in Spanish with Rosa, the latter gesturing to and fro.

Yes, the home building in South America.

Apparently, he and Rosa had come to some resolution as they both nodded heads and he gave her a side hug.

"Don' preocupación," said Bryant. Rosa smiled, wan but somewhat comforted, with another hug from Megan and pushed her cart to the next hallway. Once Rosa was out of sight, he turned to Megan. "To be on the safe side, and if it's okay with you, I'll talk with Mrs. V. in the morning and get more details. We don't know this Miguel guy, it could be true, it could be false." Megan started to say something.

"Megs, I know what you're gonna say, but trust me. It's better to get the truth right out of the gate. Don't you worry about this. I'll take care of it from here."

She had been ready to say something about trust but held it back, and she knew why.

"Megan, I need you to know—"

She stopped him, putting her fingers on his lips, and turned back toward her hallway.

Megan lay awake through the night, unable to sleep, trying to find clarity in the settling sediment of what had just happened. The anxiety wasn't with Bryant and Brittany. The scene had answered the question of Brittany's interest—and Megan's earlier unsettled feelings—clearly enough. But she wasn't worried about Bryant. Her soul confirmed to her that this was a setup, and all the tumblers had fallen into place. Bryant had done the right thing and she knew it.

No, that wasn't what bothered her. It was her reaction—childish, frightened, avoidant. What was the matter with her? Will she never stand up to this feeling, to this fear? If only she clearly knew what it was. Each moment of being with Bryant seemed to clean the fallout from last year—to release more confusion, more feelings, more refuse, revealing the way back to herself. How much of the wall was still to be dealt with?

The first brick had been her hesitancy in trusting again. Then it was about Bryant himself—was he good, was he playing, or did he truly care for her? Then it was something she couldn't pinpoint but turned out to be Brittany. So what was it now? Would it always be something? Was it simply an excuse to stay distant, to stay unhurt?

Softly, thoughts of Bryant helping Rosa stole into her mind. Once again, his take-charge manner, his ability to assess and handle the situation impressed her. So why couldn't he seem to apply it to his own life? Was his personal instability the thing that kept her at bay now?

Whatever it was, it was time to move forward, without a ready answer. This Berlin Wall she had so carefully constructed continued to come down brick by Bryant brick. She had to choose now, right now, to let it completely collapse, or it might be stuck and cemented forever, keeping her unable to tear it down with anyone.

Closing her eyes, Megan allowed the myriad of deeply buried sensations to rise. Fear. Pain. Betrayal. Anger. A swirling mass of pushing, pulsing feelings bubbled to the surface and washed over her. Tears fell thick and strong and she allowed herself to cry silently. She didn't know how long she lay that way, reliving the past pains that had remained lidded and sealed, but at last there wasn't anything left. It was as if a dam had burst and all the stagnant water had been pushed out by fresh mountain water shed. In the depth of it, Megan sensed something more embedded in the emotional bedrock, something that could not be named. Something not to be touched just yet.

But the anger was gone. The bitterness, the hurt. She wiped and wiped at the tears that had fallen down her face and into her ears. She felt strangely clean, and had no energy, or desire, to reconstruct the safe brick wall. Not today.

At 5:00 a.m., Megan finally rose, dressed in a long skirt and warm sweater wrap, and went back up on the Atrium deck. She eased into her familiar lawn chair and closed her eyes, sifting through memories of the past year, trying on ways to share it with him. As the sunrise barely peeked over the horizon, she felt a dawning awareness too. It was time to do things differently, and in the clean wake of things to make room for something new.

Megan felt him before she heard him. Solid sounds of footsteps echoed on the stairs, not running this time, sure and steady. A breeze slightly lifted her tousled hair. She felt alert and clear, more clear than she had in months. Megan knew why he was here and what he had come for. And she was ready to face it.

Bryant sat down on the lawn chair beside her, gazing out at the sparkling ocean and the early morning sky. The ocean churned steadily below them for a few quiet moments.

"Why do you run?" He said it sincerely and without accusation, staring at the sea, as if they had been in deep conversation and nothing more natural could have been asked. Megan focused on her skirt.

"Because I'm scared of you."

"Of me? You could take me down cold. I've seen you muscle Tag."

He had tried to be light but he didn't need to be. "You know me. And that scares me."

"I don't know that much. And there isn't anything scary."

Megan gazed at his profile, thinking one last time. Could she do this, could she open that door? "Do you want to know something more?"

Leaning forward, arms resting on his knees, he turned his head slightly to her, "Yes."

"Okay," she said. "What do you want to know?"

He thought. "Why did you come? I don't mean about helping Jillian. What is it that keeps you here but holding back, and not really with me?"

Megan sat very still, her long legs crossed, her skirt billowing at the base with the breeze. She stared at the endless nothingness of the sky. Cerulean blue, so clear you could float away in it.

"Because I didn't want to go home."

"Why not?"

"Because I got cheated on, lied to, and dumped. Hard." She paused—measuring, choosing. Deciding.

He remained still, his face in the math-solving repose.

"I was his house cleaner, if you can believe that. Actually, for the four of them, all good *Christian* roommates at NCU." She didn't try to withhold the sarcasm. "They paid me well for one, sometimes two days a week. And then I started adding some light cooking, nothing fancy."

"I came early from class one day, they usually weren't there. As I came in, Jackson—that's his name—was with another girl, introduced her as Tessie. They had come from the back rooms, which wasn't allowed in the honor code. I couldn't be sure what they were doing together, or if anything had happened, but they were laughing and talking low. He said she was his study partner. I wanted to believe him more than I really did, but he smoothed it over. He was good like that.

"Anyway, we started dating, I don't know how, really—studying, group dates going bowling, to the movies. Then he asked me to go hiking. One thing led to another, and another. It was easy at first, really easy."

The sounds of ocean slapping the side of the massive ship filled the pause.

"Then one week I was cleaning and an answering message came on from a Chazzy someone—it sounded important. So when he and a roommate walked in, I mentioned it though I wasn't sure of the name. It was the look that they shared. His roommate said, 'Chazzy—yeah, we know her,'—then he laughed, kind of short and throaty."

She looked down and swallowed, fixing her skirt.

"Another time I was cleaning the computer desk and accidentally hit the mouse. I saw something ... something that made me sick, and I talked to Jackson about it. He said it was his roommate's stuff and not to worry. That's what he always used to say—don't worry about it, it's all good. He had always said things, lots of things. How he cared for me, liked me ... loved me. And plans for our future. We'd be at the mall and he'd stop and look at rings and say, 'Seeing your taste, that kind of thing.' His trademark smile—he had a dimple, very slight, but right here, and he'd emphasize it when he wanted to." She stopped, seeing it clearly. "He always made comments about ... questions about kids and working and how I felt about it, that sort of thing. It had been

144

three whirlwind months and I thought we were getting very close. He actively took me there."

Megan looked out at a gull briefly landing on then rising from the ocean.

"A few times he acted funny—like we were out on a date and suddenly took my arm and turned into a store. Things like that. Or," she paused, narrowing her eyes, "sometimes he'd make me uncomfortable. The way he kissed me or, or looked at me. Allude to some things, though never outright. I just thought I was being sensitive. I haven't had a lot of—of experience with guys, that way."

"Then one day I came up to the apartment and I saw him on his motorcycle, his back was to me. A girl with bright blonde hair sat close behind him with her arms tightly around his waist. They were both looking over at something and didn't see me. She pointed and laughed and I noticed two things at once: the winter sun reflected off a ring, it was on her left hand. And she was wearing my favorite blue coat that I'd given up the year before. That's when I knew."

Megan turned to Bryant. "It was my sister."

"I started tracing things, talking to people, and found out. About him. Things that would make you sick. Things that I still can't imagine are true. And then the truth about our *relationship*." She laughed hard and short. "He'd been dating four of us, all at the same time, all for an apartment contest, ranking us on body shape first; specifically, how we looked in a swimsuit, how we cooked and cleaned, if we had income potential to work after marriage. Apparently I was ahead in the cleaning, and—" she hesitated. "Other areas." She shook her head. "It was a great big joke, but it was working. Four viable candidates. He kept us a secret until he had decided which one would pan out the best, convincing each of us separately that we'd be married by the end of the semester."

"Did you tell any of them?"

"I told my sister what I knew and she got mad. At me." Megan glanced at Bryant. "Said what did she care. He was a catch, he had a right to look for what he wanted. And he'd found it, she was the one with the ring after all. The rest of us had only been promised one."

"But then," she stopped and shook her head. "He still wanted me to clean for them, didn't see anything wrong with it." She paused, an ache in her jaw. "So I did."

Megan closed her eyes. "I just went into duty mode, and part of me didn't want him to know he'd so fully affected me. To act like I was fine, my usual way of dealing with trauma. So I cleaned for one more week and then at the end of one day, he was watching TV on the couch—some sleazy show—and I told him that I couldn't come back. He looked over from the screen and said how was he supposed to find a replacement with that kind of short notice. That a job was a job and it had nothing to do with what happened between us. That I was unprofessional and a sore loser, and"—she swallowed—"some other things."

"And I stood there, fighting to not give him the satisfaction of emotion. I told him no, in clear terms. And then I left."

Megan opened her eyes and pulled a stray hair strand from her face. "He never did pay me for that week," she said. "And I never asked him to."

Bryant stared out at the sea, his expression dark and pensive. "What happened to your sister?"

Megan looked out over the open water. She had tried to tell her sister, tried to explain what Jackson had done and how he was, with her and with others. But Kara insisted Megan was intent on man-hating him. Megan could understand that to a certain degree—it might sound that way, but it wasn't. After several attempts to reason with Kara, there was nothing more she could do. Kara had always been that way—seeing what she wanted to see, content to believe her reality *was* reality. Jackson had treated her like a queen so what had she to be sore about? Finally, Megan had given up. After hearing of their engagement through the apartment complex grapevine, she finally accepted that Kara had made her choice. And now they both would have to live with it. "They were married five months ago," she said softly, "and are staying at our house."

A gull cawed in a melancholy way above the water.

"And that," she stared at the rhythmic waves, "is why I am here."

146

The swish of the boat sounded in the silence. Bryant stared at the waves, his jaw hard. Without breaking his gaze, he reached over and clasped her hand sure and strong. She felt his warmth and tentatively caressed his tan fingers, the rough callouses—she didn't know why they surprised her. The water beat a steady cadence—soothing, gentle, no rush. He leaned back in his chair parallel to her, still staring out at the sea. She closed her eyes and pressed his hand to her cheek. With one smooth motion, he released his hand and pulled her in to the nook of his shoulder. She rested her head on his smooth, solid chest, enveloped in his strong arm.

The churning waves rolled against the ship. People's voices could be heard in chatter from the deck below—where to go at the next port, should we play shuffle board, what theme is the dinner buffet. It washed over and floated away. Megan heard the hypnotic waves, felt the warmth of his body, and soaked up the closeness. Inside, she felt empty and washed clean, like the churning white froth melting into the glassy calm expanse of the endless ocean before her.

CHAPTER THIRTEEN

For the remaining few weeks of the tour, she and Bryant spent every available moment together. It was unspoken, an almost magnetic understanding, that time was passing as quickly as the ocean covered by the massive liner. By the final week, both could feel an underpinning of something fragile coming to a close, and though they spoke in tandem conversation, in threads that continued unbroken from one day to the next, they studiously avoided the eggshell subject of home, though the tangible presence of it often made them silent.

Megan soaked up the shared time like the afternoon sun warming the teak deck—most especially the last few excursions spent together on random beaches—and always evenings after performances on their deck by the chessboards. But every now and then that ominous feeling surfaced, that thing she couldn't define or dismiss. During the early morning hours, she would often pull apart feelings as they led her through several emotional alleys, but always to dead ends, the most difficult one being Bryant and Life After the Cruise. She hated to face the truth but there it was—no job, no plan, no real life. His family sounded warm and supportive, if not anxious to have him home. Megan thought that was normal and was surprised that Bryant found it frustrating. About his father, he was decidedly silent—but what could she say about fathers. She sighed. What could she say about hers?

Despite the surfacing negativity, Megan couldn't deny the happy changes within herself. Surprising, sometimes breathtaking, she had found herself returning—not a burst, but a gradual opening, petal by petal, like time lapse. And it had felt good. Enlivening. As time had progressed with Bryant, her guard lowered, and she found a better balance between being a friend and much more. Still, questions lingered.

"Why so serious?" Jillian broke her reverie. "Thinking about Rosa?" Megan stopped making her bed and surveyed Jillian who was looking for clothes in the doll-size drawers.

"No. Rosa is all settled," said Megan. "Turned out Miguel was intending to make a run for it, pressured by others, but decided not to. He and Mrs. V. had a lovely long chat and all is well, and forgiven I think. Bryant was pretty amazing through the whole thing, actually. Translated as best he could between them, and made sure Miguel got the message, if you know what I mean." Megan smiled at the memory of Bryant towering over the short Latino man, charging him to take good care of Rosa.

"I knew we'd get around to Bryant at some point. I'm betting that was what you were really thinking about, *no*?"

Megan made a face at the Spanish inflection. "I was just thinking about the past few months, how different I feel."

"You mean how much more you're back to you?"

"Yes, that too."

"What's wrong then? You're not exactly jolly about it." Jillian finally selected a light jacket.

"The end of the fairy tale. Now reality awaits—two different states, he has no job, I have a lame one. He has no real life, and I don't like mine. I really don't know what's going to happen from here."

Jillian groaned. "So ask him."

"I have, at least tried to. We're supposed to meet tonight after the show." She shook her head. "He always tells me, 'Stop stressing about it. Let it be. Allow things to develop without all this extraneous planning.'"

"He's right. Except why do you both always have to use such big words?" Jillian pulled on her shoes. "Megs, choose one thing and go to that point and be happy. Then, if you make it to that point in your relationship, choose the next thing—hurdle, challenge, uptight plan, whatever—and be happy, and go from there."

She walked over to Megan and took her by the shoulder. "But whatever you do," she stared intently, "don't wear khaki pants and a T-shirt to my wedding."

Megan rolled her eyes and they hugged, heading out to breakfast.

After the evening's performance, most of the cast had chosen to hit an early string of good-bye parties. Brittany was rarely seen by cast members outside of performances. She was rumored to be spending time with several bigwigs and already had a possible contract on the Intrepid for the next tour. Jillian and Derek spent many uninterrupted hours together—Jillian discussing wedding details and Derek trying to enjoy the last days of unfettered life.

By mutual consent, Bryant and Megan had agreed to meet at the clubhouse swimming pool after the last curtain call. Thankfully, the clubhouse pool was generally empty at that hour due to the more popular outdoor pool and Jacuzzi on the Vista Deck.

Sitting on the low diving board side by side, Megan sat comfortably next to Bryant, her feet brushing and flicking the water. Her mid-length flowing skirt was gently tucked at her knees, though sometimes falling and spilling near the water.

"Just a couple of days. Ready to deal with your family?" said Bryant.

She knew what he meant. "Jacks—I mean, he and my sister won't be there. They're in Arizona with his family now, getting into a condo. They're not planning to visit until Thanksgiving, so I don't have to deal with anything until then."

"But seeing your mom?"

"Yes, I'll be glad to see her. She's doing good. Better."

"Better?"

"At times it's still hard for her, even though it's been so long since the divorce." The word felt weighted, floating on the top of the conversation momentarily before sinking deep into it.

"What happened?" said Bryant, with his typical ease.

Pause. "He left." She kicked the water. "With Edith—the town mayor." Bryant gave her a look. "I know, it's like a lame movie. The two of them moved to some dinky town in south Florida. We only hear from him at Christmas now. Really bizarre."

"What went wrong?"

"Your guess, my guess. Mom's guess. She doesn't talk about it much, that's just her way. But we do know a little something about the term bipolar, and a bunch of debts that Mom finally paid off a year ago. We've all made do—my brothers have finally settled down. One's at college in Arizona dating a really nice girl. Eli works on a crabbing boat on the Oregon coast and stays pretty much year-round, though he doesn't have to. Sam goes to Nevada State and comes home occasionally to do his laundry." She shrugged. "They're good boys and they adore her." She looked at him. "And me. Won't call to save their necks but very protective of who comes around."

"How did they handle the whole King Lear's Edmund thing?"

"Jackson? They dealt with it more your way. Gave him a black eye," she said, a sly smile at the memory. "In a family-friendly football game."

"Aha. All's fair on the field."

"Exactly. Sent the message, but generally they keep it low key now."

He felt the diving board, checking the make of it. "They sound like my kind of guys."

"You'd definitely get along." Megan toyed with the water and looked up discreetly at him, watching his reaction. "Speaking of ..."

"It begins." Bryant checked his watch. "At least you waited for ten entire minutes, that's a new record." He stared down at the water. "Let me guess: two different states, two different cultures—although I agree with you there, Nevada is practically its own universe. How do we negotiate it, what exactly are we?"

Megan simply laughed. "You *have* been listening." He had been joking but there was a familiar undercurrent of frustration. Over the past few weeks she'd come to know it and not be worried by it. The tone only meant he was figuring something out and hadn't found the solution yet.

"Just because I don't look into the whites of your eyes every second doesn't mean my ears don't work," he said.

Megan gazed at the white hazy pool light emanating from the green water below.

"So ... what exactly are we?" said Megan. It came out soft and contemplative.

"Two amazing people who have their lives ahead of them. Not to mention incredible and talented—okay, at least one of us."

"And dead broke, and twelve hours away, if you include freeway construction."

"There's that too." He seemed to pause for a long time. "So come see where I live."

It hung in the air.

Megan considered how to take that. "I'm not moving."

"I don't recall asking you to. Although I thought you'd prefer other living arrangements, all things considered."

"Funny." She shook her head. "It's on principle. The woman always moves, why can't the man move?"

"Okay, equal rights girl, try this." He turned to her. "We'll take turns and see which city we like best. My awesome family—with the exception of a backwards father, but with incredible cooking—or your family with the King Lear psycho brother-in-law."

Megan shook her head. "Gee, that's an unbeatable offer. Almost. Because that's your version. How do I know you don't live like the Beverly hillbillies?"

"How do I know you don't live like the Addams family? You could come out for a weekend, throw horseshoes with the relatives, and watch nonstop football on TV. What's not to love?"

Megan looked up at him. "I don't like watching televised sports. Is that a problem?"

He paused. "I'll have to get back to you on that."

She kicked up water playfully on his knees. "Okay, what about this? Jillian's wedding is in a week, perfect timing. I'll have some of my family there. And I could rig it to see you in a confining but stellar-looking tuxedo."

"You know that's a 12-hour drive for mints and a piece of cake."

"*And* a tux."

"Mine only involves *horseshoes*. Not a chance. I'll do the drive but in khakis and a decent shirt. Period."

"Deal." Megan smiled at the compromise, knowing it was an absolute triumph.

"In fact, it might even be a *plan*," he said.

"Is that a mocking tone or an actual pen-me-in?"

He looked down, touched her chin and lifted it to his. "That's a promise."

A darkness flitted over her face but she smiled to hide it. She didn't want to disbelieve he would come through but something inside her did.

He stared, puzzled. "Doth milady doubt my word?"

"No, it's just ... no, I'm not doubting you." But it came out weak. She moved as if to adjust her falling skirt. "Okay, that works. One visit to each place, and if neither works, it's off."

"Wow, you really work at relationships, don't you?"

"It's a good plan. A really good plan, actually." She glanced sideways, pushing away the doubt and focusing on the fact that he was suggesting real post-cruise ideas.

He gave her that sun-on-water smile. "Surprised again? Just because I don't verbalize my feelings every second—"

"—or look into the whites of my eyes—"

"—doesn't mean it's not on my mind."

"Well, not as much as the Lakers."

"That's true."

Megan fully turned to him, a sudden happy contentment in her soul. He looked back at her quizzically, then leaned toward her. In a quick sure motion she caught him off balance and pushed him into the pool. Laughing hard, she held onto the side of the diving board to steady herself. Bryant bobbed to the surface with a quick shake of his head to clear his hair. He gave a wicked grin and she instinctively pulled up her legs, but he swam around to the springy end of the diving board and pulled down hard and strong several times. Flying into the water she called out, "Bryant!"

After leaving the pool, they used towels to dry off their clothes as best they could, laughing and talking on the way back to their rooms. But in the back of her mind, Megan knew nothing much had changed about the real concerns. It would be different on dry land, and all that that implied. But he had promised he would come to the wedding, his first test of loyalty and reality. And she was ready to trust him, no holding back.

But somewhere in the sky of her mind, a doubtful gray feeling hovered.

The final performance was flawless. Even Mrs. Van De Morelle had clapped enthusiastically and brought overflowing yellow rose bouquets backstage for the female cast members. After stowing the last scenery pieces, the cast had enjoyed a private buffet—Megan guessed that was the "flowers" for the men—and hugs, good-byes, and last cell numbers were all exchanged.

Early the next morning, the cast ambled down the gangplank onto the pier. Megan couldn't believe it had only been a few months ago she had stood and looked up at the massive ship for the first time. She and Bryant said good-bye to several of their favorite passengers. Rosa had said farewell that morning—she and Miguel had brought them a carved wooden statue of two Turtledoves. The Bow-tie Man escorted the Senior Sensation in an old-fashioned arm-in-arm down the plank, while he carried one of her white suitcases. They stopped to give Bryant and Megan a hug and a thank you.

Surprisingly, Mrs. Van De Morelle stopped by the casually grouped cast members. She paused before the two of them.

"I'll be in touch, dear"— she leaned into Megan —"unless I see something first in the mail. Say, something sleek and gold embossed?" She winked then lightly embraced Bryant. "All right, I don't want to get sloppy, or play favorites in front of the cast." He pecked her on the cheek.

As she walked away, Megan saw Brittany cocooned by a large group of important looking people with slicked hair and expensive watches. An Indian man toted her baby blue matching luggage. She paused and glided over to them. Megan stood tall, ready for a sharp exchange but inconveniently remembered the phrase from her mother—do unto others as you would have done unto you.

"I wish you both the best," Brittany said, extending her hands to Megan, enamel sentinels at attention.

"Congrats on the Intrepid, Brittany," said Megan, trying to think kind thoughts. "We just heard officially at breakfast."

Bryant, who barely acknowledged her, simply nodded.

She had the decency to appear slightly embarrassed but recovered as a Premier Performer would. "Thank you. And good job, Megan, especially for your first cruise." With a momentary linger, she added, "See you two around." Bryant put both hands on Megan's shoulders. Megan reached up with her hand and squeezed his. Brittany got the message and walked away.

A few hours later, both Megan and Bryant headed for the airport in a shuttle, sinking into the seats and their own thoughts. Megan couldn't fight the worry, the knowledge that real life and home were waiting just one day away. What would that mean for her and Bryant?

Megan's flight left 45 minutes before Bryant's so he walked her to the D-gate. Pausing before entering the boarding line, she turned quickly to him. She didn't like sentimental good-byes.

"I'll make this short and sweet, and no mushy garbage. Call me when you land so I know you didn't pull a *Robinson Crusoe* on me."

"Daniel Defoe," he said. "Or a *Swiss Family Robinson.*"

"Johann David somebody or other."

"Wyss." He smiled. "Or, how about just 'see you soon'?"

"For the wedding," she said, more firmly than she intended.

"Express miniature ponies couldn't keep me away."

"I'm reassured."

"I always keep my word." He leaned down and hugged her close, warm and enveloping. She breathed in his ocean scent and felt his messy hair tickle her face. The reality hit her, and she released herself just as the tears came close. Tucking the luggage strap unnecessarily on her shoulder, she turned and walked into the line.

"Hey, Berlin ..."

Megan turned instinctively though she had reached the head of the line.

"I think that wall's down."

"Communist." She gave a sardonic smile, then turned and walked into the gangway.

He'll keep his word, she practiced in her mind. But somewhere inside, a deep doubt wriggled into the hollow of her stomach.

CHAPTER FOURTEEN

Gathered at the first big family dinner home, Bryant felt the familiarity of clanking dinner plates and casual chatter. But underneath he sensed an unmistakable tension. So far they had talked of everything in a superficial newsy way—his cruise experience, their life at home, even his dad's travels to Uncle Pete's, which was surprising. Usually nothing but the lumber yard or golfing with Arthur got him off his recliner. Bryant couldn't place the underlying negativity until his sister Piper coughed and stared meaningfully at her husband, and then at Mitch who sat beside his wife.

"So, sounds like the cruise was a great experience," she said. "Especially meeting great people." Piper adjusted her seat to account for her pregnant stomach.

"Yeah, the people are always key."

"And Megan, is that her name? She sounded a little bit ... key." Piper slightly raised her eyebrows, playfully enough that Bryant smiled but kept slicing his steak.

"Yes, Megan was key."

His father chewed slowly and silently, as was his way, but his mother leaned forward, elbows on the table. "Anything we can know or do we have to draw and quarter you first?"

The table conversation dropped to silence. Bryant could hear his knife slicing against the plate.

"I get it—first the fatted calf then lead the lamb to slaughter. I'm getting the theme here." He took a bite. "What do you want to know?" He played it casual but inside he didn't want to say anything. At all. It felt private and not something to discuss over steak, especially in front of his dad.

"Is she brunette, blonde, bigger than a bread box?" said Mitch, a light brown-haired, solid and serious looking man.

"She's . . ." he paused—how did he describe her in a way his family would get? "Like Gidget. Only more of a headache." But he couldn't repress the smile, so he cut another piece of steak, not missing the glance his mother gave to his sister as she sat back and folded her arms, satisfied.

"So is she going to see you soon, or is it not that serious?" said Piper.

It was inevitable. First the marriage side, then bam, it would be the lumber yard. He could almost write the script. His jaw tightened but he kept calm. "Actually, I'm going to visit her this weekend. Her best friend is getting married so I'm driving up." Pictures flashed through his mind—Megan dancing with him on the deck, sitting on the diving board, him holding her at the airport. If he were honest, he couldn't wait and would be there right now, if he didn't have to do the dutiful family bit.

Bryant looked up, then side-to-side. The tension had ratcheted up and the faces looked obviously strained. Piper sipped on her water, looking at her husband over the top of the glass.

"What? What did I say?" said Bryant.

"Well, it's just that—" Piper began.

"I've got an offer, in Seattle," said Mitch.

"That's great news, what's wrong with that?"

"I need to fly out this weekend for it."

Bryant's jaw tightened. "Can't Ross run the yard?"

His dad folded his arms. "Ross is on vacation till next week. And he's not a lead guy," he said, breaking his silence. His tiredness now gave way to the sour expression Bryant knew all too well. "It's the first vacation he's had in months."

The barb found its target. But still Bryant rebelled inside. If his dad loved the yard so much, why didn't he stop traipsing to every family member's house and stay here? He noticed the strained expression on his mother's face, glancing between his dad and him.

Bryant looked at Mitch. "What about Bertie?"

Mitch shook his head. "Come on, Bertie's good with numbers but not the hands on." He paused, looking at his wife, Trisha. "I could ask them to reschedule the interview."

Bryant knew the anger was wrong, but still it spiked, raw and intense, making him want to upend the table and slam it into the wall. He'd been on a cruise, living the life, and they'd been holding down the fort. It was a fact. But he didn't want it any more than they did. If only he knew what he *did* want—it was barely out of reach, all the time, like a taste he could remember but couldn't explain. Time was ticking and he'd drawn it out as long as possible, though why he couldn't understand. The past few years were like a stuck needle on his dad's 45s—dating the same girls, going to the same places, doing the same gigs, over and over, like an old track that he used to like.

Until Megan. Instantly, he remembered the look on her face, the doubt. Breaking this promise would kill anything between them. She could not forgive, not now when her trust factor was barely rising, and if he messed that up, Bryant knew it could be so long for good. No second chance.

He looked at the family, all waiting for a response. "I can't miss this. It's"—How could he articulate it?—"It's important."

Looks were exchanged.

His dad roughly scraped his chair on the hardwood and stood with his knuckles on the table. "So is this. We expect you to hold up your end. Nothing more."

He paused as if to say something else, as he typically would. But surprisingly, he said nothing. Turning, he walked silently toward his den.

His mother shifted in her chair, giving him a pointed, obligatory look. "That's not the only thing we need you here for. It's not your favorite, but Mrs. Landry—"

"Not another debutante thing," said Bryant, rolling his eyes.

"Not technically. But yes, hidden in the usual trappings. Just a minute—" she stopped Bryant as he made to speak. "It's a fundraiser for the girls' college and they're parading every 18- to 25-year-old in the county for a scholarship pageant. You're the beefcake. They need your charm to help co-host the pre-pageant fundraiser dinner. With Missy."

"You have got to be kidding me." Bryant looked at Piper for help. She only smiled sympathetically.

"The Landrys are one of our biggest accounts. You know their building contracts almost entirely sustained the yard during that downturn a few years ago—"

Bryant shook his head. "I've already tried dating Missy Landry, you know that. It was a fiasco. I feel like I'm 17 all over again. Out of the whole town they couldn't get someone else to play game show host?"

Shirley leaned forward. "They've practically advertised for weeks that you'll be hosting. Stella Landry said to me, verbatim, 'Bryant will make those tickets sell like hotcakes sizzling on a sidewalk.'"

Piper took another drink of water.

"She obviously thought you had curb appeal and, Missy aside, they are in dire need of the scholarship money. All you have to do is wear a tux, smile at the ladies—young *and* old—and eat rubber chicken. Is that so hard?"

Bryant looked between the five conspirators at the table—the men staring at their plates and the women with an agenda.

"It's a done deal, isn't it?" he said.

His mom looked at Piper and back to him, somewhat sympathetic but her voice urgent. "That's not all. There are two more sort of 'welcome home,' meet and greet—"

"—marry me off to the highest bidder," said Bryant.

"—one of them is the church women's auxiliary and they need—"

"Do I even get a say in these things?" Bryant sat back, exasperated.

"Bryant, honey, I'm sorry. But you knew the deal waiting when you came home this time. And we had no idea about Megan. You wrote nothing, you told us nothing. Before you left I made it clear that we wanted you to move on with your life, in several ways. And I had to tell these people something." She sat back with her arms folded. "Besides, we need you here."

But he was here, and likely would be for the next 50 years of his life.

"I'm sorry about your not seeing Megan, I really am, but have her come here, instead. We'd love to meet her." She was unusually serious, and determined. "But we need you here."

Why did she keep saying that?

Bryant shook his head. So it had begun. Once again his life was not his own—it was get married and get to the yard. And now he would have to bail on Megan, and the wedding. He fought his frustration, pictured Megan's response, and fought it down again. Between the lumber yard and his family pushing him full steam ahead, what choice did he have?

Bryant stared hard at the table. "Looks like Mrs. Landry and the ladies' club win again. And tell Dad not to worry about the yard. I'll be there." He shoved his chair back and walked in the opposite direction of his father.

In the cool early morning with the tiller rumbling beneath his hands, Bryant focused on the dark rich earth it churned out. His mom loved her garden. Year round too, though the old men in town said it couldn't be done. Bryant smiled. She'd proven them wrong every season, coyly toting a basket of winter vegetables to their counter with a, "Thought you might be up for some fresh greens, boys."

Bryant chuckled. That was Shirley. But she was a straight shooter when it came to life, so last night's ultimatum was tough. She was done patiently watching from the sidelines. He finished the row then turned off the machine with its slow whinnying sigh. He paused for a minute, leaning on the handle then took out his cell phone. It was early but he knew it needed to be done, and he'd be at the yard all day anyway. Involuntarily he scowled. The yard. An invisible noose tightened around his career neck every minute he spent there. Touching her name on the screen, he hesitated then pressed it again.

"Hello?" Megan sounded young—sleepy and quiet.

"Hey, early bird." He could see her, with hair tousled, cheeks soft, and eyes just opening, like when she had slept next to him, arm in arm, on the beach chairs in Jamaica. He had watched her for close to half an hour, had enjoyed seeing her slowly come to. A low yearning passed over him.

"Bryant? What's wrong?"

"Why does something have to be wrong for me to call you?" He checked his watch. "At 6:00 a.m."

"You woke me, and that's a punishable offense in this state. Besides, I can hear it in your voice."

How could she know that?

He knew it was best to cut to the chase. "It's about this weekend."

Quiet. He had expected that, but it still made his gut jerk.

"Look, something's come up with the yard and my brother. And some other things. They need me here."

"Oh. Really? What kind of things?"

He sighed. "Oh, these throw Bryant on the girl-town grill and serve him up kind of things. It's just how it is."

"Girls?"

"Nothing to worry about, just having to do my duty." He could hear the odd sound in her voice and knew what she'd be thinking. "It's the game they play here. I'm an eligible bachelor and there are two hundred old ladies determined to noose me. I just have to play along."

Silence.

"Megan, I'm sorry I can't make it, I know how much this means to you and I would if I could. It's just"—How did he explain the situation?—"it's just complicated."

"I understand," she finally said, but it sounded far away.

"I know what you're thinking, Megan . . ."

"No you don't. I get it, I really do. Things happen. There's a yard to run, there's a family to please, and you've been gone for a while. It's fine, really, I know."

"Megan, I'm sorry. If I could change it I would . . ."

"I know."

"You could come here, if you wanted?"

Silence again.

He could feel the timing wasn't the best on that idea. Inviting her down while he attended a bunch of girl-infested "nab Bryant" parties wasn't a great solution.

162

"Okay, bad idea. But I'll be up another time. I'm checking into it." This wasn't going like he had hoped. How could he help her understand this all meant nothing, it was just hoops to jump through?

"Sure, that sounds great. Listen, Bry, I'm really tired. I'll call you later."

But he knew she wouldn't. And guessed she did too.

Hanging up, Megan sat still, staring at the phone. *I keep my word.* That's what he had said. Express miniature ponies couldn't keep him away, right? It was one simple wedding reception. One weekend. And he couldn't even make that. Even knowing what that meant to her—not just Jillian, her best friend's wedding—but the promise he had made and the trust she had placed in him.

And he still broke it.

And for *girls*? Hadn't he told his family anything about her? Hadn't he made a stand, said something, anything, about the two of them?

The worming doubt now wriggled up to her heart. Yes, this was one time, and he supposedly had a commitment to the yard. But he hadn't committed before and now suddenly, the one time it was important to her, the time he had promised her he'd be there, suddenly he's now committed to the yard for the weekend? What about the next time? And the next? And then asking her to go there instead, while he's surrounded by giggling groupies?

Megan fought to hold onto rational thought. She knew Bryant, knew his sureness, and that meant there had to be a very good reason for him to stay. But then why didn't he explain it?

The worry about the Real Bryant Back on Dry Land that had plagued her heart for the past few weeks let loose in her mind—familiar feelings of being let down, unable to trust. Betrayed. No, that was too far. But the feeling still played at the edge of her heart.

The cell phone buzzed in her hand. Megan instinctively answered it. "Bryant?"

"Um, no, but I can go an octave lower. Expecting someone, are we?"

"Jillian? What are you doing calling so early?"

"What are you doing awake? I thought I'd catch you in the throes of sleep. They're not making you work horrendous hours at that loser job are they, or did you finally cave and decide to go full-time?"

"Not yet. I don't know. I haven't made a decision."

"Well, that sounds familiar as of late." Through the phone Megan heard a scraping sound. "What are you waiting for, the perfect opportunity? Speaking of, were you expecting the Bryant Boy to call?"

"He just did." In a flat voice she recounted the conversation.

"Truly, I'm so sorry, Megs. But you're not holding this over him, are you?" Silence. "Megan Genevieve McCormick, that is so unfair. You don't know what happened or why. And of course his family is going to have him doing stuff like that, that's what moms and old biddies do with single guys. What's the matter with you? You used to blow things off easier than this. It's like *you've* become this little old lady. I'm gonna start sending you Medicaid pamphlets."

"It was a promise."

"Yeah, and so are lower taxes. Things happen."

Megan paused. "I know." How could she explain the reality to Jillian? She was sure of Derek and knew where they stood. They're relationship had been tested in all kinds of situations and had come out solid. But she didn't know Bryant, not really, not in daily life. Brittany had said he couldn't commit long-term emotionally, that he jumped to the next thing when his focus changed. Mrs. V. had said he couldn't commit until he knew what he wanted, and that took a while. She couldn't just ignore these things like she'd done with Jackson. Choices were warning signs, and if she didn't pay attention, she'd make the same mistakes all over again.

"Look, if I know him, he'll be up here the second he can get away from the yard," said Jillian. "And aren't you the one that wanted him to settle down to a job and be responsible?"

Yes, she did. But responsible to their relationship promises first. Otherwise work would always be an excuse to be first. She'd seen that firsthand with her dad. It was, "But I have a conference, we'll celebrate our anniversary when I get back." But he never did. It was always onto the next big deal, pleasing the customer, ignoring the family. This wasn't about Bryant being a dedicated worker. This sounded too much like convenience and not making waves.

Another scraping noise through the phone from Jillian. "I don't know why you're putting so much stock into this one promise. He's in a no-win situation, it sounds like to me—pulled by old women and working for the family. You can't have it both ways, wanting him to be a responsible working man but loyal to you, in another state. If you keep at it, you're gonna split him down the middle."

"That's a pretty picture. What is that noise?"

"What noise?"

"That scraping sound?"

"Oh," Jillian hesitated. "I'm going through a kind of ice cream phase again."

"What? It's three days before the wedding."

"I know. And this is my second."

"At six in the morning?"

"*You* try getting married. It's no picnic." Last scraping. "Which brings me to two key points in this entire banal conversation. Stop messing with him like you're a three-year-old. If you keep stringing him out and up and down with this nonsense and expectations, he will walk. I'm not kidding. Why don't you go see him? I mean, what exactly keeps you here? It's certainly not job fulfillment."

"For starters, he lives 12 hours away, Jillian. And besides, that's so final. If I follow him there, it's the scarlet D for desperate. The last straw of my dignity. I'd be throwing myself at his wood pile saying, 'Marry me.'"

"What's wrong with that?"

"The man should do the chasing."

"You sure have a lot of rules about what should happen when." Jillian swallowed. "Look, when I realized Derek was the one for me, I got scared too. Do you remember?"

"I recall another definite ice cream phase."

"Major phase. I ate one of those humongous Styrofoam ice cream cups every single day for two weeks. Gained like five pounds. And all because of the brakes."

Megan shook her head and sat up. Sometimes following Jillian took work. "What brakes?"

"I put the brakes on, Meg. I put them on in the relationship, but in a fake way. When you force something to stop that should keep going, it's not good. For one thing, it's exhausting."

"And for another, it makes you consume copious amounts of ice cream."

"My point exactly. So, stop putting on the brakes."

"But aren't I supposed to be wise? I'm in a healing phase right now, isn't that something like the fourth step on the grieving pyramid or whatever?"

"Healing is as healing does, Meg," she rattled on, perfectly satisfied. "You've had time and now, you're forcing it into something that it's not. It's time to trust, to move on, to not get freaked out by every little movement. I know you can feel it. You just won't let yourself."

"Because what if I'm wrong? Maybe, let's say for argument's sake, I'm better and my heart is ready and I can trust myself to be right. But I thought I was before. What if I'm completely wrong about him too?"

"Megs, what exactly are you afraid of, have you asked yourself that?" said Jillian. "I mean, we're all afraid of something about falling in love. But we have to still get out there and live, not curl up and die in a corner, trying to pretend we won't get hurt."

Megan paced her bedroom floor, fully awake now and holding the cell phone while gesturing with her other hand. "I have to face facts, and the cold reality is that I hardly know this man. We sang, we danced, we were on a cruise ship. It sounds ludicrous, it has to even to you. Am I really going to put my life in the hands of someone who ultimately can't decide what job he wants? Who actually *has* a great job for the asking but just doesn't want it? Or who makes a promise to me and right out of the gate changes it up because of pressure from some old ladies? The cruise life was great and it all looked good on paper, Jillian, but this is real. Marriage, children, mortgage—these are the things that make up real life, not snorkeling and buffet lines. He's a great guy. He's the best guy I've ever met, and when I'm with him"—she shook her head, blinking back emotion—"I just feel right—I—" Her voice felt tight. "And then I know it's coming, like climbing the rollercoaster on the first hill—it's exciting and great. And the second, and the third. But then you get to the twister, and you can't breathe. I can feel myself want to let go but I'm stuck before the twister, holding back the whole car, because I've spun out of control before and I didn't like it. I didn't like it at all."

"Megs—"

"He's a patient man, but he's not that patient. No one can be. But I can't figure out what signals to pay attention to and what to ignore. I want to enjoy the relationship ride but I have no idea what it will take to let go like that. I just can't yet. It's scary. It's too soon to get hurt again. If I do it wrong, I might never want to love someone again, ever."

Jillian remained silent, thankfully letting Megan release the angst and worry without impatience. Megan rubbed her eyes to eliminate the blurry tears. It was complete child-like fear, irrational to a point, but it was so real. A scene flashed in her mind—kindergarten immunization shots. She had never forgotten it. Listening to that little red-haired girl in the room ahead of her, half hidden from where Megan stood in line, but clearly heard throughout the building. Screaming and writhing, the little girl had sobbed through the entire experience. Megan had been almost paralyzed to walk in next, but her mother half-dragged her, promising it wasn't as painful as she thought, and that it would be over in seconds.

Megan didn't believe her, not after the red-haired girl. So she fought, cried, screamed, kicked, and even upturned one of the side tables. But still, the solid-looking nurse hadn't faltered for a moment, securing her to the chair and chattering about the new kangaroos at the zoo. Then she smiled. Megan hadn't understood until she said, "First one done." She hadn't even felt the shot. After that, it wasn't so bad.

Megan sat down hard on her bedroom chair. How was she ever to get past this? "Jillian, I'm stuck. And either I deal with this or I'll be an old maid working at the library indexing book titles." She paused. "Or in an asylum."

"I'll come visit."

"You always were a good friend."

"You'll figure it out, Megs, you always do. Now if you don't mind getting off your whiny horse, I actually called for a reason and it's a really good one. I have a floral emergency."

"Yes, the wedding!" Megan felt her face go hot. She'd been bawling about her pitiful love life when her best friend was getting married in three short days.

"Ah, she remembers. Listen, my cousin has backed out *last minute* on finishing my corsages, the loser. Her Christmas gift is officially out for the next five years. So I am in definite need."

Floral. Megan thought for a moment. "Wait, do you remember Mrs. Watts from the high school? She was always roped into doing corsages and boutonnieres for prom. I'll talk to her."

An hour later the floral emergency was contained. Megan had called the talented Greta Watts, a perpetually permed gray-haired woman with 50's glasses and an instant knowledge of all community happenings. She had not only agreed to solve the floral crisis but to involve two other ladies. The success of the problem-solving energized Megan. And more than that, just connecting with Jillian and hearing her voice, her excitement, and the fact that she would even think of Megan days before making the most important decision of her life, made her feel purposeful and loved. It also didn't hurt that Jillian knew how to deal with her post-Jackson mood swings—that she minimized Bryant's no-show and helped her step back and put things in perspective.

At least for now. The tugging in her heart remained, even when she willed it to leave. Shaking her head to physically make it go away, Megan looked at the clock. Her roommate worked graveyard and would be home any minute to sleep. It had been a gift to find an apartment so quickly, and with only one other roommate. But it wouldn't be for long—the contract was up at the end of December.

Megan sighed. She should be getting ready for the day, even though work was only five minutes down the street. But nothing compelled her to begin.

The thought of going back into the pale yellow office with a parade of angry, tired, or apathetic faces made her want to pull the covers over her head. In one decisive motion, Megan reached for her running shoes. A few minutes later she left her apartment and drove to Putnam Pines Trail.

Megan breathed deeply. Though not the Ruby Mountains, Putnam Pines was a mini man-made park version. Here the elevation gave the tepid Nevada air a crisp freshness. Step, step, breathe; step, step, breathe. The pungent pine smell enveloped her as did the tall lush evergreens on either side of the path. Earthy moss and fallen brown needles softened by the last rain quieted her footfall. Each step brought her closer to a mental picture she couldn't yet define. Was it of Bryant? Of her, or of her life?

Thumping across the forest floor, Megan covered the familiar ground. It was her favorite trail, the trees reaching high to the sky, yet the earth solid and sure beneath her. In a few more turns Megan would need to make a path change. Right for the higher but shorter route she had never taken that rounded an undiscovered corner, or left for the narrow but beautiful familiar path. Having been that way many times before she knew the spectacular views of the mountain landscape were worth the run.

Thump, thump went her shoes, rhythmic and steady.

Jillian was getting married, and she knew—knew—that Derek was the right one for her. Anyone could see it, could feel it around them, they were two halves of a whole. And Megan was truly happy for her. But what about *her* life? What was in store for her? School was done, she had a dead-end job, and a temporary apartment. The picture in her mind of something coming was the only thing she knew, except that she couldn't shake the mixed feelings that meshed and twisted in her stomach. In the meshing was a dark and foreboding feeling that she instinctively turned from. But another feeling—light, soft, and welcoming—threaded through it as well.

Megan breathed deeper. Were the conflicting feelings part of the same experience, or was it a choice to make between the two? Thump, thump, thump on the soft pine needles. In the distance she could see the expected fork in the nature path. Running toward it, Megan felt a sense of decision before her. What was she going to choose?

Coming upon the split, Megan paused for a moment, jogging in place and eyeing both directions. Neither looked particularly ominous or promising. Which should she take today? Like Alice, Megan needed a Cheshire Cat. Hadn't he said that it depended on where she wanted to go? Well, where did she want to go?

"Like an old lady," that's what Jillian had said. Or more like one of the forest birds, hopping from branch to branch and unable to make a decision or think. What had happened? Yes, she had burrowed deep within herself this last year but the summer had changed her, she knew that much. Feeling the dappled sunlight warm her face, she knew Bryant had opened that place in her again—the light, the good, the trust—enough that she couldn't bar it shut tight like before.

Bryant.

And now he wasn't coming. But did that matter? What would she have done three years ago? Even two? She would have gone forward anyway.

Megan eyed both paths. In a burst of choice, she ran to the undiscovered right, feeling a coolness in the immediate elevation as she ran up the incline and around the corner. Full clustered pines lined both sides of her path. She breathed deeply. She was still Megan, and returning to herself wasn't a bad thing. And hadn't she become a better version of herself through the summer? Memories flowed to her—wearing skirts, putting on makeup, being in a swimsuit again. She smiled without thinking. Splashing Bryant on the diving board, dancing on the deck, holding each other while watching the hazy sunset. She had learned to joke again, to play, talk, and kiss, all in a way that felt real.

Again, Megan breathed in the fresh forest smells, deep and cleansing. Yes, she was the same Megan, but more—better, stronger, improved. She didn't have to reject one over the other, she was both—the same but not. And regardless of where Bryant fit in the equation, she would continue to be so.

Megan dipped to miss a low-lying branch. Coming back to the present, she looked at her watch, surprised how quickly the time had passed and that the trail ended in about 50 feet. She hadn't known the end was close and the trail so short. Setting her face like she'd done in the 4 x 4 race in high school, she eyed the gate at the trail head and ran full on, sprinting like the final championship depended on it. Breathing deep and pumping her arms, she soared through the gateway, this time with her arms flung behind her, head tipped high. She slow-jogged around a small cul-de-sac of dirt and trees, finally stopping and taking in large gulps of air. Megan looked up, took in the sky high pines, the clean stripped Nevada air, and the freshness in her lungs.

She knew exactly what to do.

An hour later, showered and dressed, Megan rapped on the door of her boss. "Sylvia?"

An Asian-looking woman raised her head from between stacks of paper on a desk. "A little late this morning, are we?" She smiled with her pen poised.

"Yes, so sorry about that. A little"—she thought for a moment—"forest therapy." Sylvia nodded, but waited expectantly. Megan had proved herself enough to warrant some leeway. "I was just curious if the full-time hours were still available?"

"Want them?"

"Absolutely."

Sylvia cocked her head. "I thought you might have bigger plans for this fall." Megan only shrugged so she said, "Okay, they're yours."

"And if you have a minute, I have a few ideas for the weekend staffing issues," said Megan.

"Great, come on in."

As she sat in the chair beside Sylvia's desk, Megan knew this wasn't her dream job, not even close. But she was going to start doing again, choosing the higher route with no guarantee of what was around the corner. Smiling confidently, Megan ignored the unbidden image of dancing with Bryant on the Jamaican beach.

CHAPTER FIFTEEN

Bryant paced expectantly, phone in hand.

"Oh yes, is it Bryant?"

"Yes ma'am, Bryant Johnson." Bryant felt sweat bead on the sides of his temples. "I'm sorry to bother you, Mrs. McCormick, I just wanted to talk to Megan for a minute."

"Call me Loralee, please. And I'm so sorry, she's gone to a wedding this weekend until late tonight."

"Yes, it's her friend, Jillian's, right?" So Megan hadn't told her mom he was supposed to come. "It's just that I can't reach her on her cell."

"Oh, after the couple left, the group all stayed at a cabin in Tahoe for the sort of party after the party. They don't have reception."

"At a reception?"

"That's good Bryant, very good." He could almost see her smile by her tone. "But I can leave a message for her as soon as she returns, unless you want to try again?"

"No, I mean yes, great, a message would be great. And I'll try again." They exchanged some more pleasantries and Bryant was about to hang up when she paused.

"Bryant?"

"Yes, ma'am?"

Pause. "I'm sure I'm stepping outside my permitted territory—she's so testy lately—but, though I don't know a lot of details, I do feel to tell you ... she's a pillow. Really, a downy soft grandmother's pillow. You might get pricked by parts of the chicken feathers but there's a whole lot of softness inside for the patient person."

172

"Okay."

"Just don't get scared by the poky chicken feathers, all right? That's all I'll say. No more. My lips are zipped."

"Thank you, Mrs. McCormick, I'll keep that in mind."

"All right, talk to you soon."

Bryant shook his head. Chicken feathers? He chuckled, just as his sister ambled into the room holding her large stomach. "Anything for a starving pregnant mother to feed on?"

He leaned down and kissed her on the cheek. "Just roasted a pig. That should keep you for an hour."

"Ba ha." Frowning, she grabbed a loaf of cinnamon swirl bread on the counter.

"What's up, sis? Waistband getting too tight?" Slicing the pieces roughly, it was as if she hadn't heard him. "Hey, Piper—you okay?"

She looked up, pausing with the knife. Then she smiled, but it was a practiced one, the kind his mom put on for company when her feet hurt.

"Oh, don't mind me. I get this way in my last trimester. And who were you just talking to?" she said, segueing the conversation. "Was that a legitimate smile I saw just now?"

Bryant leaned against the counter. "Megan's mother."

"Ah, the Mysterious Megan." She popped a piece of bread in Bryant's mouth. "So, has she forgiven you for not coming to the wedding?"

"Probably not. Probably won't speak to me again," he said, chewing roughly.

"Not likely."

"Piper, you're the only one who would get it. I need to go see her."

She stared at him. "But you heard Dad. He needs you to stay at the yard."

"The yard, the yard, it's like a huge lumber idol." He grabbed a nearby dish towel, pulling and snapping it. "You guys are always pushing me to get married, not that I'm saying this is it. But for the first time in years, I really want to pursue someone. And now because of some 2 x 4s, you're all saying no?"

From the corner of his eye, he saw someone in the kitchen doorway. "You don't have to eavesdrop, Mom."

"I know I don't. I heard you from the garden." Giving him a quick peck on the cheek, she placed a garden basket of fresh chard, tomatoes, and zucchini on the counter by the sink. Piper picked up her plate of bread slices and headed for the safety of another room.

"Chicken," called Bryant.

"No way, I may be pregnant but I'm not stupid." Piper made a face and a quick exit.

Shirley began washing the first bunch of chard under the faucet as Bryant moved next to her, leaning against the counter.

"Does she mean that much to you?" said his mother.

Bryant looked at her. She'd changed. "You doin' okay, Ma? Usually you'd be spitting nails or breathing fire, or something cliché." He said it lightly but it was true. She used to joke and laugh but this was different. Her eyes had lost a bit of spark and looked tired at the corners. For the first time, it was hard to see his parents age.

"It's been busy."

"You're making me feel guilty."

"Me, your mother?" She smiled as he moved beside her, drying the tomatoes she handed him.

"Mom, what's wrong?"

She was quiet for a moment. "For a while now you've had this wanderlust, for whatever reason. But that's part of who you are at times, and you've always been able to ultimately keep it in check." She paused, considering. "Until the past few years. I've kept thinking it's a phase, but, honestly, we haven't known what to do with you."

"I haven't known what to do with myself."

"I know. And that's why we've given you time. It's been so unlike you." She shook her wet hands and dried them in the hand towel. Turning to Bryant, she took him in, as if reliving many years of memories. Reaching up she smoothed his hair, shaking her head. "But I know you'll figure it out. You always do, and as soon as you do, watch out. But we're just asking you to figure it out . . ."

". . . a little faster. Believe me, I know. Think I want to be twenty-seven and living at home?"

Shirley leaned against the opposite counter from Bryant. "What is it that you need?"

Bryant thought for a moment then became serious. "I have a plan but I have to see her, really be with her. I can't explain everything about it, but I know what she needs, what I need. I think this could be it, Mom, and the only way to know is to risk it. But Dad, and the yard . . ."

Shirley nodded—thoughtful, frowning. Then she sighed. "Okay, do what you need to do. But *after* this week of making the social rounds. And I'll take care of your dad."

"Seriously? It'll be okay here?" A small flame kicked on inside him, like lighting the winter furnace.

Shirley smiled, tired but bantering. "Yes. But go make yourself useful with those weeds right now. Somebody's got to earn their keep. And don't breathe a word of it to your father. Not 'til I've warmed him up." She swatted him with the dish towel and turned back to the vegetables.

Bryant left the kitchen with a lightness in his step, heading to weed whack the lawn with a renewed zest. He tried to ignore the concern about his mother. Did she think he wouldn't settle down, commit to something? Of course, he could understand why, but she knew him, better than anyone in the family. Knew he had bigger plans in mind than a lumber yard, always had. Even in college when he'd gone for simulating large-scale engineering projects, huge bridges and skyscrapers, so sure this was his dream. She'd understood when he had lost his interest, when he'd realized it was more drawing boards and schematics than hands-on creation. And she'd understood his deep down fear, the worry that he'd never find what he was meant to do, always tiring of it in a few years. It wasn't exactly a good prospect to offer the future Mrs. Johnson.

Suddenly came the image of Megan on the Jamaican dance floor, looking up at him, trusting him, loving him. The feeling shocked him, the warmth and security. He shook his head. She was definitely not showing a lot of warmth or security right now, except to her dead-end job. Yet something compelled him still, but what he couldn't say. All he knew was to pursue this until he could figure out the solution.

Hopefully, his plan would work. If not, it was the yard for good.

Monday mornings always felt a little bleak to Megan but especially with no exciting event to look forward to. After the wedding celebration, all last week the office had seemed particularly dismal, much like when she had returned from the cruise. Megan looked around and shook her head. Her first few days back she had been shocked by the familiar state of the office—it was as if she had never left. Same yellow on the walls, pale and worn. Same computer that Tina couldn't get to work. Same fax machine that stuck on the number nine. It wasn't bad, it was just—the same. And she wasn't.

Facing another seemingly mundane day, Megan put her purse below the desk and switched on her computer. Bryant had called only once and texted twice during the past two weeks, having been "busy" at the yard and with "other stuff." The lack of communication only confirmed to her what Brittany and Mrs. V. had said—personal communication was not his forte. Neither was his understanding about promises. So far, Dry Land Bryant was not stacking up to Cruise Ship Romancer. Megan was seeing the light and not liking what it showed.

After a few hours of sorting through job requests, placing six individuals, and faxing a ridiculous amount of paperwork, she looked up at the sound of the bell on the front door.

Her mouth fell open. Bryant entered the waiting room with that almost arrogant smile on his face. He knew he'd surprised her. Big.

Bryant? Here?

It took her a moment to comprehend what she was seeing. His wavy hair—cut shorter and more business-like—his rugged build, his tanned face. He was here, in Harperville, Nevada, standing in her office.

Megan felt her insides swirl. Just the sight of him conjured those familiar giddy feelings—cuddling on the deck, kissing on the dance floor. Within seconds a slide show of memories flashed through her mind and heart.

But then came the memories of the past two weeks. Reality. And the tightening in her stomach from the concerns she'd felt and feared. No, she told herself, she would be smart. Safe. Rational. She would not be detoured by those sudden bursts of romantic feeling. Even if he did drive 12 hours, just for her. Through construction. And look so dang good doing it, too. She gripped the side of the desk.

Be. Strong.

Putting on her professional demeanor, Megan called to him in the foyer without rising from her chair. "May I help you?"

He paused mid-step, holding his keys and looking around the empty waiting area. "I sure hope so. I'm looking for a job."

"Just take a seat and fill out an application clipboard on the table. I'll be right with you." She spoke as smooth as honey butter. He looked puzzled at first but then smiled again and sat down, grabbing a clipboard from a stack in a box.

Megan scooted in her chair so that he couldn't readily see her behind the small service counter and began making phone calls. She fought to cling to reason. Couldn't make it to the wedding? Couldn't call or connect during the past two weeks more than a hello? Couldn't call her now to let her know that he was coming?

He could wait.

Megan repeated this in her mind like a mantra, trying to focus on paperwork and keeping a functional attitude, but finding herself sneaking looks into the foyer. He busily completed the application, the math problem expression on his face. Several times she fought the urge to run to him, hold him, tell him how ecstatic she was to see him. But deep down she knew this set the future precedent. How she handled his broken promises and poor behavior today would determine how he respected her down the road.

Right?

A full half hour later, Megan walked to the service counter and yelled out to the still empty waiting room, "Next," and sat back at her desk.

Bryant stood, stared at her, then stepped through the swinging door next to the counter and sat across from her at the desk.

Megan reached for the clipboard and perused his papers. *Okay, pal, I'll play along until I figure out just what you're doing.*

"So, why are you really here?" she said.

"I told you, I'm looking for a job."

"That's slightly humorous."

"I'm serious." He still retained that knowing I-surprised-you look around his eyes, like a little boy who had scored something good. "What incredible job opportunity could I expect to experience, I mean, with your fantastic placement abilities?"

"I'm not sure." Megan fought again between reaching across and hugging him, and yelling at him for dissing his promise and making her worry like crazy. Was he really here for a job or was this a joke? And he had left the yard? For how long?

As if in answer to her question, he sat forward, his blue eyes intense. "I'm here for one week, Megan—one week to see if I can make it work here."

"You mean, find a job?"

"To make it work on both fronts." He looked at her meaningfully. "If we can see this is real, outside of cruise ships and curtain calls, then we'll know where to go from there, right? One week here. Then you can take a week off and come see how I live."

Megan stared, thinking through it. "I don't know what to say. What about the yard, did you decide anything?"

Bryant's face darkened. "It's taken care of. For now."

So he hadn't decided on anything yet. Megan breathed slowly, trying to calm herself. Yes, he was here, showing how he felt about her. And it was a romantic and sweet gesture. But then again, what did one week do? It seemed more of the same, an unrealistic situation. Just like the cruise ship, being here for a week was temporary. Nothing solid, nothing solved. She wanted steady, sure, a plan. He'd had weeks on the ship to figure out a solution and still nothing. Then he canceled his first big commitment to her, unable to leave the yard. Then suddenly he up and leaves the yard in a grandiose gesture but without even talking with her about it. She wanted to think happy thoughts but Jackson was too fresh for her to ignore. This wasn't the kind of steady relationship behavior she was looking for. Sandy beaches and Vista Decks were over, it was time to knuckle down to real life. But could he?

She pursed her lips, tapping her fingers on the desk. "Well, let's take a look, shall we? What exactly are your skills?"

"I make a mean breakfast." He raised his eyebrows playfully. "And give great Valentines."

She kept a straight face. "Fabulous. I'm sure the girls in hometown Channing, California, could tell me all about it."

His eyes narrowed but he only shrugged, missing her opening for him to apologize, or further explain.

"Well, with those skills certainly there are loads of jobs perfect for you," she continued. "However, the Chippendales calendar is already out, so let's look at something a bit more challenging, shall we?" She scrolled her computer lists, passing up exec jobs, media prompter, etcetera.

Bryant leaned back with his arm resting on the top of the chair, the arrogant smile on his face. "I think I can pretty much handle what little Harperville, Nevada, might have to offer."

In the blink of an eye, the way he sat in the chair, his confident air, Megan felt transported to those last moments with Jackson. Intuitively, she knew it was unfair, that the comparison wasn't real. But it still stuck to her, gnawing at her doubts.

Her cursor passed over a particularly unpleasant job title. Megan felt the beginning of an idea. "Aha, I think I have the perfect fit. Just fill out this paperwork."

"More paperwork?"

"The blessing of honest toil."

Yes, she would give him the week, definitely. But not fluffy temp jobs and homemade dinners. She'd give him the reality of what "little Harperville" had to offer, and see if he could hack it, day in and day out. Deep down she desperately needed to know he was in it all the way, not just when it was pleasant or convenient, but when real life waited. He had said let's see what it's like outside of cruise ships and curtain calls. She couldn't agree more.

Megan realized he was waiting. "Where are you staying?"

"At the Motel 6."

"By Lucky D's casino?"

"That's the one."

She whistled softly. "You might want to pack something. I mean other than clothes."

"So I've been told." He seemed aware she was softening, and did the wrong thing by smiling that I-know-how-to-get-you grin. "Better than a wedding reception, don't you think?"

"We'll see." She was back to business. *Yep, that was men. Blow off not keeping a promise with a bit of boyish charm and a ride in to save the day.*

"Okay, be at this address by 7:00 a.m. tomorrow." She handed him the paper. He took it without glancing at it, steadily smiling at her. Then nodding his head, he turned to go.

Megan watched him leave, fighting not to run after him.

We'll see if you're still smiling tomorrow.

"Is this the right address?" Bryant said to the old woman at the door, surveying the decrepit street.

"Oh yes, indeed," she said, warbling cheerfully. "We've needed some insulation now for, oh, I don't know how long. It's right up here in the attic." She opened the creaking door and told him, as they slowly trudged upstairs, that a "few things" needed fixing before they could begin the insulation.

Walking into the five-foot-high attic, he realized at once he was in trouble. Chairs, boxes, trunks, and knickknacks of every sort filled the space. Add "moving man" to the job requirements, he thought wryly.

"I don't see a blower," said Bryant.

"Oh no, we don't use those kinds of new-fangled things. We'll do it the old-fashioned way." She smiled and patted his arm. "I'll have some lemonade for you in a few hours."

Already the sweat broke out on his forehead. It was going to be hot, back-breaking work, all by hand. He thought of Megan, shook his head, and started moving the closest boxes.

At 5:30 p.m., Megan pulled up to the old house. Bryant was covered head to toe with sparkling bits of insulation, obviously wrapping up a conversation with the homeowner at the door.

Megan waited by his truck.

"Hey, boss, a personal visit?" Bryant strode over to her. "To what do I owe the pleasure?"

She willed the flutters in her stomach to be still. "You need to turn in your time card each day. I thought this being your first day I would save you the trouble."

Annoyingly, his eyes sported an arrogant bring-it-on look. "Aha. Well, isn't that nice, the boss thinking about one of her lowly workers. Well, seeing as you're down here, wanna catch a movie? For employee morale and all that."

She shook her head. "I don't date employees. But I'm sure other plans won't be hard to find."

"What, around here?" Bryant gestured expansively at the broken down neighborhood. "This is a great place. There's like one movie theater with three whole movies, it's great. And if I get really bored there's a Piggly Wiggly down the way—ice cream sandwiches, three for a buck."

"Sounds like your night is made."

"Oh, I'm set." He stared her down, the challenging air still present. "Right after I pick out the small, burrowing pieces of insulation glass in the numberless pores of my skin. If I rub my arm just right, it feels really good, like a piranha is eating my limbs."

Megan kept a straight face. "Gee, that sounds like fun. Well, I'd better get going. I'll put you down for eight hours, and here"—she tore off a white sheet and handed it to him—"is the address of your next assignment. Be there at—"

"—7:00 a.m.?"

"You got it. Thanks, Bryant."

"Anytime, Megan."

She felt him watch her leave, knowing he still wore that ingratiating smile.

The next afternoon, although her work was finished, Megan found herself hanging around the office, just in case Bryant dropped by his time card. It was crazy to even think about it—literally crazy. She was giving him the worst possible jobs available in the greater metropolis of Harperville and Wells, Nevada, and still she was hoping he'd come by to see her? Yes. Because she had to know his staying power, his ability to commit.

And deep down she knew it wasn't just that. This was buying her more time to figure out where the two of them could go from here. With no signs of any major changes in his life—no settling down, no clear plan—it was just the same situation as on the cruise ship. What exactly was she looking for, then? She had no idea. Just something solid, decisive—something that said he had his life figured out and not just a quick fix or placating people.

And yet, the Old Megan part of her knew she was being hard on him. It wasn't his fault she'd experienced Jackson. Or her dad leaving. It wasn't right to make him go through these emotional tests just to make her feel more secure. But, at this point, she didn't know how else to do it. Trusting her instincts alone wasn't working, hadn't worked. She needed something solid to hold onto, something that said he was a sure thing before going any further.

Sighing, she closed down her computer just as the doorbell jingled. She scooted out of her chair but smelled him before she saw him. Megan came from around her desk and saw Bryant standing in the reception area. His body was soaked in something all the way to his chest where an irregular horizontal line delineated the dry. Within minutes the stench completely permeated the room.

"Just came to turn in my time card," he said, holding out a piece of paper. Megan walked through the swinging door, holding her nose, and gingerly took the time card from him. She could have sworn he had smeared it on purpose.

"I'm sorry, Bryant, you'll need to leave. What you're wearing is not clean office attire."

"Oh, okay." In one smooth motion he pulled his shirt over his head and dropped it on the floor.

She bit the inside of her cheek to keep from smiling. Still holding her nose, and without even acknowledging his ripped bare chest, she slowly walked to the hat rack and grabbed a large pink sweater with an even larger crocheted daisy on the front and tossed it to him.

"A shirt is also required office attire." She nodded for him to put it on. He stared her down for a few moments then swung it around his shoulders leaving his bare chest clearly seen.

She deliberately folded her arms. "And how was the job satisfaction today?"

"Oh, definitely a 10." He stamped his foot, leaving a brownish residue on the carpet. "Sorry, there was something on my boot. Busted pipe in the sewer main, so Harvey and I went down in through the manhole, the two of us working on it, when it completely broke loose. Was a great day. Maybe even an 11." He smiled and tipped an imaginary hat and walked out, pink sweater and all.

Through the half-closed blinds, Megan watched him get into his truck and pull away, a smile tugging at her lips. Day two of worst possible jobs and he had stuck it out with no complaints. So far, so good. She grabbed the air-freshener and still holding her nose, used the other hand to spray a five-foot radius, trying not think about how much she missed him, and how ready she had been to say yes to a movie.

Bryant arrived at 7:00 a.m. on the dot, exited his truck and groaned, deeply. Dozens of men in bright orange vests swarmed the US 93 like ants. The asphalt truck was already running, smoke and steam billowing from its enormous yellow belly. A bearded man with a sizable gut whistled to Bryant who was now walking in that direction.

"Hey boy, are you the temp? Get your butt over here. You're two hours late." The man sported a wad of chew in his lower lip and spit flew each time he spoke. "You ever done this afore?"

"Well, one summer we put in—"

"Good enough. See that big guy over there, the one with the pants hanging off his butt? That's Doley. He'll get you raking the asphalt, and don't give him any lip. Lunch is at two." The man turned and hollered to the operator of the huge yellow asphalt paver.

Bryant did as he was told, taking the orange vest and contemplating how much he cared for Megan.

At five o'clock, Megan stepped out of her car and scanned the roadway for Bryant. Finding him, she walked toward the cluster of construction workers. A few whistled, which made Bryant glance and return to his work, then, on recognition, stand upright to look at her again. More whistles came but she remained impassive behind stylish sunglasses. She could have sworn Bryant turned and gave the guys a dirty look.

He thoroughly watched her walk toward him.

"Thought I'd pick up your time card," she said.

He stared at her. "It's not 5:30."

"I know. I wanted to close up early today." They both knew it was an excuse.

"Carl, hold this, will you?" The man with a semi-toothless smile tipped his hardhat to Megan and said something to Bryant that made him shake his head.

Bryant took her by the elbow and guided her to the side of the road. "You'd best stay out of the way. It's mighty dangerous for dainty boss ladies such as yourself." He knocked his hardhat.

Megan smiled at him then surveyed the scene, her feelings soft, like her old self. He'd done the jobs she'd given him without a fight, and she could feel him showing he would do whatever was needed, and that he was sorry about his no-show presence the past few weeks. On the one hand it was ridiculous to put him through this and she hated needing so many reassurances. But she had promised herself not to get swept up in the emotion of loving against her better judgment. Living through the domino effects from her parents' divorce was a constant, piercing reminder that love was better viewed realistically.

"So, how was work today?" She looked up at him, taking in the blackish sweat rivulets running down his face.

"This was a fun job. In fact, maybe my favorite. The toxic fumes, the way my eyes burned, and that warm, grilled feeling of being a chunk of barbecued chicken."

She bit her lip. "I wanted—we wanted to say—that you're doing wonderful work. Sylvia—my boss—is really pleased with how, um, diligent you are. How dependable."

"Sylvia says, huh? I'm thinking that might mean a bonus is in order?"

"Maybe." A small smile escaped. "Something at the Piggly Wiggly. My treat." She was officially extending the olive branch.

Bryant tipped his head—grinning, understanding. "The Piggly Wiggly, huh? That's what I call a class-act company."

He stood still, taking her in—she could feel his look almost drinking her up. Combined with his sweaty face and tall rugged frame—and knowing he was doing all this for her, making it up to her—made her feel attractive and womanly. Involuntarily, she smiled bright and full. Without hesitation, he reached down and kissed her generously.

"Ew," she said, finally laughing and pulling away from the tar and sweat.

"That's from a working man." He winked and trudged back over to the roadway. "I'll pick you up at 7, that's p.m. And it's an ice cream sandwich, so wear something pretty."

Megan couldn't help smiling the entire drive home. It didn't answer where to go from here, but that would come tonight.

CHAPTER SIXTEEN

Zucker's Pond was famous for its man-made pool and nature-made 100-year-old oak tree. Under the sprawling branches overhead, Megan and Bryant ate sub sandwiches and laughed about childhood pranks. As he talked she watched his face—animated, relaxed, happy—despite the horrible jobs she'd sent him on. Megan sighed inwardly. He was amazing, so good, and yet something still held her back from fully trusting him, committing to him. What was it that didn't sit right? Was she doing what Jillian had said, "sabotaging her happiness"?

"What, do I need a car chase in here somewhere?" Bryant had been talking. He teased her but his face was serious.

"No, I'm sorry, just thinking about—about life."

"In other words, I should have gone with the car chase." He balled up his wrapper and tossed it in a big garbage can about 10 feet away.

"Nice."

"That and $40,000 will get you a scholarship."

"So what happened with basketball?"

"Sore subject." He rested his arms forward on his bent knees. "My senior year, Dad kept me at the yard. My stats stunk—not enough practice time, not enough sleep, too much arguing with him about the whole thing."

"That was a long time ago, Bry."

"Of course it was, but *he's* still back there," Bryant said. "It's all about the yard, like it's another child or something. Although, to be fair, he's hardly been there since I've been home, not that I've been home that long. He's traveling a bunch, up to my Uncle Pete's and some different places. Big surprise to me."

"Maybe he's learned something. Maybe he's changed."

Bryant shrugged. "Things always change. Employers who give you heinous jobs ..."

"Employees who are cocky and annoying ..."

"Girls who reject awesome men that want to date them. Lots of things change." He leaned back against the tree. "Speaking of change, you realize you've got two days left."

She sat still. The puffy white clouds had passed over the sun and they were in a momentary shade. "Yes, I do."

"I checked back home and there's a temp place, if you want to see their situation. Have you talked to your supervisor for the time off?"

"I'm working on it." She was, but only in her soul. She hadn't breathed a word to Sylvia.

"Aha." He sat up. "Anything you want to tell me?"

"No," she said then looked up at him. "Yes." She gazed at the pond. "I guess I'm trying to understand how this will help us know where to go from here. I mean, how does a week in each other's cities fundamentally change anything? Have you made any decisions about the lumber yard or something else?"

The question was unexpected. He just looked at her, processing. "No, no decisions yet. At least on that score. But it's only been a short time. There are some things worth figuring out as you go along. Together."

She touched his hand, interlacing her fingers. "It's not in me to dive into something without knowing what's below. When I go in, I dive deep, and it takes a while to resurface again."

"A bit serious, aren't you?"

"Well, we're not kids. It's not prom and hanging out at the Tastee Freez, though I really would have enjoyed the ice cream sandwich. It's real life—balding hair and car payments."

He burst out laughing. "That's jumping ahead."

She sat up. "Laugh, but it's real, and I'm not going to sit in pretty sunlight and pretend it's not."

"No, you're not."

"That's exactly how it starts, all starry-eyed and we'll make our own future together. 'Things will happen as we move along, Loralee, and it'll all work out.' I've heard that before. And then it doesn't. People can't make promises like that, because they don't know. And when bad things happen, someone says, I got a bum deal. I don't want pretty stories and it'll all be fine. I want to know what's coming, and take it with my eyes open."

Without hesitation, he brought his mouth to hers, surprising her with his warmth. He kissed her again, softly, then pulled her in—asking, receiving. Like a glacial thaw, warm air rolled through the crevasse. She breathed it in. Why was everything clearer when she was with him? Or was it that nothing else mattered?

But hadn't she felt that before, someone becoming her world? Ignoring the warning signs and thinking it would all work out?

When he pulled away, he tipped her chin toward him. "Did you know that was coming?" She tried to smile but couldn't so she looked down.

Leaning back, he tugged her shoulder and she nestled into him.

"And your eyes weren't open, either."

"Oh, shut up."

He lay his head back on the prickly bark, grinning.

They stayed until the stars began to pop in the sky. The Nevada nights were still warm and hazy, and they chatted all the way to their separate cars.

"And what exciting career choice do you have for me tomorrow?"

"Oh, you'll like this one." Megan spoke normally but felt pained at the unmistakable lightness in his voice and manner. He had done his part, completely, and now it was time to go. And he had no doubt that she would follow him to California, just as she should.

But she couldn't. Because it wasn't about him. It was something else, something that stopped her from going farther without a guarantee. Each moment Megan pushed back the reality of what she would choose and what she would say. Bantering back to their cars she felt a pressure fold in on her. She would have to decide, again, which path in the road, and she didn't want to take either.

Thursday.

Megan checked her watch, looked at the clock, and checked it again. Nausea pulsed through her, knowing that today was it, and she would have to tell him the truth. If only she knew exactly what that was. In one decisive move, she scooted her chair back from her desk. She would leave and not be here. He could drop the final time card on the desk. Carrying her things, she opened the door, just as Bryant entered.

"Oh, I was just—" In one glance he took in her coat, keys, and expression. Standing in the dusky light of the doorway, she knew there was no excuse to invent.

"Going somewhere?" He said it quietly.

"Yes."

He stared at her, the air seeming to hold still, her heart thumping hard and loud and flushing her face.

"But not with me," he said. It was flat and final.

Megan looked evenly at him. "I can't go with you, Bryant." His jaw hardened. "I should, I know I should—you've done it for me. Heaven knows, beyond the call of duty. I don't understand it, but it can't be love."

"Or maybe it's selfishness."

"In that case, you don't want to be with me."

She watched his face, looking for the anger, the tirade he rightfully deserved to express. He had taken so much. But he simply stared at her with a puzzled, tight expression. He folded his arms over his chest and looked out into the parking lot.

"Do you care?" He turned back to her. "Do you even want to make this work?"

How could she help him understand when she didn't yet understand herself? Not knowing what to do, she fell back on being business-like. "The truth is, I don't know what's wrong with me. And until I know, you need to move on with someone who isn't so emotionally unstable." Brisk, analytical—it

190

was her only protection. His face, that open vulnerability before her. It was excruciating and she knew in moments she might throw herself at him and say inane and gushing things.

They stood immovable, both filling the entry, each standing down their sides as the silence thickened and pounded. She could see him at any moment turning and leaving.

Surprising her, Bryant sat heavily on the corner of the low entry oak table and pulled her to his lap. She couldn't fight the gentleness.

"Bryant, I'm so sorry." The tears would have to come now. "You shouldn't want me."

"Okay, that helps."

"I'm working through things emotionally but something's not right and I just don't know what it is. Until I do, I can't go forward. I've thought about it—going back with you—about nothing else, really."

"Except for outstanding jobs to give me."

"That too." Megan smiled wearily, fingering her keys. "I know I should go with you, and it's wrong not to, but honestly, I can't."

"Won't.

"Can't." How could she explain that it wouldn't let her, that restraint in her soul? A thought came. "When I was eight"—she gave a deprecating smile to his grimace—"I was riding my bike in the gravel and I slid sideways and fell. I gashed my leg really good. At the time I was in a dodgeball tournament, but Sam—my brother—said to let it heal. But the other players said I was the best and convinced me to play. So I played, and the gash ripped open again. My brother said, 'Meg, you need to wait for the muscle fibers to knit together.'"

She took his hand. "That's my heart. It needs to knit. You've swept it out and the pain is gone. But I can't rip it open again."

"Do you think I would do that?"

"Just being with you sometimes hurts." He looked concerned, worried. "Because I so want . . . I yearn to"—she had almost said love—"to like you, fully, as me. But it's a weak version. My heart, this part to care, feels so fragile. So many times I don't have a clue what I'm feeling or why, and that means I'm going to hurt someone while I figure it out. I have to let my heart heal before I can fully give it to anyone. Especially you."

She prayed he would understand everything she hadn't said.

Bryant caressed her hand, thoughtful, but his eyes focused on something else. They sat that way for how long, she didn't know. The evening shadows fell across them, there in the entry way, sitting on the table, her head leaning against his shoulder. After a long silence, Bryant brought her hand to his mouth and kissed it.

"Okay then, that's that." In one final motion he stood up with her then walked through the agency door, got in his truck and left.

Megan couldn't speak, her throat felt thick and sore. Part of her almost screamed at him to come back, that she was wrong, but she couldn't utter a sound.

Lying in bed that night, she thought through their conversation like a looped reel, over and over, what she should have said or done. Why couldn't she get past this already? A chime from her phone said she had a text. Looking at the screen it was from Bryant:

You have one more week. We can figure this out. But that's it. Final.

And no more lame jobs or I file a formal complaint.

She smiled and held the phone to her chest, a warmth spreading through her insides. Could she figure it out in a week? She would. She didn't want to play games but her soul didn't sit right, not yet. But it could. When, she had no idea and no guarantee. But moving closer to it made her feel bolder and more able to make it happen. And she knew just what to say to Bryant tomorrow. Grinning, she lay back as several thoughts flitted through her mind, most of them involving some form of a picnic, and a skirt, and fresh made lemonade.

The country highway was practically empty as Bryant drove back to the hotel after his last temp job of the week. Friday, he was relieved. After a quick shower, he would head out to Megan's real home about an hour from her apartment. He'd been specially invited—something about her brother coming home for the weekend. The sound in her voice had been unmistakably happy. But the joy of it was held in ransom for him until he figured out what to do.

He'd told her one more week without telling his family. Bryant shook his head—he already knew what they'd say. If only she could hurry up and figure out where she stood, to commit. It wasn't such a difficult thing.

Intuitively, he knew she wasn't playing games for the fun of it. Something held her, deep down, and kept her from committing to him. In past relationships, that had usually been his problem. It didn't feel so good coming from the other side. Maybe that was it—his ego. Or impatience. Once he knew what he wanted, it was a done deal. But she was excruciatingly slow, and confusing. Why he stuck it out, he couldn't understand. How much more he could take, he wasn't so sure.

Bryant heard the familiar ringtone from his cell phone and smiled. Taking one hand from the steering wheel, he reached to the side, feeling under his work jacket until he found it.

"Hey, little sis."

"Big sis to you."

"I guess you got that right, especially now. What are you, five months?"

She laughed. "Almost eight, so don't mess with me. I can't take you down but I can sit on you."

Bryant frowned. She had joked but the laugh wasn't in it. "Everything okay?"

"Yes and no."

"Tell me about no."

She sighed. He could see her ease into the chair and hold her belly. "Mom will kill me but I think it's way past time you knew." Bryant tensed. "Dad's sick."

"Oh," he relaxed and scanned the highway. "You scared me there. What is it, the flu?" Not that great but still, nothing to get worked up about.

"No, Bryant," she said, low and serious. "He's sick. He's been sick for the past six months."

Something numb and cold started from his stomach and like an ink stain spread up to his throat. He swallowed, awkward and loud. "What's wrong?"

"They didn't know." She paused. "Second batch of tests just came back yesterday. Bry, it's a brain tumor, small, but a very good chance of being cancerous." Her voice wavered. "We thought he just had the flu, or was tired, or age, but then weird things would happen here and there. He'd forget Jakey's name, or sometimes speak gibberish. Or act like he was going to speak, then walk away."

His mind pinballed a hundred questions. "How long has he been like this? Did you get a second opinion? Why didn't you tell me—was this before the cruise tour?"

He could hear her blow her nose. "Right before you left, I wanted to tell you but you know Mom. She thought the tour would be good for you and you had agreed, which shocked her. Then you met Megan"—she sniffed and blew again—"so she didn't want to ruin anything. And neither do I, really, I'm not complaining. But Bry, it's just too hard. The hours are getting longer and I'm so tired. And hormonal. And with Sarah and Jakey—who has been a handful lately."

Bryant pushed his mind to process it all. "You're not working, are you?"

"Mitch and I have taken turns and pitched in all we can, and it was okay, but we're so worn out." It tumbled without stopping. "And Mom is leaning on me, she's so scared. Mom's never scared. And Dad—he says, 'Nothing's wrong, Piper-girl, just getting old.' Ha." She spat it out. "But he can't remember his own grandson." She was talking in between soft sobs. Bryant waited for an opening. "Uncle Pete's helped schedule him for surgery already. He's the one that sent the results. Dad's been there up a few times getting testing and resting up."

The traveling. And Bryant had thought his dad had just been golfing. Suddenly it all fit—his mother's pinched look, her lack of spunk, Piper's irritability and fatigue. Dad's worn face and hardly being around.

"And now Mitch and his job offer. He's stalled them as long as he can, but it's with Brinkerhoff."

Bryant gripped the steering wheel, the tumblers falling into place and fighting a rising anger. Why hadn't they said anything before now, why hadn't they explained? And then he knew. The e-mails. The letters. Casual but there had been that tone, the underlying message that he'd heard, and heard wrong. All wrong. They weren't trying to rope him into anything—they were shielding him. He thought of Piper, eight months pregnant, with kids, and doing the books. And Mitch with three kids and student loans, running the entire yard. They'd shouldered the whole load, and he'd been singing on a cruise ship.

He hit the dash.

With a single smooth motion, he barely slowed down and squealed the truck into a u-turn, barreling down the empty highway in the opposite direction. The shower would have to wait. "Piper, it'll be okay. I'll be home in twelve hours. When's the surgery?"

"What? No, Bry, listen. Monday if you can do it, that's when he's scheduled. But I'm not trying to stress you out."

"Twelve hours, maybe less."

"But what about your job? What about Megan?"

"I'm taking care of it. Right now."

Speeding heedless of consequences, Bryant screeched into the McCormick's driveway forty-five minutes later, skidding to a stop and sending gravel spitting into the air. A soft blonde-haired woman holding a green garden hose turned to the sound.

Hopping out, Bryant quickly scanned for Megan's face.

"Bryant, that must be you," the woman called in a cheery voice. Seeing his darkened face, she said, "Is everything all right?"

That had to be her mom. "Nice to meet you, Mrs. McCormick. Is Megan here?"

"She's inside," said her mother, wearing a worried expression. "Do you want me to—"

He took the distance to the house in long strides. "I got it, Mrs. McCormick." He stomped onto the porch and opened the door.

Megan turned from the fridge with a bowl of cut apples in time to see Bryant enter the room.

Her face flushed with pleasure. Recovering, she put down the bowl and said, "Free food, I knew you'd come early."

Bryant strode into the room and stopped dead in front of her. "That," he said, chest rising and falling, "stops now. And any other sarcastic or hostile comment you're possibly about to make."

Megan opened her mouth but nothing came out.

"For months I've done everything I can to show you how I feel. I've dug ditches, cleaned sewer pipes, did whatever grunt job you gave me." His eyes, she couldn't turn away. They burned, electric and crackling. "I've listened, and I've tried to understand, even when you pushed me away. And I am done."

He stepped closer, his face inches away. "I need to know. What do you feel for me?"

Searching him, she took in his eyes, his energy. "I—I don't—"

And then he pulled her in, with one arm, then both, and kissed her full and strong. He completely enveloped her senses, declaring his feelings, demanding an answer. Megan couldn't help but respond, feeling overwhelmed by a rush of sensations—heady sparks and tingles that gave way to a deep, rising yearning for a closeness she'd never felt before—until she finally pulled herself away to catch her breath.

He bored into her eyes. "It's not complicated. I love you. I want you, with me, by my side." His voice was low and pulsing with emotion. "I'm leaving, right now. When you figure out what you're doing, you call me. Maybe I'll be around. Maybe I won't. But I am done."

With one final penetrating look, he turned and strode across the room, slamming the door behind him.

196

CHAPTER SEVENTEEN

Eleven hours later, Bryant got out of his truck just as Mitch met him in the parking lot of the lumber yard, looking worse than Bryant felt.

"You're a sight for sore eyes," said Mitch. "I heard you drove through the night—thanks."

Bryant shrugged it off. "Where's Dad?"

"He's at the hospital for his last appointment, but he'll be home tonight. Ross says he can take care of things for a couple of days, but—"

"Yeah, I know how Ross is. Don't worry about a thing."

"Listen, about the offer, I can ask them to hold it, they know that Dad's sick." He paused, hesitant. "I need to wait until I know you're in."

"I'm in right now. Go call them."

"Are you sure?"

"If you make me beg, I will, but it isn't pretty." Bryant grabbed the hardhat from Mitch, then took his outstretched hand and tugged him in for a slapping bear hug. "I'm sorry, Mitch, that I wasn't here. Real sorry."

Mitch stood back. "Well, you're here now. And just in time. I about fell asleep on the chop saw yesterday."

They walked into the yard, Mitch pointing and catching him up along the way. All the while hard, angry feelings balled inside Bryant. Megan hadn't rejected him outright, but her not coming, not budging, was a rejection sure enough. In a way he could feel it wasn't her fault, but still, she wasn't willing to get rid of whatever it was a little quicker, and he couldn't wait forever. Suddenly he wanted to hammer something. Hard.

Stepping up into the trailer office, Bryant followed Mitch inside then let the office door slam shut behind him, closing the door on Megan McCormick.

197

Megan ignored the knock from her mother on the small bedroom door. You wouldn't have known it used to be her room, almost all signs blocked by cardboard boxes holding her family's history in decorations and knickknacks.

After a night and most of the day since Bryant's stormy good-bye, Megan still didn't know what to do—well, except one idea. Her mom had taken on her usual all-is-well demeanor, still humming in a falsely cheery mood while cleaning the house. She was no help. Jillian was semi-officially still on her honeymoon. Megan offered yet another silent prayer to understand what to do next.

Her chest hurt with feeling things, conflicting things. One minute she felt his kiss from last night—never had he been like that with her, so encompassing she could hardly breathe. And feelings shooting and tingling all over her body—it had been shocking, thrilling, overwhelming. Then the pain of watching him leave, actually walk out the door and be gone, for good. No text, no call, nothing. He was truly gone. And then the ache began all over again, spreading from her ribs down through her stomach, through her veins, through her limbs, until she felt heavy and immovable. It was her fault, all of it. And yet, she didn't know how to stop it, how to solve it, how to make it go away and have it be all better.

Then the anger. Smoldering from some place low she had felt it start to burn, and rise. Not anger at him or herself, but at the doubting gray feeling that kept her holding back, kept her confused.

But this time, she could feel something else taking over. The Old-New Megan was not going to need three months on a cruise ship to get it together. No, the desire to do was there—but exactly what, and what wouldn't worsen the situation—those were the questions.

She pursed her lips. The idea came to mind again. It was worth a shot. And it certainly couldn't make things worse.

Calling directory assistance, Megan hoped she had the right one. She had tried his cell phone but no answer—this was the next best idea. Finally, dialing the home number, she willed her hands not to shake and took a few deep breaths.

"Hello?" said a woman's voice.

"Hello, Mrs. Johnson?"

"No, this is Piper, her daughter. May I ask who's calling?"

"Piper, oh!" Megan burst out unintentionally. "I'm sorry, it's Megan, Megan McCormick. You don't know me but—"

"Megan, of course I know you. Well, not in person, but certainly from the few juicy tidbits we've been able to squeeze from Bryant. Just a minute—" she could hear the sound more muffled. "Jakey, honey, that's a no. Put that back, that's Grammie's. I know. Share your trucks with Sarah." Then back to the phone. "Sorry about that."

"Are those your children?"

"Yes, only two—and so fun—but some days it feels like I have ten. Anyway, where were we? I think Bryant's at the yard. He didn't go to the hospital because Dad will be home after the appointment, although things sound a bit more optimistic now for a successful surgery. Such a relief, and we're so glad Bryant could get here quickly. I'm sure it was a shock for both of you."

"Hospital?" Megan stood very still, unable to think fast enough. His dad? Surgery?

"Well, yes, isn't that why you . . . Megan, didn't Bryant tell you?"

"No, he told me nothing, except—no, nothing."

Pause.

"Oh. Wow, I really put my foot in it. I—um—well, the cat's out of the bag now, although I don't get why he didn't say so." Another pause. "Megan, I'm sorry to be the one to say it. Bryant's dad is sick. He has a brain tumor, well, we just found out. He's going in for surgery on Monday. It's—"

Then she couldn't speak and started crying. "I'm sorry—really, all this with Dad, and I'm eight months pregnant, and the little ones aren't sleeping so it makes me hormonal and weepy all the time—really, I apologize."

Megan's knees began to buckle and she slid down the side of her bed to the floor. Waves of emotion passed through her. She had kept him selfishly here while his family needed him home. That was why he had been so angry, that's why they had wanted him back. She felt sick and swallowed it down.

"Piper, I'm so sorry. If I had known, I would have told him to go home days ago. I didn't know he was coming here at all."

"I know. He wanted to surprise you. He's so—I've never seen him so focused on someone before. But don't feel pressure"—she laughed short through blowing her nose—"we're just intense like that. Like me—hi, nice to meet you, here's my life story."

Megan wanted to reach through the phone and hug her. "Piper, I feel terrible I didn't know. What can I do, how can I help? I feel so, so—"

"Helpless? I know, we all do. Just pray, Megan. We're down to only that. We've got the best doctors, and Dad's being a trooper, in his own way, though he despises hospitals. He's only been in once before and that was an experience we all try to forget—Jakey, water stays outside. Anyway, there's nothing more that can be done. I'm sorry to blubber, it just is what it is."

"How's your mother doing, if I can ask?"

"Mom's great—she's always great—just worn out, not like herself. But she'd go in and do the surgery herself if they'd let her, that's the way she is. The rest of the family is coming down late Monday night, some of them Tuesday morning for a few days, so that'll help. Except for feeding them. Johnsons like their food, let me tell you." She sighed but tried to laugh.

That's when Megan knew what she needed to do. It was clear and sharp, like the beach days on the cruise deck—blue sky, no clouds, full steam ahead.

"Piper, I have an idea. I really want to know if it's okay but I think I could help—in a lot of ways—if you'll let me."

"Sounds mysterious. If it comes with a back massage, I'm all for it."

Megan shared her plan and though at first unwilling, Piper eventually agreed. After hanging up, Megan showered, packed, told her mom the plan, and hopped in her car.

A green highway sign came into view—sixty miles to Channing, California. She had stopped at a roadside hotel and slept for four hours, then returned to driving. The sun peeked between two mountains and Megan checked the time—she would be at Piper's in less than an hour. Megan felt excited at the prospect, at being able to help instead of hinder. She would be there for his family, but only as a friend. No strings attached. She would help Piper, be a nanny for a week while his sister took care of her dad and family, did books at the yard, and got a needed break.

Having cared for her nieces one summer, Megan looked forward to doing this, especially as a sort of penitence for Bryant being away from them while seeing her. She didn't even know them and yet she was anxious to serve them. And though she and Piper had only spoken a short while, his sister's warmth and genuineness had made her feel close to them already.

Initially, Piper had only agreed to have her come and be a support to Bryant, positively insisting on her staying with them. But Megan was determined to make up for being a distraction, and so difficult, though she hadn't wanted to be. Throughout the conversation she had an insistent desire to be an extra pair of hands, to help cook, clean, babysit, whatever was needed to alleviate the stress. She remembered when her father had left and the load that had transferred to her mother. How it helped when neighbors stepped in to care for them. This was something she could do.

Megan shook her head, thinking of the past two days. Thank goodness for Sylvia and being used to the whole temp agency, last-minute lifestyle. And that they'd known each other for two years. She'd been good about letting Megan go, with a slight mischievous smile no less. But even with everything falling into place, Megan had no idea what to expect from Bryant. If he were truly hostile she might be making a 24-hour round trip.

Bryant. Despite the lengthy drive and time to think, Megan still couldn't understand the hesitation within herself to fully commit to him. As she considered their best times—on the cruise ship, the excursions, at Zucker's Pond—she could see the pattern: relaxed, open, connected. As soon as she froze, things got complicated. And yet, the coldness didn't necessarily come from her. That gray doubt remained an obstacle to be dealt with.

But for now, she was clear about one thing—her role here and now was to serve. Whether Bryant would allow her to do it was something she'd find out.

Megan looked over at Piper's home phone, at her own cell phone resting on the kitchen counter, then to the front picture window. Surgery had been at 10:00 a.m. this morning. Three hours and still no call, no word about how it had gone.

"Okay, you be red this time," said Jakey. A tousled-headed five-year-old boy in worn jeans and a white T-shirt made car noises on the "Our Town" mat situated on the floor. The carpet mat was decorated with colored pictures of storefronts and parks and highways. Dozens of play trucks, cars, boats, and transportation vehicles were strewn over it.

"Sounds good. Or should I be the backhoe?" said Megan. "I saw some digging at the pond in the park." He stopped, thinking this option through.

"Yeah, okay, I guess." More car noises. "I'm going to the gas station and get me some gas." He sped away with his car, making gas pumping sounds of dings and glugs.

Megan couldn't help smiling, and wondering how she could feel so comfortable in a mere 24 hours. She'd yet to see Bryant, having arrived early Sunday morning, just in time to help a protesting Piper get her two children breakfast. After church—Bryant and his mother stayed home with his father at the house—it had been early supper and naptime all around. Later, Megan had insisted that she tend the children while the adults gathered at their parents' home. Piper ultimately relented, grateful to process the emotions without having to worry about the kids.

Abruptly, Piper's phone rang, bringing Megan back to the present. She stood up to answer it.

"Hello?"

"Megan, it's Piper. We're done and he's doing so well. The whole thing went like clockwork," she said, a tremor in her voice. "They're certain the tumor isn't cancerous, though they're testing it to be sure—thank goodness for that. They've removed all they can find and said he should recover well as far as they can figure."

"Piper, I'm so glad, I can't tell you how wonderful that is to hear." She hadn't even met the man, and yet she truly felt it in her heart. Bryant must be so relieved.

"How are Jakey and Sarah?"

"Doing great. Sarah's napping still and Jake and I are taking on the town."

Piper laughed gently. It felt good to hear her sound lighter. "Thanks so much, Megan. It's so funny, and please take this right, but I never let my children stay with complete strangers. It's just that you don't seem that strange to me."

Megan laughed—yes, she was Bryant's sister. "Well, you don't know me yet. I'm sure Bryant can tell you a few things." She stopped—she hadn't meant to mention his name.

"Oh, I'm sure you'd love to hear what Bryant's told us," she said slyly into the phone. "And he says hello, though he has conspicuously said nothing about you. Which clearly means he can't wait to see you. We'll be coming home in a few hours. Thanks again for taking care of them and give them my love."

"Will do, don't worry about a thing," said Megan. Hanging up, she felt relief—tangible and light—knowing not only that his father was well and the operation successful, but that Bryant didn't despise her completely. Not yet.

After playing a while longer, Megan sat a just-awakened Sarah in the high chair and Jakey at the counter to stack Legos while she prepared a big batch of spaghetti. Just before dinnertime the door opened.

"Jakey buddy!" His father, Brandon, walked through the door, opening it wider for Piper.

"Daddy!" Jakey jumped off the counter stool and ran pell-mell, jumping into his father's arms.

"Whoa, you're getting so big, buddy," said Brandon, a tall dark-haired man in his thirties with an easy smile. "Something smells good."

"We made sgetti."

Piper walked over to Megan. "You honestly don't have to, Megan. Besides, you're gonna make me look bad. It's been a lot of tuna sandwiches and foraging from the sideboard lately."

"I'm not eight months pregnant," said Megan, nodding to Brandon. She felt a satisfaction in being there, being useful. "If you're hungry, it's ready. I just need to—"

A quick courtesy knock at the door and it opened further.

Bryant.

Megan turned back to the sink, reaching up to discreetly feel her suddenly warm face.

"Bry, where's Mom?" said Piper.

"She's still at the hospital. She sent me here." Bryant defended himself. Megan could hear him taking off his jacket. "You know Mom. She said I was cranky—"

"—she's got that right—"

"—and needed to rest, and they were just fine without me. Pete and Janelle are staying at the hospital with her. Denise and Robert are staying at the house for whoever might show up."

Megan stayed unnecessarily busy preparing plates for the table. She plunked large dollops of noodles on the center and ladled generous portions of meaty tomato sauce on top. Piper and Brandon helped bring the dishes to the table. Bryant approached the counter.

"Need any help?"

Megan looked up at him, the first time she'd seen him since . . .

"You can take the salad, if you want." She handed him the bowl. Their eyes met but his without any indication or feeling. If anything, there was a distinct coolness in his manner.

After saying grace, the table broke into the noisy sounds that a three- and five-year-old can make while being made to eat. Megan sat across from Bryant and ate mostly in silence, listening to them recount the surgery, the prognosis from here, and what remained to be done. The mood was upbeat. They had weathered the worst and the initial results were already more positive than they had hoped.

"Matthews is one of the best there is," said Brandon. "He got all of it, and without traumatizing the rest of the brain. He's amazing. Said that Dad should only need to stay a week or so."

"That short? For brain surgery?" said Piper.

"Did you see Dad? Even drugged he already had movement in his mouth, which means his motor skills are looking good. Therapy and all that is supposed to start day after tomorrow."

"They don't waste any time," said Piper, helping Sarah keep the spaghetti on her plate and not in her hair. She wriggled in her high chair to protest.

Reaching for her milk, Megan noticed Bryant staring at her, but he returned to his plate and cleaning its contents.

"This is really good, Piper," said Bryant. "Is this another one of those crockpot things?"

"It *is* good, isn't it," said Piper, grinning. "Megan made it."

Bryant looked up—Megan looked down.

"So, everything good at the yard with Ross there right now? Got any plans for the week, Bry?" Piper said. The room went very still except for Sarah and Jakey's noises. Megan noted that Brandon shook his head, smiling, as if to say, "Don't meddle, sweetheart."

"You know Ross, he always needs a hand," said Bryant. "Spends more time on his backside and his cell phone than he does actually working." He took another piece of bread. "It'll work for when I'm at the hospital."

"Now that Dad's good, I'm gonna stay with the kids. Megan needs a break from being on Sesame Street, I think."

Megan began to protest.

"Don't even think about it. Bryant can show you around the yard tomorrow. You can get out and get some fresh air, then go see Dad." Seeing Megan shake her head, Piper added, "The boss has spoken—and that's me. If you don't believe it, ask Brandon. Any woman in her eighth month is the boss. Isn't that right, dear?"

"Whatever you say, sugar," said Brandon, and winked at Megan. He whispered to her, "Got one word for you—hormones."

Megan pushed noodles around with her fork, feeling Bryant's stare between her and her sister, and hearing a slight chuckle in Piper's voice as she spoke baby talk to Sarah.

CHAPTER EIGHTEEN

Megan's stomach churned as she tidied breakfast dishes with Piper who chatted amiably until Bryant arrived. At the last moment, Megan convinced Piper to let them take Jakey, whose favorite thing next to the Our Town mat was the lumber yard. Not only would it give Piper a break, but hopefully soften the situation. What would she even say to Bryant, to explain about her being here?

Bryant entered Piper's doorway, his face set in a stoic expression. Megan swallowed down the feelings that immediately surfaced—sadness that he was done dealing with their relationship, angst for what she'd put him through, frustration that she couldn't get over her emotional issues quicker, and longing to be with him like they used to be.

Bryant swung Jakey up for a hug. After a bit of small talk and details of their dad, they said good-bye.

He opened the truck door for Megan and an enthusiastic Jakey. She noted it seemed much cleaner than it had been before. It took them a minute to get the booster seat just right, their heads awkwardly meeting in the process. Still, he didn't look her in the eye.

Heading for the yard, Megan knew she had to say something, seeing as she had been the one to arrive at his hometown, unannounced and uninvited.

"Bry, I need to talk to you." She looked down at Jakey who was driving his yellow truck across his legs.

"Not so fast."

"No, not about that." She definitely didn't want to discuss their romantic situation, especially in front of Jakey. "It's just that I'm not here to mess things up. I only want to help. You helped me this summer—so much—and I didn't realize, fully, the sacrifice, especially finding out about your dad. I just wanted to make it up to you and your family."

From her periphery, she saw his eyes narrow. Megan frowned. She'd been careful to not imply any romantic overtones to the visit, now that she'd told him clearly she wasn't emotionally ready to commit to him, and he had as clearly said he was done waiting. The last thing she wanted was to further confuse him. Why couldn't this be simpler?

"My plan is to stay out of the way and let Piper rest. She's obviously put in a lot of time at the yard office. I don't know how she's done that and kids. But this way she can do it without being so tired."

"That's your plan, huh?"

"You know how I like to plan." She tried to be light.

He nodded—a short tight movement—and they rode in silence. Inside, she felt the distance and the hurt from him, and wanted to make it better but didn't know how. Sighing inwardly, she chatted with Jakey about his truck.

The first thing that struck Megan about the lumber yard was that it was big, bigger than Bryant had led her to imagine. And loud. Saws buzzing and a few forklifts hauling lumber back and forth with the reverse beepers going on and off. Two large warehouse structures stood facing each other. Like a protective soldier, a smaller office type showroom stood in front and between them.

As they entered through a wide opening between the warehouses behind the showroom building, Megan heard "Wood pile!" Jakey, who had been happily holding each of their hands, took off like a shot in the direction of the far end of the first warehouse. Apparently, this was a familiar play place. Megan squinted, watching where he ran.

Bryant walked to some hooks on the side of the warehouse and grabbed two hardhats, handing one to her.

"Seriously?" said Megan.

"Worried about your hair?" He had tried to joke but it was forced. His eyes smoldered with a serious intensity she didn't know how to take.

"Can we still see Jakey?" said Megan, looking ahead.

"Yep, that's why the sand box is situated there, by the office. Piper's idea. Besides, Jakey knows his way around." Bryant continued walking with her between the two warehouses, pointing and perfunctorily explaining some things. The inside structures revealed four floors of wood bays, holding varieties of wood planks. Men in hardhats moved confidently from bay to bay, or to waiting forklifts for loading.

Megan put on the hat, feeling conspicuous as he walked her through the middle of the open space. The men turned and stared—some with open interest—but no one jeered or catcalled.

As they approached the alcove, Megan saw a large weather-beaten sand box littered with Tonka trucks situated next to a grungy woodpile. She wondered if Jakey had had a tetanus shot.

Bryant took a hardhat from a hook on the wall and bent down, handing it to Jake. "Hey buddy—your hardhat." The little boy looked at Bryant and gave him a thumbs-up, which Bryant returned.

"Hey, Ryan?" Bryant called to a young man in a flannel shirt stacking wood in the next bay. "Keep an eye on Jake, will you? We won't be long."

The man nodded at Jake. "No problem, he's my man."

Turning toward a worn white double-wide trailer on cement blocks, Bryant was about to say something to Megan when the door opened and a dark-haired young man dressed conspicuously in a nice shirt and slacks exited. He walked toward Bryant but with his eyes fixed on Megan.

Bryant nodded in greeting. "Bertie, this is Megan. She's come to visit while Dad's in the hospital."

Bertie shook her hand while giving an appreciative smile. "Wow, great. How long are you staying?"

Bryant turned to face him and said meaningfully, "Until Dad is out of the hospital. Don't you have some accounting issues to deal with?"

Awareness dawned and he adjusted his glasses. "Sure, yeah, nice to meet you, Megan. Um, see you around." With one last warning look from Bryant, Bertie walked in the direction of the front showroom.

Climbing the rickety steps, they entered the well-used office with large windows, giving a clear view to an old field on the east side, and most of the yard on the west side.

Papers were stacked everywhere—in trays, file folders, and some strewn openly between two different desks, a sideboard, and two bookcases. Near a snack counter sat an old coffee maker on a cabinet stand with cheery ceramic mugs, a hat rack, and a boot shelf. A plaque hung over the door: "If women don't find you handsome, they should at least find you handy." Various family photos were sprinkled throughout the trailer in stands, frames, and stuck hodge-podge style on a magnetic board. It was worn and comfortable, like a favorite chair, with smells of freshly sawn wood, earth, and working men.

"So, this is command central?" said Megan.

"Yep, this is where it all happens. Don't be jealous."

She put her purse on the nearby desk and glanced out the west window at the constant movement. "It's great—the yard, your family, really, it's all amazing. From what you said, I guess I pictured something different."

"Like?" He sat in his obviously regular leather armchair, leaning back.

She turned around to face him, leaning against the other desk. "Small, boring, going nowhere kind of thing. This is not that picture."

"We're holding our own."

"I think a lot more than that."

He only shrugged. The sounds of a young boy's cries could be heard. Megan instantly turned back to the window to see Ryan with Jakey in tow. He opened the door and they stepped inside.

Megan went right to Jakey, lifting him up on her hip and giving him a hug.

"Oh, he's good, just got a sliver from the side of the sandbox," said Ryan. Bryant nodded and the young man patted Jakey on the head and left the office.

"I have the perfect thing for slivers," said Megan, who toted him over to her purse. Searching through it, she found her make-up tweezers and a hard candy. "Can you suck on this magic pill while I get rid of the sliver?"

Jakey's tear-filled eyes looked at her solemnly. She unwrapped and handed him the treat, then took his other hand, searching for and finding the small sliver. Bryant distracted him with teasing questions of where was his magic pill, and, wasn't Jakey going to share, so that Megan had pulled the sliver before he could make too much of a fuss.

"There you go, buddy," said Megan, giving him a quick hug. He returned it, putting his arms around her neck, which surprised her. He held on while she hugged and rocked him, seeing that he was getting sleepy.

"I think it might be close to his naptime," she said quietly.

Bryant stared at her with a peculiar expression. He didn't respond right away and she almost repeated it, thinking he hadn't heard her. But then he said in a gruff voice, "Okay, sure, I need to get to the hospital anyway."

Ultimately, Megan had begged off of coming to the hospital—it still felt too personal—and made the point she needed to help Piper with the kids. She had felt a shift in Bryant since being at the yard, though she couldn't name it. Not distant but thoughtful and brooding, even barely remembering to say good-bye to her. All she could think was that it bothered him she was here, interfering with their personal lives and spaces. She was more determined than ever to stay low-key and out of the family's way.

Megan offered to fix lunch. Piper had been grateful, her only request was that it be anything but macaroni and cheese. Afterwards, while Sarah and Jakey napped—Sarah in her crib and Jakey on the floor of his Our Town mat still clutching his yellow truck—Piper headed over to the yard to finish up some necessary paperwork. Megan quickly cleaned the bathrooms and kitchen, and mopped the floor.

At Piper's return, she announced a surprise. "No worries on cooking tonight, Megan my girl. It's at the big house." Megan opened her mouth to which Piper raised a wagging finger. "Not one word of refusal. We're bringing the kids so you're committed. It's sort of an impromptu gathering. Most everyone has arrived by now. And, Dad actually talked today. So, it's party time, like it or not."

Megan looked stricken, to which Piper laughed outright. "Don't worry, it's only a big load of people who can't wait to gawk at you. What's not to love?"

Yes, she was most *definitely* Bryant's sister.

Arriving for dinner, Megan took in the outside of Bryant's family home. A good-sized lovely house, not pretentious or fancy, with a fresh-looking craftsman style in olive green and sharp white trim.

Stepping through the door, Megan realized immediately that Piper had not been exaggerating about the family. Streams of people and children seemed to flow from every opening. Two large golden Labradors the size of small horses roamed freely between the humanity. Megan had no idea Bryant had so much extended family, again surprised at what he hadn't shared, although maybe living in it was so familiar. To her and life in a quiet home with a few absent siblings, this was like the mall on Black Friday.

Wading through people, she smiled and answered the inquiries: "Hi, who are you?" and, "Good to see you. Whose clan are you with?"

She bumped into Piper once. "Been initiated into the family reunion?" she said. "Mix, mingle, have some food. Enjoy the inquisition." Chuckling, she ambled by, toting two plates. Megan took up her own plate and spent a safe amount of time spooning dishes onto it. She found a quiet corner, tucked away in the family room, but it wasn't as secluded as it seemed. For the next hour women of all ages found their way to her like a trek to the Dalai Lama, asking all sorts of questions: "Where are you from?" "How do you know Bryant?" "Oh, you're Megan. And how long are you staying?"

Two ladies chatted next to her. "You know it's about time Bryant settled down," said the first one, looking suspiciously at Megan.

"I know," said the other. "Dating everyone in the county, and these stage mothers—so pushy."

"If that isn't the truth. And sometimes it's the mothers themselves, the single ones of course." They both nodded knowingly.

Megan almost touched her forehead to be sure there wasn't a sticker saying, "Wed Me."

Occasionally, she saw Bryant from a distance, wearing that supercilious half-smile as he watched the women descend upon her, clearly unmoved to rescue her. Megan noticed a fair amount of 20-somethings continually finding their way to him as well. Piper had commented earlier about it. "Don't let them scare you, there's always been a sort of following for Bry. He got tired of that a long time ago."

But he didn't look tired of it. In fact, if she were being honest with herself, she'd say he was rather enjoying it. Someone feeding him from a plate, two other girls laughing at whatever he seemed to say. Well, he was free to do as he pleased. She was strictly here to help the family. Nothing more. Frankly, she had no one to blame but herself, and her ridiculous emotional state. If only she could jump over it like one of her track hurdles. Boom, boom, boom, finish line and done. It just wasn't that simple. She didn't have the experience or tools to navigate this. It wasn't stats. It was figuring things out, and that took time and understanding. Two things she'd already pushed to the limit with him.

Abruptly, Megan rose and excused herself on pretense of finding a bathroom. Her heart hurt and she needed some peace. In the hallway, someone tugged her arm. Turning, she saw Piper with a sympathetic expression. "Had enough? Go upstairs, last room on the right. It's the quietest. And Bryant's old room." She winked and pushed her gently toward the stairs. Making her way, Megan gratefully ascended the stairs, anxious for a moment of solace.

Piper snagged Bryant's arm as he walked past her, shooing one of the dogs out the front door. "Listen, I've been watching you watch Megan the whole time. Before your eyes fall out, how about you do something fun with her?"

Bryant's face hardened. "Not the time, sis."

"Look, Dad's doing great. He's got more babysitters than he can count, and can't stand any of us right now. He's good, the yard is good, it's all good. Go take her up to the mountains. You know, look at the *views* ..."

Bryant narrowed his eyes. "The nights are cooler now."

"So build a fire."

"Will you stop?"

"Only if you get going." Piper smiled, smoothing the front of his hair. "She's here, Bry. Here. Obviously, whatever the deal is, she's swallowed her pride to show she cares."

He shook his head and kissed the top of her hair. "You are relentless," he said, walking in the opposite direction of the stairs.

Megan lay on the bed, unable to rest, never mind knowing this used to be Bryant's old room. It felt too intimate, though he couldn't have stayed here anytime recently. She got up, silently walking around the soft blue room, carefully organized but stuffed full of life's paraphernalia. Bryant's life.

Countless gold and silver trophies stood proudly in different sizes for various sports—football, basketball, wrestling. Pictures in frames crammed the shelves—a young helmeted football player dwarfed by shoulder pads. Had to be Pee Wee football. She fingered the frame of a crew-cut junior high Bryant standing short between two basketball players, a cocky smile saying he didn't care about that. A messy-haired high school Bryant standing tall, front and center of the basketball picture with arms behind his back, no smile.

Then the females. Lots of dance pictures with oversized corsages and pretty girls with dated hairdos. Bending to the pictures, Megan saw they were obviously from a popular set. The displays, with coordinating ribbons and accessories, said Mom preserved these.

Bryant had obviously been driven and successful and yet now, he drifted, hating his job at the yard but with no real vision for his life. Megan shook her head. Both she and Bryant, each with their own emotional boulders in the road to move aside, and yet seemingly unable to. Maybe they just needed time away from each other to solve their problems and come back together a little more whole. Could it be that easy? Was it ultimately timing that stood in their way?

The sound of a cell phone ringing brought her back to the present. She looked around before realizing it was in her back pocket.

The number didn't look familiar. "Hello?"

"Hello, Megan? Is that you? Listen, I'm on shore for a short time and wanted to call you from a landline—thank you, Keenan, I'll just take an herbal tea—how are things back in the US?"

"Mrs. Van De Morelle? This is a surprise, a big surprise. Yes, I'm doing well. Things are good." Why would Mrs. V. be calling her?

"Good, good. Listen dear, I've only a few minutes—you know how it is— but I have a proposition for you. In case you weren't aware, I hired Rosa and frankly, she is worth three of you and any of those Performing Premiers, I can tell you. Very smart and quite funny, always trying to teach me Spanish and correcting my English—yes, Keenan, show them in and I'll be right there—sorry dear, are you still there?"

"Yes, yes, I'm here."

"All right then, my offer is this. Would like you to come work for me and help manage a new department? I'm going to try my hand with legal immigration as it were—imagine that—helping some of the well-qualified ship employees into long-term working situations. Mostly in the US and Canada. I'm thinking—yes, Keenan, lovely, be right there—I'm thinking to offer you a gloriously healthy salary, say upper five figures, to tempt you away from that fabulous temp agency you're slaving in."

Megan shook her head in awe. "That sounds amazing—you're actually placing the workers on the mainland? Honestly, that's a fantastic idea. But do you mean I would work from the ship?"

"On the ship, at different ports, whatever is needed. Travel, cruises—but working ones, mind you—truly a dream job if there ever was one, if I do say so myself. But work it is, don't kid yourself that you'll be tanning all day. So what do you think?"

Megan's mind felt like popcorn, her thoughts exploding all over the place. "I'm not sure. How exactly would that work?"

Mrs. V. gave her several details, all of which sounded slightly warbled in her mind. The whole thing sounded fabulous and surreal, yet something pulled at her mind and heart. "Mrs. Van De Morelle, this is incredible, and I have to say, a bit overwhelming."

"Well, let me add a little more to completely overflow it. I'm asking Bryant to come on board as well."

Bryant? Megan's stomach swooped.

"I have need of his Spanish translation and diplomatic services. I tried his cell phone but no luck. Perhaps you can pass on the good news and have him give me a ring?"

"Of course, that's great news for him."

"So? Will you jump on the offer or not?"

That was so Mrs. V. Offer a life-changing deal and want an immediate response. "This is amazing, and I'm so glad you called. But may I have some time to think it over and talk with my employer?"

"Absolutely, but don't make me wait too long. Think it about it and get back to me in what—a few days, no more than a week?"

Megan's mind whirled. "Terrific. And thank you, I'm delighted, and flattered you'd even think of me—beyond flattered. Yes, I'll call you in a few days."

They exchanged good-byes and hung up. Megan sat on the edge of the bed, tapping the cell phone on her chest, staring into space and processing the conversation. A spectacular opportunity. Unbelievable. Doing something she'd love to do, with good people, in an incredible environment. And being paid an excellent wage to do it. A dream come true. Why wasn't she jumping at the chance? Why hadn't she already said yes, a resounding yes, right then?

And Bryant in the deal, too? Megan's mind jumped to images, the two of them spending time helping others, being together on the ship, on the shores. But, she pulled back to reality. He was just getting settled here—his dad, his family. Would he leave again so soon?

A knock on the door, and Bryant poked his head in. "What's this, checking out my private life?"

Megan smiled, surprised that he was talking to her. She quickly surveyed the room. "Very telling, I must say. Bryant with a basketball. Bryant with a tennis racket. Bryant at the Sweetheart Ball, draped by yet another lovely lady."

He rolled his eyes, walked over and sat on the floor across from her with his back against the wall. But even with the grimace, he looked different—softened, as if tentatively extending an olive branch of some kind. But why, she had no idea.

He looked at the cell phone she held close to her. "Talking to one of your adoring fans?"

"Only over 60." She said it slowly, carefully, reading his expression.

His eyebrows furrowed, then lifted in understanding. "Mrs. V?"

Megan numbly affirmed. Bryant's eyes narrowed, as if he knew something was coming that he didn't want to know.

"She's offered me a job." It came out flat, like a bad cold.

Bryant nodded slowly, then automatically grabbed an old basketball on the floor next to the dresser and tossed it between his hands.

"A good one?"

"Amazing." She watched his reaction, a consternation that clouded his face. "But it gets even better. She offered you one, too." His eyebrows went up. "It seems your translation skills are needed."

"Seriously?" His eyes processed the possibilities and she could almost read them—spend time together, work with people who needed help. But the yard, his family. That math problem look pervaded as he absently tossed the basketball. He conspicuously didn't ask the myriad questions she knew he had—would they work on the same ship, could they work together if she still was in relationship limbo, would it be as unreal a future for them this time as it seemed last time?

"When would we start?" His voice sounded far away.

"End of October."

He nodded. Six weeks. She knew it was going through both their minds.

Later that night, Megan lay in Piper's old bedroom, next door to Bryant's old room. Curled up on the bed against the wall, she stared across at the three girl cousins, now asleep in sleeping bags on the floor. Smiling at their contentment, Megan rolled over to face the wall. She wished she could sleep that easily. Reaching up, she touched the bumpy orange-peel white paint, realizing this wall connected to Bryant's old room, who at the moment was also sharing his space with several boy cousins in their sleeping bags. About 1:00 a.m., she could tell from the lack of noise that the boys had finally dropped off. But in her soul she knew two people were wide awake, with only a wall separating them.

It used to be two states, Megan thought. It might as well be. He had said nothing about the job offer, not one word. And she had no idea where he stood with her for the future, except that he had started to thaw somewhat, at least to be cordial.

Should she take the job? Mrs. V. had said it was a two-year minimum commitment. If she didn't take the job, it would put clear pressure on Bryant, i.e. "I'm giving up this amazing opportunity to hopefully have something work out with you here, in two different states. Even though I've said I'm not ready yet and have been completely horrid to you." And, as her mother was sure to say, she'd miss out on a once-in-a-lifetime tailor-made opportunity, never mind a great financial situation.

But if she did take it, and Bryant did too, it would say "I want to keep our relationship possibility open even if it hurts you to be with me while I figure it out." If she took the job and Bryant didn't, it would send a different signal— "I'm leaving for two years and we're done, for good."

Ping, pong, her thoughts and emotions went back and forth.

The ticking of the dresser clock showed 2:15 a.m. Megan groaned. When would this all be over and she could just *be?*

CHAPTER NINETEEN

Megan raked more leaves from the corner of Piper's small front yard.

"How about you finish over there, Jakey?" she said. The five-year-old had his miniature-sized rake and had spent at least 15 minutes on the same spot, taking time to examine certain leaves, trip over the rake, and track the movements of an unwitting slug.

Megan stood with her rake and smiled. For the past few days, she had spent most of her time with Jakey and Sarah, making meals and keeping their home tidy. With the two little ones, that had proved to be an almost full-time job. But she also had weeded the front yard, with "helpers," and made herself indispensable to the point that Piper had already asked her to stay on for salary. Megan had laughed at the suggestion but felt warmed by the praise.

She would really miss this little guy. And Sarah. And Piper. And—she frowned. I'm not here for him, or for us. Since talking in his room, she and Bryant had shared only a few superficial conversations, though she'd seen him frequently enough—he was in the house right now, saying he had to talk over some accounting things with Piper.

Over the past few days he'd still been cool, though not as angry. More as if processing. Megan wasn't sure but it felt like he was weighing things—her, the job offer, the yard. She yearned to talk with him about it, the possibilities, but didn't want to open up any wounds. She had promised this visit was about serving the family, not about them. But she could feel his struggle, too. Several times in the middle of a typical interchange his expression had shifted and the pause in the conversation made her think he was going to share something. But he didn't.

Megan knew either way, it didn't matter, as her time was coming to a close here. His father was doing incredibly well, better than the doctors had hoped. One nurse said it was because he was a fighter. Another nurse said that was code for crotchety. As the weekend approached, most of the family had left and returned to their lives knowing their dad was in good hands. The yard seemed to be running well. Bryant was a natural, Piper said, who seemed happier and with better energy, laughing more often and sporting color in her cheeks. There was no reason for her to stay longer.

"Sounds like the yard is good," said Piper, easing herself down on the couch. "How about you? Made any decisions?"

Bryant gazed out the big front window watching Megan rake the leaves and talk with Jakey. "Yes and no."

"Tell me about no."

Bryant turned his head, grimacing at the word play. "She got a job offer, an excellent one, for both of us actually. But for her more of a dream job of a lifetime. I can't stand in the way of that, not when she's already told me she's not ready for anything more relationship-wise, with me at least."

"But she's here."

"Because she's like that. She helps people. I can't take this any other way just because I want to. Sitting in her office, clear as crystal, she told me where she stood. She needs time and doesn't know how long. And I have to respect it." He swallowed. "I've thought about it twenty different ways. I know the best decision for me, and for her, and I don't like it. But any way I look at it, it's the right thing to do."

Piper nodded slowly, understanding. "Have you told Megan? She leaves tomorrow."

"No. Not yet."

"How is she doing?"

Bryant turned back, watching Megan laugh at something Jakey said, helping him scoop leaves into a garbage bag. "Don't know. I haven't seen much of her."

"Yeah, I noticed," she said. "Not much, except stopping by my house all the time, and looking out this window, and always being where she generally is."

He shook his head, a small smile tugging at his lips. "You cannot be trusted, sis."

"Wanna tell me why you're pretending you don't care?"

"Because she needs a good kick in the pants."

"Charming."

"It's better than what I originally wanted to say."

"Which is?"

Bryant squinted from the natural light, folding his arms tightly. "Because I can't stand to be without her. But I can't let her know. She has to make her own decision, without me in the way." He shrugged. "Besides, a little humble pie has been good for her."

"I see, so helping me hasn't been one of her favorite things?"

"No, not that. She's jerked me around so much it's good she gets a taste of it. Not that I blame her completely."

"That makes no sense."

He looked down at his confused sister, wondering how much to share. She patted the couch next to her and he sat, pausing then rubbing her feet while he relayed all Megan had told him about Jackson.

Piper stared at him. "And you've put her through this over the past week? I thought we taught you better." She removed her feet. "Megan can't control being scared. And that's how she sounds—hurt and scared, nothing personal. Do you understand she's cooking and cleaning, like she used to for Jackson, and now she's doing it for you? Sure she's at my house, but you know exactly what this is, an apology, prostrate on the ground, for something she can't fix yet. Can you imagine how that must feel to her?"

He stood up—restless, angry—looking at Megan outside. "You think it's been easy for me to stand by and watch? Wanting to help, to make it easy for her? To hold her and I can't."

"And that's your sacrifice?"

"Yes, and it feels right," he said, turning away from the window. "And I'll be glad when it's done."

In the early morning quiet, Megan stole out of her bedroom, inching the door closed. She had made the bed, tidied the room, and written a thank you note for the Johnsons. Good-byes to everyone had already been said last night. She tiptoed down to the creamy white and blue kitchen.

Stopping at the bottom of the stairs, she saw Bryant through the barely open French doors leading to the back deck. She debated. Her idea had been to leave without a good-bye, no anger or tears, and let things be as they were. Apparently Bryant had other plans.

Walking through the open doorway onto the deck, the soft morning light blanketed the small English cottage-type backyard. Every corner teemed with foliage and pastel flowers interrupted with curving primrose paths all supervised around the perimeter by tall pines. It was an atypical amalgamation, but somehow it worked. Megan took in the postcard picture, pulling her hoodie closer. Though warm for the September morning, she felt a chill inside.

Bryant turned at hearing her footfall. "Leaving early?"

"Thought so, I—" She had been about to say couldn't sleep but only said, "Couldn't waste this kind of morning." Which was true.

He stood up and gave her his chair, then sat one leg on the corner of the large wooden picnic table, his arms folded. Megan sat down, both of them staring out at the garden—golden light filtering through the variegated leaves, the cobblestone paths, and old stone fountains now still.

For a few minutes they enjoyed the garden silence.

"My mom and sister appreciate all you've done," Bryant said.

"It's not been much."

"And with Jakey," he said, as if he hadn't heard her. "I think especially with Jakey."

Megan smiled. "He is so like my brothers." Thinking it sounded too personal but not knowing what else to say, she crossed her legs and looked out at the lush landscape. When had it become so hard to talk to each other? Probably since they got the job offer. And she had told him to leave Nevada. And made him pass all kinds of ridiculous made-up tests that now made her cringe.

A bluebird chirped from the lonely copse of Aspens. A tension began to fill the small space between them, a humming kind of feeling that seemed to suddenly crackle. She could feel something coming and began searching for a way out.

"It's gonna be hot today," he said.

"I know. I should really get a head start," she said, and rose to leave. He sat where he was but reached out one arm to the side to stop her. "Just a minute."

She paused, and turned her face to him, not moving closer. Gently, he wrapped his arm around her waist and pulled her to him. She leaned into his chest, looking out at the intricate garden. Where did they go from here? It was all winding paths and forks in the road, and she desperately needed to know which one to take.

He paused then said in a slow clear voice, "I'm at the yard now." He dipped toward her head. "For good."

Like a punctured ball, her insides folded into one another. Megan knew what he meant. He'd made his decision. And ironically, it was the stable choice she had originally wanted. Before Mrs. V.'s job offer. He was saying she could do whatever she liked, take whatever job was offered, he wouldn't stand in her way. But he wouldn't wait around for two years while she figured things out either.

Of course not. Now she had to choose for herself—be that freedom-fighting Megan taking the new road without letting a guy determine her life, or work through her emotional stuff in small-town USA and hope in the process she could ultimately keep Bryant.

Either way, time had officially run out for her. The tears were expected—though she'd never let him see—but the squeezing sensation in her lungs surprised her. She focused on breathing normally.

It occurred to her that he was waiting for a reply.

"I understand," she said. But she didn't. Not any of it. Not him, not what he said, how she felt or why she couldn't throw her arms around him and never leave.

They stood in silence for a moment. Nestled close to her hair she felt him nod, curt and final. Still they stood, neither opting to go. The same bird called to its mate, a lonely, mourning kind of sound. It didn't fit with the shimmering sunlight and evergreen branches.

He kissed the top of her head. The squeezing in her lungs became unbearable. Disengaging, she turned and walked robot-like, picking up her travel bag, focusing on the door, then the front stoop, then her car. Like a dream, she pulled out of the driveway, ignoring the image from the corner of her eye—of Bryant now standing on the stairs, watching her go.

Six weeks.

Leaning back in the old office chair, Bryant looked out the west office window but without seeing. He knew that wasn't much time to decide what to do about Megan McCormick. Six weeks and she'd be gone. Mrs. V. had said it was a two-year commitment. Either he let her go fulfill her dream, or he did what he really wanted to do—drive up and drag her back like a sheik claiming his harem prize. That seemed to be the only thing that could work with her.

Bryant tossed a miniature hard basketball onto a matching miniature backboard hanging on the trailer wall by the window. It bounced back to him. He bounced it several times on the same worn spot and each time it came back. He surveyed the busy yard. Same old yard, same old day. Same old problem with Megan. And no real solution in sight. Yes, he could go and stand in her apartment and beg her to be with him. But he was sick of begging. If she wasn't ready, she wasn't ready. And all the pleading in the world wouldn't change that. He had to face the truth: this was out of his control and there was nothing he could do about it but wait or move on.

Neither option looked good.

Bryant swung around, staring at the dust-covered office. "Command Central" Megan had called it. He laughed, a short, deprecating one. The "office" had been a double-wide trailer, which had been added onto and make-shifted into an office space. His dad hated to spend money. "Why build a new office when this one works just fine?" Except in winter, when the heater malfunctioned. Or summer, when the fan blew nothing but hot air.

The whining sound of buzzing saws and men hollering back and forth came to him through the closed window. He heard the beep of the forklift as it backed up to load another order of lumber. Bryant put hands behind his head, thinking about the years of working in this same office—since he was five. He could remember running in and his dad saying, "Get a hard hat on son, this ain't no play-place here." And Ross, with his big belly even way back then overhanging suspender-held Wranglers—always Wranglers. And his worn out cowboy boots, and his kicking off the dirt by smacking the stair tread every time he entered. Ross had a year, maybe two left, especially after his double bypass. Already it was hard for him to work part-time.

Bryant shook his head. Whichever way he sliced it, this yard was part of his future, like it or not. Now it was time to accept it. Still no major solution had come from the sky, though he'd been looking. If only something pulled him, made sense to him, something that said yes, this is what I should do with my life.

Megan.

Surprising him came the clear picture of her sitting by the lake, laughing about their childhoods. Megan sitting on his lap at her office, eyes wide and childlike, telling him she couldn't go. Megan pulling the sliver from Jakey's hand, talking to him sweetly, right over there on that desk. Megan standing in his arms on the deck, leaving. Always Megan. Always leaving. Why did she resist so much? Why did he care so much? There were a hundred girls who showed interest. Well, not a hundred, but more than her, and more predictable, that was for sure. She was like the late summer sky—warm and inviting one minute, crackling thunder and lightning the next. Who needed this kind of stress?

He shook his head. Where did he go with either choice? He didn't want to work at the yard, but that's where fate pushed him. He wanted Megan but she and fate actively pushed him back.

The metal door swung open with a squeak. Bertie entered and stood in a kind of hesitant nervous way. At 24 and looking like an Ivy League computer nerd, he was completely out of place at the yard. But an internship two years before had made him useful in the legal department and indispensable in the accounting department, as he was the only employee in both.

"What's up, Bert, my man?"

"Well, I've been thinking." He looked around the office and through the window to his right.

"I've told you before, Bertie, that'll get you nowhere around here."

He half-heartedly smiled. "If you have a minute, can I run something by you?"

Bryant pointed for him to have a seat. "Hit me with it."

Bertie took a minute, looking at the rolled up scroll of paper in his hand, then decisively said, "Where do you see the yard going, in the future, I mean?"

Bryant sat up. "No idea. Why?"

He took a perceptive breath then let it fly. "Well, I have some ideas, if you're interested. The yard is in decent shape for now, financially and physically, though it could use some upgrades. But if we want to compete, really compete, we need to go online, get more technology involved on the lumber side, and network with local and regional connections to push sales."

"Okay," said Bryant slowly. "What would that look like?"

Bertie's right leg started moving up and down. He played with the paper in his hand. "We could start with a few things, just to get the wheels really rolling. Now that we're selling directly to more retail stores, we could build a more loyal clientele by being the connection to the products. Work with better wholesalers up and down the west coast. There are five right here in our local region, another eight within twelve hours of us to the north and south. These are solid suppliers, people who could get us better and niche lumber for cheaper prices, all depending on their market prices."

Bertie's legs were bobbing up and down so quickly Bryant thought he might take flight.

"We could personally visit the stores, hand pick the specialty ones, and do like a mass road trip. Go meet and shake hands, schmooze and tell them the kind of business we do yearly and what needs we have. It's a scratch-the-backs kind of deal: they get us better prices, we deliver more orders. If they make us their number one go-to, they become our first referral to customers."

Bryant nodded—thinking, envisioning. "The only problem is I'm not a salesman. That's Dad's job."

"You've been a salesman for the past three years."

"And hated every minute of it."

"But you can *sell*."

"Since when?"

"Since you were twelve. You're a natural. People trust you and you know what you're talking about. And that's why the technology angle has to involve you."

"Me?"

"Yeah, we need a personal touch to it. We can have online access for customers at the retail locations. Here too," he gestured to the window at the showroom. "At a touch, customers can see the wood samples and not just in small squares but a whole room in a house. By pressing a button they can see exactly how it would look in a large space. But the personal touch"—he was sweating the excitement was coming so fast—"is you. You're the connector. 'Ask Bry, the Lumber Guy.' What do you think?"

Bryant was speechless.

"You've got that kind of face that chicks and old grannies love. You'd be wearing an official Johnson Lumber shirt and a friendly smile, right there on the home screen. And the women push that button right below it and bam, their home dreams come true."

"Wow." It was almost nauseating but he couldn't dismiss that Bertie had a point—several, and on a few fronts.

"Listen, your dad is a good man. He likes things done the old-fashioned way, and that's fine. Mitch is a great guy too, but he's been busy with his kids, and I know he's been job hunting so he's basically been pinch-hitting. But I'm thinking, now that you're here, you've got some energy, some vision. You could do something with this place."

"A mass road trip, huh?"

"Five or six days tops. Nail it down with the wholesalers and store managers, in person."

"What about the yard?"

"Ross can deal with it, a lot better than he lets on. Of course, actually walking around and doing something might put him in traction for a week afterward, but that's life."

Bryant tapped his fingers on the chair handle. "This is sounding pretty good, Bert-man. What about the online side. I know zero about technology on that level. And to be honest, it sounds expensive."

"Look, it's either that or eventually we die on the vine. Or in the yard. Literally. I've been doing the numbers for a couple of years. The cost for change-ups isn't too bad when you think of the results. A simple website based off a blog template is cheap and easy to manage. Customers make their choices using the online information, e-mail for a consult, or pre-order after they've already done most of the work. If they want to come here, you bet. That's where the 'Ask Bry' buttons come in, big ones that we all wear, like a bright orange or green. It's unusual—I mean, Bry, what kind of a name is that, right? Well, I mean—"

"No offense taken."

"Okay then." Bertie shifted again. "I've got a friend who could do the site, easy." Bryant looked doubtful. "Seriously, he's home from MIT. He's got a couple of weeks before he starts his new job, and he could use something fun, really power up a site this simple."

"This would be fun?"

"You haven't met my friend. Nerd does not begin to do him justice."

Bryant leaned forward on the desk. He should run it by Dad, but he was in the hospital. He would run it by Mitch, but what could he do with it? It was up to Bryant, bottom-line, and about time he acted like it. "Okay, Bert-man. Work up the numbers, the time frame, contacts, all that jazz and if it looks good, let's do it."

"Seriously? Man, that's great, wow, that's . . . I'm telling you, a few months from now you'll be living the life."

Bryant shook his head. "I'm holding you to it."

Two weeks later, Bertie hurried up to Bryant in the middle of the yard, bundled up in a parka and woolen beanie though it was 65 degrees.

"Bertie, you look like you've had one too many sodas. What's got you all worked up?"

"It's done, Bryant, the whole thing." He handed off a red presentation folder to Bryant, who quickly thumbed through it. "If you can swing it, go to the office, I've got it online. The computer desk stuff for the customers is supposed to come this afternoon, and check these out." Bertie opened a black duffel bag to show DVDs, binders, and new color hats, shirts, and "Ask Bry" buttons. Standing like a high-schooler waiting for his test score, Bryant glanced at the products. He was impressed. Very impressed.

"I think you deserve a bonus, Bertie," said Bryant, grinning. "I'm taking you to Arby's."

Bertie's face fell. Bryant laughed out loud as he grabbed him by the shoulder and headed to the showroom.

Four days later, Bryant was in yet another hotel room. Bertie grabbed his shoes and said, "I'm getting food. Be right back."

"Something without oil. Or gravy."

"Don't I know it. I've been backed up since Tuesday."

"I'll confirm with Mike for tomorrow morning." Bryant sat on the chair with his feet stretched out before him. He could have slept right then and there, but something kept him restless. He clicked the remote and channel checked. Nothing good on, not even a good game. Turning back to his cell phone, he skimmed the addresses looking for McIntyre and thumbed past "McCormick."

Megan. He sat for several minutes, staring at the name, the number, his finger millimeters from the button.

Bryant scrolled on to McIntyre and pressed it.

CHAPTER TWENTY

Sitting on her bed, Megan sighed and picked up the cell phone. She paused, double-checking with herself one last time that this was the right thing to do.

After saying good-bye to Bryant, and knowing his final decision, there was nothing to be done. For whatever reason, she wasn't able to commit, and he wasn't waiting. Not that she blamed him. Megan clenched her fist around the phone. Why couldn't she get over this? What was it that still held her back?

Timing. It had to be timing. And there was no forcing that. Abruptly, Megan remembered making bread alone for the first time as a young girl. She'd had all the right ingredients but the bread still fell flat. Loaf after wasted loaf, she was about to give up until one day she realized the yeast was the problem—it was out of date. It then made sense why there hadn't been the froth, the chemical reaction she'd expected. After correcting that one issue, making bread was a cinch.

Yes, timing was crucial. Which meant a stalemate as far as she and Bryant were concerned. On the drive back from California, Megan had been sure that meant a yes for Mrs. V. and a new chapter in her life. And yet, the peace had not come. Until she considered turning the job down.

Megan looked down at her phone, thinking of the job offer. It had been five days and no real answer. But something told her if she took the job, she would be pushing that too. A perfect opportunity, with the right ingredients, but the date was all wrong. Praying that this was the right answer, she dialed Mrs. V's number.

"Hello?"

"Mrs. Van De Morelle? It's Megan McCormick."

"Megan, dear, I've been looking for your call and finally, here you are—yes, Keenan, it's all right, it's on my direct number. Sorry, dear. All right, well, let's get down to cases, shall we. You know how I despise the chitchat. Have you thought about my offer?"

"Yes, I have."

"Wonderful! Believe me, dear, you will be just what the doctor ordered." She went on to detail several notable people already involved in her new plan and Megan could hear the new energy in her voice. Every moment became harder for her to say what needed to be said, especially when she wasn't completely sure of it herself.

And yet. Hadn't she known from the first what she should do? If she were honest with herself, yes. Now it meant being courageous, doing the difficult thing, taking down other typical Megan wall bricks of Job Security and Future Plans. Well, that was all right. She was the Old-New Megan McCormick, and she could do hard things.

"—and the committee is completely on board with the idea. You'll fit right in—have I been talking too much? I'm not overwhelming you, am I?"

Megan smiled into the phone. "Mrs. Van De Morelle, you are always a delight, and I mean that sincerely." She paused. "I can't express how much this offer has meant to me. It's made me feel like myself again, back to being capable, and of bigger things. It's clicked something for me, something important. So I want you to know that, and feel that from me. And," she swallowed, "I have to say something difficult."

"You're not taking my offer."

"No, I'm not taking your very generous and lovely offer." Megan exhaled. Two bricks down. Maybe a whole section. "I know it's unprofessional and, in fact, insane not to, and I can't really explain my reasons."

She heard a deep and elderly chuckle through the line. "Oh, I think I know. Bryant is a very good man, I've told you that before. And even though he's not taking it either, and I am deprived of the help I want, I believe you're both right, my dear. You two have something to develop right there at home."

"No, no, it's not entirely that. I don't even know if anything will happen." Megan faltered. It felt hollow and sad to articulate but the conversation was giving her answers, even as she spoke the words. "There's no guarantee, is what I'm saying, but this time, I don't feel there needs to be. I'm hoping, and trying, and still running around the next corner I guess, seeing where it will take me. And I don't want to do anything that would keep me from making the best choice for what I really want."

"And what's that, my dear? What is it you really want?" She had that grandmotherly voice, and Megan could almost hear the pearl glasses tapping her chin.

Megan thought for a moment. "Peace. And to be loved by someone good. I want ..." She wanted Bryant. A warmth, sure and blanketing, filled her insides even as she thought it.

"Then you're absolutely right. Let me tell you, dear, all this"—Megan could see her gesturing before the cruise line cabin—"is not worth more than my Harold. He made it fun. Now, it's just a chore, really. Always the handout, the connections, everybody wanting something all the time. Harold gave it meaning. Whatever you do, Megan, be with someone who gives it meaning."

The elderly woman sighed. "All right then, I'll take my double losses. I'll return to my committee and discover yet another spritely, intelligent couple who can immediately replace you both. No harm done, my dear, but if you should have any news, of any sort"—she heard the deep laugh again—"don't hesitate to give me a call. Or an invitation."

How Megan loved this nosy, elderly woman. They said their good-byes with promises to keep in touch, and hung up. Part of her felt relief and clarity, the kind that comes from discovering what you feel only in the moment of saying it. And part of her felt . . . she couldn't say.

Megan surveyed the room. So, what now?

Thinking, she walked downstairs to the kitchen, weighing her options. Facing a full-time work week at the temp agency with its pale yellow walls and worn foyer furniture was not a joyful prospect. And yet, the decision to reject the cruise offer felt right. She knew it. But what did that mean from here?

Okay, God. No exotic cruise job? Fine. What's the next best thing?

Opening the fridge, she pulled out the orange juice. Pouring and drinking a glass of it, she stared at nothing in the kitchen—thinking, wondering. Should she call Jillian? With Derek's job in Arizona and Jillian a new wife, connection hadn't been as frequent or easy. But with Thanksgiving weekend approaching, Jillian would be here visiting her family, and they could see each other at least for a few days. Together they could think of *something.*

Besides, Megan had bigger things to deal with. Kara and Jackson were visiting for Thanksgiving too, and already a thin dread wound up through her esophagus every time she had to talk about it. So, she didn't.

Megan sipped her juice, looking aimlessly at the cozy kitchen in its red and white gingham curtains, scrubbed white walls, and knickknacks of deep red ceramic roosters and green apple placemats.

Slowly, she put the glass down. Clear and simple, Megan knew exactly what to do. Picking up the cell phone, she pressed Sylvia's number.

Before the week was out, more than one brick would come down.

Several weary days later, Bryant and Bertie ambled into the trailer office. Ross swiveled in the office chair and laughed at their rumpled clothes.

"Well, well, you've returned with the spoils of plunder, I hope?"

Bryant sank into the nearest chair. Bertie slapped his portfolio and briefcase down on the desk, flopping into the chair next to Bryant.

"'Victor and Victorious,'" said Bryant, and closed his eyes. "I never wanna see fast food as long as I live."

"So?" Ross leaned back with his cowboy boots on the desk. Bryant stirred, eyes closed, unmoving, raising his hand in a thumbs-up. "All 11 stores, on board."

"Well, ain't that something," said Ross, laughing softly. "Now there's nothin' left to do but the work."

Bryant and Bertie knuckled each other, barely opening their eyelids.

Bryant breathed in the smell of pine—at once it reminded him of Megan, that quiet morning on the back deck. He wondered for the hundredth time if she had ultimately taken the job, which he was sure she had. And how she felt about it, if she thought of him, of them, and had made any headway with her emotions at all.

Bryant shook off the questions—it was over. She wasn't calling to say differently and he had made it clear where his loyalties were right now. He watched Mitch work over a small fire pit in the clearing, the tall crowded mountain forest surrounding them. Mitch's wife had sent them up with homemade chicken potpie. That, the pine trees, and a slow fire were just what he needed after being cooped up in a car and hotels.

Mitch hopped up next to Bryant on the tailgate and offered him a bottled lemonade.

"Congrats on the sweet job offer," said Bryant, clanking his bottle with Mitch's. "Got life by the tail, man."

"Give or take," said Mitch, but his expression held a clear contentment. "I'll be glad when the move is over. It's just a few days now."

"No sympathy here. Especially when they're moving you. And paying housing the first year. Not bad at all."

"What about you? How'd the road trip go?" said Mitch.

"Pretty good."

"Really?"

"Ah, the tone of surprise," said Bryant. "Better than good, to tell the truth, but I can't take the credit. Bertie is God's gift to lumber." He shared some details of the trip and Bertie's master plan.

"Who knew." Mitch looked genuinely impressed then took a swig of his drink. "Good job taking it to the next level, bro."

Bryant's face reddened. "Mitch, you had a family and were running a yard. You were basically hanging off a cliff. Somehow I don't think innovation was high on the list."

"Yeah, it figures you'd find easy street after I leave."

"Hey, I'm actually working here."

"A first for everything." He lobbed a large wood chunk from the pile in the truck into the fire. "I'm proud of you, Bry. Stepping up, taking care of everything the way you have. You're sure making Dad happy, being here full-time, taking the reins."

"Well, smile maybe."

"How's he doing, anyway? I haven't seen him in a few days."

"Stable. Sometimes he still doesn't recognize Jakey, remembers me three times out of five. But he seems to have mellowed for good, which is incredible, and not giving the home nurses grief. So the operation did something good."

"Speaking of something good, heard from Megan?"

With one word, Bryant's heart clenched like the wood floor grips in the yard—squeezing, pressing, strong and unrelenting.

"No," he finally said, and watched the firelight fingerlings as they reached up and sideways. The sun dipped low in the background.

"Sorry, bro."

Pressing, pressing.

"It is what it is," he said, taking a drink from the bottle.

"Gonna do anything?" said Mitch. "Or you just gonna let it go?"

"Already have."

Mitch shook his head. "Sounds like it's stretching you, B-man. That's a good thing. Trust me, marriage is pretty much all about that. It's good to get a bit of it beforehand. Helps you know what's coming and not be so frustrated when it does."

"No one's getting married here."

Mitch smiled.

"I can't even get her to seriously date me. Not exactly progress after five months."

He kept smiling.

"Besides, it's time to acknowledge it's not going to work and move on. Focus on the yard. Date the Clawson girl."

Mitch looked surprised. "Well, this is a turnaround. All the same things Mom said last year."

"Yeah, but don't tell her. She'll never let me hear the end of it." The sound of his own words—the yard, the Clawson girl—hung in the air, a heavy blanket covering his heart. The yard was going great. Kelly Clawson was great. But neither of them felt great in his soul. Neither of them filled that hollow hurting curve in his heart. He tossed a wood chunk.

Mitch nodded and leaned against the side of the truck edge. "You know, Trisha played a little hard to get. And I didn't like it, not one bit." He chuckled. "She'd been dating some guy, one of those wannabe muscle shirts with the big head, but I just knew she was for me. Can't explain it. So I saw them at this bowling alley on a date, there was a whole group of us guys and girls. And I made a beeline straight for her, with muscle shirt standing right there, and said to her, 'You might be with him today, but you'll be going home with me tomorrow.'"

Bryant laughed into his drink. "So did she?"

"The guy turned around with a bowling ball in his hand. What do you think? But she was impressed anyway. Called me up, said okay slick, you've got one date. And that was that."

"Your point?"

"You gotta humiliate yourself."

"Been there, done that. Not enough."

"If she's not with you, something's missing."

Bryant glanced at him sideways. "I can't control this one, Mitch. She's not playing hard to get, it's something else. I'm thinking for once it's not about me. It's like a waiting game for her to figure it out. But now she's got this job and I just can't play it anymore." It hurt too much, but that wasn't something he'd say to Mitch.

"So let her figure it out. Give her some room and she'll come to her senses."

"Yeah." The tone was final, without hope.

They both sat in silence for a bit, each steeped in their own thoughts. Mitch shifted. "Well, I better get home or Trisha will have my backside. No peace, man. You single guys got it made."

"You know it—stale pizza and sweaty socks. I'm living the dream," said Bryant, finishing off his drink then hopping off the tailgate to put out the fire.

Bryant knew what Mitch was trying to do but he had heard the satisfaction, the energy in his voice. Mitch was about to start a great new job, with a wife he adored and three kids he craved to be with. Life was sweet.

What did Bryant have? Would he ever feel content like that—have the sweet life like that? Megan came quick and clear to his mind.

No more. It was done, over. She'd gone, without one word of asking to stay, or to work it out, or to find a solution. Now he had to accept that too.

Could he?

CHAPTER TWENTY-ONE

"You are Employee of the Decade, did you know that?" Sylvia stood in the office foyer with a bag of fast food sub sandwiches, gazing in open astonishment. "This is gorgeous, absolutely beautiful."

Wearing a blue head-kerchief and satisfied smile, Megan rose from her bent position of painting the lower far wall, and surveyed her work. It had taken a few weekends but the pale sickly yellow walls now sported a two-tone of warm honeycomb and light brown. Sam was coming later that night to put some white chair rail around the room where the two colors met. Fresh white slat blinds now graced the windows—that had been the one big money splurge—and Megan's mom was almost finished sewing the curtains and valances in cranberry, tan, and gold for the windows. They would go up after the paint dried.

Megan nodded. Yes, she was pleased. Very pleased. At least she was getting something right in her life. "And the furniture is coming Monday, which gives this plenty of time to dry."

Sylvia stepped gingerly on the plastic floor covering. "Are you going to tell me the overages, or do I not want to know?"

"No, no, we're right on budget," said Megan, laying the paintbrush on top of the can lid. "The couches were at the Salvation Army, in amazing condition. And my neighbor had the coffee tables in her basement. They weren't even being used." Megan smiled. And Mrs. Watts was making silk flower arrangements for the foyer even as they spoke, which would bring it all together.

Sylvia shook her head. "Honestly Megan, I don't know what to say. It's needed to be done, but I certainly couldn't face it." She gave her a hug. "Or those putrid yellow walls one more day. I've looked at them for 14 years, did you know that? And I hate lemon yellow."

Megan laughed.

"What I'd like to know is where are you getting the energy?" Sylvia doled out the food. "What's gotten into you?"

"No idea. But I'm going with it until I find the cure." Megan sat in the middle of the floor with her, trying not to think about Bryant, about closing that door.

"Well, don't find it too fast. There are some plumbing issues if you get the notion."

Chatting, they unwrapped their sandwiches and reveled in the success of the new look. Megan focused on the joy of the moment, forgetting temporarily about losing Bryant, or the foreboding she felt about the impending visit of Kara and Jackson.

After all, how bad could it be?

Megan felt good. The sun streamed in through her bedroom window. She stretched her arms above her head in a lazy gesture. Sunday mornings were her favorite. And finally, life was cheerful. She was helping, she was happy, she was progressing. Maybe whatever it was that had felt like emotional ankle weights had begun to lift, to leave her forever. Possibly?

Her cell phone buzzed and rang at the same time. She lazily grabbed it and pressed the button.

"Hello?" she said.

"Megan?"

Bryant. Hearing his voice, saying her name. Megan felt that familiar liquid honey spread through her. Only this time, her hands began to tremble. Just when she'd forgotten about him, or told herself she had.

"Megan, are you there?"

"Yes, I'm here . . ." she couldn't say his name aloud or she might lose every bit of composure she owned.

"How are you doing?" His voice was tight, somewhat unnatural, but upbeat.

"Good, really good," she said, her voice a little high. Was that a lie? No, she had just been thinking that not five minutes ago.

"That's good. Really good." Sounds of clearing his throat echoed through the phone. "Hey, Piper wanted me to call and tell you. It's a little girl."

Piper—the baby! She sat up. "She had the baby? That's fantastic news. How are they both doing? Did everything go okay?"

"Great, both of them. The baby's healthy and strong, sleeps and eats all the time so I'm guessing she's pretty happy."

"What's her name?"

"Serenity—Serenity Shirley, poor kid. But she's got a load of curly blonde hair, she's amazing." His voice cracked. "Anyway, Piper's doing good. She was great the whole time though she about kicked the doctor in the teeth when he didn't give her enough pain meds."

Megan laughed, with a wall of tears just behind it. A sudden fierce yearning for him flooded her. She wanted to reach through the phone and pull him through, all six foot two rugged self of him and muss his hair and feel his skin. Megan closed her eyes until the pain of it passed.

"That's such fabulous news, truly, I'm so happy for them. And how's your dad?"

"Back to bossing us around," he said, but with a smile in his tone. "Or tries to, anyway. Doesn't have the fight he had. More mellow. He's absolute mush with Mom, will do anything for *her*."

"And the yard?"

"Good."

"Really?"

"What's with everyone's surprise? I haven't burned it down, if that's what you mean."

She laughed again in spite of herself, dabbing at the corner of her eye with her finger. Was it possible to have two conflicting emotions—joy at hearing him, pain at missing him?

"No, I meant you actually sound happy about the place," she said. Bryant quickly shared about his recent foray into sales and the changes in the yard.

"Bry, that's incredible. You've found your niche, right back where you least expected it. 'To arrive where we started and know the place for the first time . . .'"

"T.S. Eliot, I think. I wouldn't go that far, but it's working out all right."

Megan heard loud noises of conversation and clanking noises, like dishes.

"Oh, sorry about the noise, some of the neighbors brought food, and more food. We think Piper should have another baby just for the celebratory feast. I'll go in the other room."

Megan heard a coquettish voice calling him—that wasn't an old neighbor lady. She thought about the lineup of county girls. Yes, she would just bet it was a continual stream of friendly casseroles and batting eyelashes.

The air space felt suddenly awkward. They had talked about all the safe points, skirting the thin ice of conversation.

"That's better, not so loud. So"—his tone changed—"are you packed?"

"Packed? Oh, packed." Pause. "Well, I decided—it seemed like—" Megan looked at the ceiling and shook her head. May as well bite the bullet. "I told her no."

"No? You're not going?" The outburst sounded more like him. But then, "That's a surprise. Why not?" Back to measured and cool.

Why not? Thoughts entered her mind like freeway cars. Because it didn't feel right. Because I don't want to be that far away from you. Because it was too final. Because, I really don't know. Her throat tightened, making it hard to speak.

"Oh, it was a timing thing." She put her finger on the receiving microphone so that he couldn't hear her ragged breathing. Next, she would be crying, so she fought it.

"A timing thing. I see."

Pause.

Another call of his name. "Well, I better head out. We're going back to the hospital. She's already asked for some contraband Ben and Jerry's and is apparently anxious to get it."

"Tell her I said hi, and congratulations."

"Will do."

Pause.

"Take care," he said.

"You too," she said.

And then the dial tone.

Megan held the phone, curled in a fetal position and ignored the knocks from her mother until the late afternoon shadows fell over her and she finally drifted back to sleep.

CHAPTER TWENTY-TWO

Standing at the kitchen counter strewn with various salad ingredients, Megan glanced at the clock while mixing a large bowl of their traditional three-bean salad. She quickly calculated how many more salads would be needed for a group of unlucky thirteen. Compared to the last few holidays, this was a houseful. Her mother's sister and husband had come down at the last minute, bringing their two teenage children. Plus Jillian and Derek, Megan's three brothers, and Kara and Jackson . . .

She glanced at the clock again.

"When are they leaving?" Megan's brother Sam strode into the kitchen, a tall, well-built young man with brown hair and deep set eyes. He smiled mischievously at her while he grabbed a chip to dunk in the dip.

"They aren't even here yet," she said, playfully slapping his hand away from the bowl. "It's only 24 hours. We can buck up."

"Okay, little sailor," he said with a wry smile. "Maybe you can, but I've got plans for watching the game without Jerk-son involved. Don't expect me to act like everything is chummy."

"Got it, thanks for your support." She tossed the salad, giving him a look.

He got serious, walked over and put his arm around her. "You don't have to either, Megs. And if he gives you any grief—" he made a motion as if to throw a football, with a gleam in his eye.

Megan put down the salad spoon. "I know. And I'll make myself scarce too, don't worry. He's only an annoyance." She said it confidently but the nausea gurgled in her stomach.

He winked and stole another chip before she could reach his hand. Finishing the salad, her thoughts strayed yet again to Bryant. He hadn't called, not once. Not in weeks. It was her fault. She knew it was crazy to think that a man would take any more of the same treatment, that he would call or come around after how she'd repeatedly told him to leave. But still she hoped.

Jillian entered the room, making a beeline for the vegetable tray spread on the counter.

"Your mom says Kara called"—she made a face—"and that they were about thirty minutes out." She crunched a baby carrot. "I'll tell you what I'm thankful for—car trouble. Or you would have had to spend the entire weekend with them."

"Don't I know it."

Megan felt the luck of it too. She had been physically ill Thanksgiving morning until hearing her mom talk to Kara. The engine had blown a gasket. With everything closed up, and Jackson not exactly the best mechanic, they said they'd had to wait until a shop opened. Now it was Sunday and the visit was inevitable. But the trip would be blessedly short, hello and good-bye. Megan had wondered why they would even make it, except that Kara had said she missed the family so much. So she said. Megan suspected she wanted to pry some money from her mother to cover the car repairs, or the newlyweds' overindulgent habits.

But that was Kara. Even in high school, she was unapologetic about her wants. It was nice things and hot guys, and she didn't seem to grasp the collateral damage that went with getting what she wanted. Like Beth. Megan had defended Kara—no way would her sister sneak around with a best friend's guy. That was, until they had both come clean. He had the decency to be somewhat embarrassed. But Kara had believed it to be for the best, boldly saying he wasn't right for Beth but perfect for her—everyone knew it, and Beth would find someone better. Though on a certain level it had proved true, it didn't make it right. Beth had been a good friend, a best friend, always able to overlook Kara's constant need for attention.

Megan sighed. It was those kinds of experiences, and others—like leaving her stranded at college after promising a ride—that made it hard to understand Kara. Sam had made a three-hour round-trip to get her, but Kara didn't blink an eye. As Kara became more immersed in her own social world, she and

Megan drifted apart. By the time Megan left for college, and even when Kara attended Nevada Groves, they had little contact, though Megan had repeatedly tried. It was a void that left her with a lingering sadness. Megan shook her head to clear the negative thoughts and returned to the salad. "Where is everyone?"

"Your mom and Patty are looking at quilting patterns in the spare room. The teenagers are basically plugged in like an IV to the Xbox in the living room. And Derek is in with your brothers watching the game. You know what football gorillas they are." She scooped up another carrot. "Speaking of nice men, is Bryant coming?"

"Nice try." She slammed the salad bowl harder than she had intended. "Nope, he's not." Megan remembered the phone call, his voice, his lack of response to her not taking the job.

"You okay?"

"I've got bigger things to worry about." Which was true. That nauseating gurgle was spreading like snake poison through her insides.

Jillian came around and gave her a hug. "I'm here. Use me as an excuse any time."

"Thanks for coming, really. I know you've had to squeeze it in."

"What, free food on Sunday that I didn't have to cook? Where's the sacrifice?" She smiled and grabbed a spoonful of salad. "I'm here, k? Whenever, whatever, I can deck him on the spot. Give me the look and I'm your girl."

"Wow, Charlie's Angels *and* a dinner show diva."

Jillian grabbed her hand and squeezed it. "You'll be fine. Just be yourself, Megs."

From the front entry Megan heard rather than saw them first. Kara's loud voice proclaimed what a nightmare the drive had been, how the weather was so treacherous, and what a sacrifice it was, all to spend time with family.

It begins. Megan took a deep breath and put on her best company smile.

After the couple had made the initial rounds with her mom and mother's sister, Patty, Kara and Megan exchanged a perfunctory hug and kiss. Megan only nodded to Jackson. He stood with his hands in his pockets, feet spread apart, surveying her with his spiky model hair and designer jeans with the shirt tail stylishly left out.

"Meggies," said Kara. "Come outside and see our new car. Can you believe it?" She flounced the creamy soft fur collar of her tight white winter coat.

"I thought you were getting your old car fixed?" said Megan.

Kara rolled her eyes. "Oh, the mechanic said it would be better to start with a clean slate. That way it wouldn't cost so much in the long run." She nodded knowingly to her mother. "And we got the most amazing deal. Holiday purchases are really such a bargain. And Jackson is sooo good, such a salesman. Had the guy talking through his nose—saved us *three thousand dollars* schmoozing him. Isn't he amazing?"

Kara linked arms with her mother and all four of them went outside. A sparkling red Camaro sat like an ornament in the driveway. Her mother spent a good ten minutes giving obligatory ooh and ahh responses and questions, while Megan wondered how they were affording it. Well, it was none of her business.

Feeling something ominous, Megan looked up to find Jackson at her side. Where had he come from so quickly and quietly? He stood uncomfortably close, practically touching her shoulder with his.

"What do you think? Sweet ride, huh?" His voice was low and throaty—she knew that familiar tactic. But why was he using it on her? He was married.

"It is a beautiful car," she said. "Work must be going well." She spoke calmly, even with a bit of irony, but the panic began to rise uncontrollably, like a mercury thermometer. The foreboding she had felt weeks earlier seemed to manifest itself by degree now.

"Yeah, work is going great. I'm top salesman, Meg. Things are going excellent for me." He turned to look at her, his face so close she could feel his breath on her ear. Megan faced straight forward, showing no signs of affectation.

"That's great, Jackson." Why was he telling her these things? Why was he standing so close? A cold shudder passed over her. Something about the way he looked at her, spoke to her, stood next to her. Nothing she could put a finger on—typical Jackson—but she could feel it. Suddenly, Megan felt grateful that Kara and her mom were here with her though she couldn't define exactly why.

Megan moved, ostensibly to look at the car from a different angle, but allowing herself more distance from him. She wished her mom and Kara would hurry up and finish the extended interior tour so they could return to the house.

Watching the fading afternoon light shining on the TV, Bryant reflected again on Mitch's words: Trisha played hard to get. Humiliate yourself. Don't give up.

Everyone had gone home and today he was alone. His mom had taken Dad to Piper's. After three solid days with family, Bryant had had enough and wanted a break. But he hadn't expected what free time would do to him. Everywhere he turned, everything he saw reminded him of Megan.

She hadn't taken the job. Unfathomable. Why wouldn't she? There could only be one reason, at least in his mind. Was that what Mitch meant, why he shouldn't give up? Had she finally figured out what she wanted? But then, if she had, why hadn't she said so? Why hadn't she called? Bryant felt wary of jumping to conclusions. And yet. She wasn't going. His heart lurched beneath his ribs, a hopefulness that he'd kept compressed in that hollow space. But now, it inflated without permission. Maybe, just maybe.

Bryant looked over at his cell phone, narrowed his eyes, then turned back to the TV. Keeping his hand on the remote, he tried to focus on the game.

After returning to the warmth of the house, Megan quickly gathered the group's winter coats. Her mother took Kara and Jackson to the living room while Megan made her way to the safety of the laundry room that served as a coat closet.

Closing the door, she paused in the small space with the dryer tumbling in the background. Her face felt unnaturally warm—not a romantic flush, more like a finals exam. The nausea had turned into something tight and suffocating. The gray confusion in her mind kept pushing in, making things fuzzy and cold. What was wrong with her? Why wasn't she stronger? He meant nothing to her now. Nothing. But Megan hung the coats with shaking hands. Could she still care for him, even after all this time, after all he'd done? The feeling was a tremor of something she knew but couldn't recognize. It didn't feel like caring, it felt like . . . Megan looked at her shaking hand.

It felt like fear.

With the turkey almost ready, Megan and her mother spent the next thirty minutes preparing the last minute dishes. Megan spent part of the time readying things that didn't need to be before they all sat at the Thanksgiving meal in the dining room. She surveyed the incredible load of food—golden basted turkey, orange yams with oozing marshmallows sliding down into the bowl, piping hot rolls with glossy tops, and three kinds of salads. This was an unusually hearty holiday table, and not one bit of it looked appealing.

Her aunt, uncle, and their teenagers had somehow landed at the far end of the table so Megan listened in on the conversation with her mother, three brothers, and Kara who talked about redecorating their just-purchased condo.

"The color palette, honestly. It looked like someone vomited paprika on the walls," Kara was saying. And all about Jackson's work. As an intern for a local advertising firm his last year of college, he'd apparently made his mark now by rising to assistant ad exec. Since graduating, he'd spent a good deal of his time and money on the road and at party functions "networking," he told them.

"Honestly, you'd think you could get decent furniture," Kara continued. "We're in Scottsdale, Arizona, not Podunk, Arkansas," said Kara, drinking from her glass between bites. "Did I tell you the deal I got on these Ferragamos?" She raised her ankle above the table height. "Absolutely a steal at $165. You really need to visit, Mom. I could take you to the most outrageous places with absolutely incredible prices."

Loralee answered politely and tried to involve her sons when they weren't scowling at Kara's remarks or making sarcastic remarks. When Kara began hinting about needing cash for the holidays, Sam's look was almost murderous. Jackson stared at Megan through most of the meal, enough that she finally had nowhere else to look but down at her plate. After an hour, Megan's head throbbed and she got up on the premise to clear space for pie.

"Oh, we can clear that later, Meg," said her mom. "And let's have dessert in a little while."

"I'm for that," said Sam, patting his stomach. "Got to work it off, watching the game." He winked at Megan who made a face.

"I'll just clean up a few things," said Megan. As she walked out with full hands, she heard the chatter begin to break up with talk of watching the rest of the game. After loading the top tray of the dishwasher, she looked up to find her mother and Jackson.

"Megan, would you mind driving down with Jackson to get some Tylenol? We're completely out." She tried to appear cordial but her voice was strained. "Jackson has kindly offered to get it if you can show the way. You know how tricky those turn-offs are to McMillan's."

"Doesn't Kara want to go?" Megan's confusion was aimed at her mother.

"She's anxious to show Patty and me the pictures from redecorating their condo. It might be a while." She smiled apologetically. Megan understood the familiar company face of let's-keep-everybody-happy, that was her mom's way. But at the same time she read Jackson's purring look of triumph. She tried to catch her mom's eye to communicate this was a very bad idea, but Loralee had already nodded at Jackson and turned back into the hallway.

Jackson swung his keys around his finger a few times. "Shall we?"

That same smug model look—how had she ever found it attractive? Megan forced her thoughts to the situation. Getting in the car with him seemed unwise at best, but neither could she scurry away like a coward.

"That should be fine," she said, more confident than she felt. "But let's hurry, I want to spend some time with Patty before they leave."

Jackson nodded in an "Of course" way and opened the front door for her.

Driving the country roads, he kept glancing at her from the side of his eye, a kind of leering look, and most often at her legs. Megan took to looking out the window, counting the minutes until they arrived at the mom and pop store.

"So, this cruise ship thing," he said, soft and throaty. "That doesn't sound like you. But it's got me interested. Why did you do it?"

Because you're a lowlife scum and I moved on, with three-thousand ocean miles between us to make it clear. "Oh, you know. It seemed like a great opportunity, and it was." Thoughts of Bryant suddenly crossed her mind, at first eliciting joy then momentary pain. Covering her emotions, she pointed which way to turn.

Jackson nodded. "Oh, I see." She was afraid he had. "So, did you meet anyone interesting?"

"Lots of people."

"No, I mean someone really interesting." She blushed. "Aha, I can still read you like a book, Megs." He rested his hand on her leg, giving it a friendly squeeze.

"Really?" Megan tried to smile in a relaxed way, forcing herself to be bold. "Are you reading me now?" She lifted his hand and put it back on the gear shift.

His face darkened slightly as he throttled down the car and hugged the next corner. "What's his name?"

Megan almost shook her head. Typical Jackson, he hated competition. But it was creepy that he even cared about that now. He was married, something he seemed to continually forget.

Suddenly, a very clear thought pierced her mind: *he is a collector.* Jackson didn't care about Kara, or her, or the other women he dated. He cared about winning, about *having.* Dating four girls at once had been a status symbol, a challenge, and from the college stories, nothing new. And she highly doubted a gold band on his finger would stop the craving for constant feminine adoration. With this realization, Megan felt deeply sorry for Kara who likely had no idea what was in store for her.

"Just make the next right and we're there," she said.

After pulling up to the store, Megan practically jumped out of the car while saying she'd grab the Tylenol and be right back. After making her purchase, she hurried back, catching his expression through the windshield—a moody, furrowed brow kind of look, almost menacing. Until he saw her approach the car, then it was dimples and smiles again.

Pulling out and back toward home, Megan gave simple directions again. When he intentionally missed a turn, Megan felt a sense of panic. What was it about him that made her feel this way? Like a pacing lion ready to strike, Megan could feel him working up to something, but exactly what she couldn't say. "You were supposed to go right back there."

"Was I?" He lazily turned to her, one eyebrow raised. The hair on the back of her neck stood up.

"No problem," she said, "we can still turn at the next one."

"We *could* take a drive, it's nice out today."

Megan felt her throat constrict. What was his game? She hated trying to guess his moves, never mind navigate them. Pretending more confidence than she felt, Megan said "Look, Jackson. I told you, Patty is leaving and I want to say hi. If we don't get back soon they might leave. Or even call Earl to see if we've had an accident, you know how paranoid Patty gets."

Jackson squinted his eyes. "Who's Earl?"

"The county sheriff. She's so funny about things like that," said Megan, sounding conversational but making the point. "She calls him about the smallest, slightest things. Doesn't make Earl too happy either."

Jackson paused then slowed down at the next right, thinking. For some reason even the relief that they were headed home didn't totally comfort her.

Entering the house, Jackson headed to the TV room and Megan went upstairs to give her mom the Tylenol, offering to finish the dishes while the ladies chatted. With the kitchen to herself, Megan gathered up the remaining plates, feeling a foreboding, but shaking her head and telling herself to be calm and mature.

She had almost finished loading the dishwasher when something made her tense. Glancing at the doorway, she saw Jackson enter with a few side plates in his hand.

"Thought I'd help out a little, work for my supper, that kind of thing." He smiled, all charm and smooth, his dimple showing. It still shocked her how good he was, how naturally enveloping he could be. Like one of those exotic green plants that shine and curl and look breathtakingly beautiful, until they snap your hand off.

"Oh, I'm good here." Megan leaned down to secure the detergent, her heart pounding and the nausea reaching her throat. She felt trapped. In the u-shaped counter to her left was the sink, to the right was the dishwasher, and Jackson was coming toward her at an angle, blocking the only escape.

"Let me give you a hand." He approached and leaned over the dishwasher with her. She took the side plates from him to have something to do, then filled the detergent holder as if nothing was wrong. Her heart hammered against her breastbone. Why was she reacting this way? It was only Jackson.

But she felt herself hiding behind the familiar wall, what remained of it, with her eyes mentally squeezed shut and wishing he would just go away.

She closed the dishwasher door but still felt him near. Standing up, Megan saw that he had stepped closer. Her back was against the corner between the sink and the counter.

"You know, you look great, Megs. I don't think I've ever seen you look so amazing. The cruise must have been just the ticket for you," he said.

"Yes it—it was a good summer."

He stepped closer, leaning outstretched arms on either side of the counter, glancing down from half-closed eyes with that look he used to give her.

"I can tell it was good. I've missed you, did you know that? Missed lots of things about you." He eyed her up and down leeringly and stepped in one more time. She could see the intentional stubble he left on his face. She could see his eyes, smoky green with the long fringed lashes. And she could see his lips in that smoldering smile, talking to her, telling her things he thought she wanted to hear.

It happened faster than she could have imagined. He bent down, putting one hand around her waist and pulled her in as his face came to hers. Instinct was all that moved her. She slapped his face—hard and sharp—and pushed him back.

Breathing irregularly, she pointed at him. "Don't ever touch me again. Ever."

He only smirked, rubbing his face. "Or what? Think a little spunk will make a difference? Think you can push me back forever?" It was silk, and deadly. Now she knew why the dark feeling, the nausea and the fear. She knew what he was capable of, instantly remembered what she had learned, and had chosen to deny. *Things I can't imagine are true.* She could imagine them now.

"Maybe not," Megan said, pointing a shaking finger to where her brothers watched the game. "But they can."

Bolstered by that truth, Megan felt a shift—physically and emotionally—and the last bricks fell for good. In one sharp moment, she saw him for who he was. Saw his anger at refusing him, standing up to him, at no longer being swayed by what he thought or said. Like a shock to her system, the truth made everything clear: it had been him all this time, that feeling of fear and holding herself back. All she had needed was to stand up to him, like this, to hold the emotional upper hand. And she had done it—out in the driveway, in the car to the store, and now in the kitchen. From her repeated rejections, it was obvious to both of them he had no more power over her, and she was finally free.

She advanced towards him, suddenly strong and energetic so that he involuntarily stepped back. "I see you." And then she laughed. "I *see* you. You're small—just a small, inconsequential fish in your own little pond. And you can *never* intimidate me again."

A sound at the kitchen entry made them both turn. Sam walked in holding an empty chip bowl and stopped still. A cheer went up from the TV room—something good had happened.

Sam's right empty fist clenched low by his side. "Everything okay in here, Meg?"

"Couldn't be better," said Megan. She pushed Jackson aside and walked quickly over to her purse. She had one last thing to do and it was now or never. Standing by Sam, she turned back to Jackson.

"And you still owe me $150 for that last week of work. Got a problem with it, you can take it up with the university complaint department."

Her last view was of Jackson standing in the kitchen, between arrogance and confusion, and Sam seething. She'd let the two of them work that out.

CHAPTER TWENTY-THREE

Driving in the dark, Megan knew she could push it for two more hours then she would need to find a hotel, but only until dawn. After that she would be there in a couple of hours. What had Jillian said to her before the cruise? The old Megs would have jumped at the chance. Well, she was jumping now, a definite Old Meg move, but it was right. She knew in her soul, with a pristine clarity, that this was what she should do. Finally, she felt the balanced yin-yang of her Old and New self—improved, tempered, and perfectly clear on what she wanted.

Bryant.

During the hours-long drive, Megan had gone over in her mind their relationship—from despising him, to letting down, to being friends, to being everything. Then letting go, leaving, yearning, and losing.

She shook her head. Incredible. The ride had been unplanned and almost unbearable, but he had borne it. And now, she was done. No grayness or fear, no anger or hostility. In a few short months with God's help and Bryant's patience, she had become whole again, free and clear. Her nose tingled and the tears welled in her eyes. Everything in her spilled over with feelings of gratitude for Bryant's patience, his understanding, his wisdom. How she loved this man.

Loved.

Yes, she did. "I love you, Bryant," Megan whispered, allowing the words to escape like a thin stream into the car air. Then louder.

"I love you, Bryant Johnson!" She yelled it to the windshield, then laughed. A cascade of emotional glass shattered inside her breastbone. She could almost touch her heart, feeling the beat of it steady and sure. No doubts, not one. She felt the realness of the love, so thick and full, like a safe downy blanket that encased her, with a yearning to wrap him inside.

Megan pushed the accelerator.

Bryant pushed aside the silver tinsel and placed the cup under the fountain lever, watching it fill, then taking a long swig. He stared out through the dusty window with his typical surveying glance. From the showroom he saw Bertie quickly thread his way toward him through the moving equipment and beefy lumber guys.

He shook his head, chuckling. Bertie had been just what he needed. And now things were taking shape. Orders were coming in fast and steady on the fax machine, several every half hour instead of one every few hours. Ross was spending more time networking on the phone, his favorite thing anyway, always leaning back in the chair with his cowboy boots on the desk. And Mitch was settled in Seattle, having started a few weeks ago with Brinkerhoff. A feeling, quick and sharp, nipped through him. He missed Mitch. He hadn't realized how much the past few months had meant to both of them, talking more, just being. It had been like old times. Better than old times.

Bryant walked over and turned down the new heater unit, letting himself fall into the chair. He looked out at the field to his right, the newly poured cement footings showing. The new office would be just what this place needed, finally.

Even Dad was doing good, thought Bryant, and not just physically. They had begun talking, not a ton, but enough. Bryant was surprised how much they could communicate playing a game of Snap and saying a total of ten words.

Bryant swiveled in the chair and stared out through the west window. Running the yard had proved surprisingly satisfying, something that he hadn't anticipated but welcomed. Seeing the place progress under his care had given him the purpose he'd been missing.

Yes, everything had fallen into place. Except the one thing he wanted more than the rest of it combined. Bryant's jaw tightened. Nothing to be done about that now.

The door banged open and Bertie entered, eyeing Bryant lounging in the chair.

"I told you, a month with me and you're doing the executive push up." He took a seat in front of Bryant's desk. "Another month and you'll be golfing in San Diego. Speaking of fun"—he shifted in his seat nervously—"want to go out Friday? I mean with a girl? There's a nice girl that I know who is totally your type. She won't say two words to me but she'd be all over you. I mean, not in the literal sense. Well, maybe, I don't know, but she's definitely not into nerds."

Bryant let his head rest back on the chair, wearing a pained expression. "I'm sure she's nice, Bertie. They're all nice."

"What's wrong with you and dating, man, you're a natural. You're smart, good looking—except at the yard of course." He shook his head. "If I had your looks and style, I'd be booked out for months."

"It's not like that, Bert-man. You think it's exciting, meeting someone new—maybe she'll like you, maybe she won't. It's not like that." He looked out the grimy window. "It's like playing the same song on the CD player, over and over. You like it at first—it's upbeat, it's interesting. But after about the 45th time of that same song, you wanna reach in, pull out the disc, and smash it on the gear shift."

"Okay, good to know. But Megan didn't seem that way, what's up with you and her? I mean, if I can ask."

Man, he hated that question. "Absolutely nada. Nothing. Zilch. That about spell it out?"

"Yeah, that sums it up. Is that why you're so dang moody?"

"Easy."

"So what's the problem?"

"I don't know." Bryant swiveled in his chair toward Bertie, throwing his hands out. "You tell me, Bert-man, you're a Stanford graduate. You're full of knowledge and wisdom. You tell me."

Bertie shook his head. "Dude, if a girl even wanted to go to dinner, I'd be asking her to marry me, so I'm not the one to ask. But plain and simple, Megan is a catch and a half. She came here and cooked for your sister, like the whole week, and brought in those muffin things that were awesome. She's a babe and a half, and smart enough to make you chase her. I'm telling you, I'd kill a deer and eat it raw if that's what she wanted."

"Wow. Find that on a greeting card?"

"If you don't go for her, let me know when the coast is clear."

Bryant couldn't repress a smile. It was so easy for him, so clear cut. She was great, Bryant was great—why couldn't they get together? From that point of view it *was* easy. He was done thinking about it. All it did was make his head hurt. And his heart.

"Talk to me about something else."

Bertie looked out the window. "Uh-oh, must be a rookie."

"No hat?" Bryant groaned. "Man, I feel like I babysit twelve little boys every day of my life."

"*You* do?" Bertie put on his hardhat. "I'm not saying a word."

Bryant grabbed a hardhat, still muttering under his breath. He walked down the short steps from the trailer, heavy and slow, scanning for the offender. There he was, big parka and baseball cap.

He shook his head. *Rookie.* "Yo, buddy, you need a hardhat."

The guy had his back to him and didn't move. Bryant strode towards him.

"Hey, buddy, I'm talking to you."

Megan turned around and faced him. "I'm sorry, boss, I guess I don't know the rules."

He stepped back in shock. *Megan, here?* Instantly his mind raced. If she was here, there had to be a reason. And she wasn't crying or angry, she was smiling, so it had to be a good one. He squinted down at her. "Where's the skirt?"

"That depends—if you want me for grunt labor or light typing."

Bryant's face took on the math-puzzle look. "I'm working hard to figure this out. What are you here for? Is this a joke or for real?"

She shook her hair free from the blue baseball cap. "Absolutely real. I'm here, Bry, for you and you alone. I'm in, one hundred percent, nothing held back." Her voice cracked and she tried to keep the tears from starting. "You've been . . . how can you begin to know what you've been to me? You've made me Megan again, whole and healed. And I'm all yours, beginning to end. Whatever you need me to do to make this work, I'll do it. Because I love you, and I don't want to be away from you. Not now, not ever again."

In one motion, he dropped his hat and clasped her to him. Heedless of the others and fueled by the pent up emotions he'd kept at bay, he kissed her full on, his warm, urgent mouth to hers. Burying herself into him, Megan wrapped her hand around his neck, bringing him closer to her, leaving no doubt of her feelings. Enveloped in his arms again, she finally felt the sureness and the peace she had longed for. With Bryant, she was home.

Workers lazily walked by whistling and shouting, "That's right, B" and "Hey, where's your hardhat, man?" Laughter and buzzing saws echoed off the buildings. Bryant finally pulled away and looked at her with that sun-on-water smile. "Welcome to the family business."

Megan smiled and pulled him back.

THE END

ACKNOWLEDGMENTS

My love and gratitude to my family for supporting my "creative" habits,
and to my Heavenly Father for the joyful, fabulous feeling of
creating something that didn't exist before.
And, of course, to Jane Austen
whose books and movie adaptations have
for years planted romance writing seeds
in my imagination's soil.

BOOK CLUB QUESTIONS

1. Trust is a main theme woven throughout the story. Who were the people Megan was hesitant to trust? How did her progression of learning to trust various people help her ultimately heal?

2. What are some of the traits that ultimately attract Bryant to Megan? How are basic virtues, regardless of physical attraction, a draw to the opposite sex?

3. Megan "tested" Bryant's feelings for her to make her feel more secure in his love. Was she right or wrong to do this? What did she learn from the process, about Bryant and about herself?

4. What similarities did you see in Megan's responses to Bryant (negative, hestitant, testing, etc.) that you've experienced in your own romances? What did you learn from those prior experiences that has helped you see things differently now?

5. If you were Megan's best friend, what advice would you have given her in responding to Bryant, and to Jackson?

6. At the end, Megan sees Jackson for who he is and is no longer bound by his influence. Have you had that similar experience, learning to standing up for yourself and to no longer be afraid of a situation or person you had feared or avoided? How has it affected you?

7. Throughout the story Megan learns to appreciate what the past has taught her as well as apply it to the present and future. She doesn't have to stay stuck, and she doesn't have to try to be something completely different, either. Have you experienced this in making personal changes? In discovering who you are, how do you choose what to keep from the past and what to add from the present and future?

ABOUT THE AUTHOR

Connie Sokol is a mother of six—expecting her seventh—a national and local presenter, and a regular speaker at Education Week. She is a monthly TV motherhood contributor on KSL's "Studio 5" and is a former TV and radio host for Bonneville Communications. She is also a former columnist for Deseret News and Utah Valley Magazine. Mrs. Sokol is the author of Faithful, Fit & Fabulous, Life is Too Short for One Hair Color, and Life is Too Short for Sensible Shoes, as well as talk CDs and podcasts. Mrs. Sokol marinates in time spent with her family and eating decadent treats. For current blog, podcasts and products, visit www.conniesokol.com.